Praise for

THE HOUSE ON FRIPP ISLAND

"Kauffman's keen, atmospheric follow-up to *The Gunners* explores class, friendship, and dark family secrets . . . Inevitably, events spiral to a shocking conclusion. Kauffman's characters leap off the page . . . Readers will devour this suspenseful summer drama."

—*Publishers Weekly*

"Rebecca Kauffman has long been one of my favorite writers, and *The House on Fripp Island* is her best novel yet. The story of two very different families brought together for an unlikely vacation that takes a dangerous turn, Kauffman's latest is a rare and gripping combination of gloriously observed prose and three hundred pages of pure suspense. I loved it."

—Julie Buntin, author of *Marlena*

"A novel full of secrets set in a stunning beach house is my definition of a perfect summer read. I was stunned by the twists and turns of Rebecca Kauffman's masterful novel, *The House on Fripp Island*. Bring plenty of sunscreen when you take this book to the beach . . . you'll be reading all day long."

—Amanda Eyre Ward, author of *The Jetsetters*

"A sharp, modern story about the wilderness of family life."

—Adrienne Celt, author of *Invitation to a Bonfire*
and *The Daughters*

THE HOUSE ON FRIPP ISLAND

ALSO BY REBECCA KAUFFMAN

The Gunners

Another Place You've Never Been

The

HOUSE *on* FRIPP ISLAND

Rebecca Kauffman

MARINER BOOKS

Houghton Mifflin Harcourt

Boston   New York   2020

For information about permission to reproduce selections from this
book, write to trade.permissions@hmhco.com or to Permissions,
Houghton Mifflin Harcourt Publishing Company, 3 Park Avenue,
19th Floor, New York, New York 10016.

hmhco.com

Library of Congress Cataloging-in-Publication Data
Names: Kauffman, Rebecca, author.
Title: The house on Fripp Island / Rebecca Kauffman.
Description: Boston : Houghton Mifflin Harcourt, 2020. | "A Mariner
original."
Identifiers: LCCN 2019026087 (print) | LCCN 2019026088 (ebook) |
ISBN 9780358041528 (trade paperback) | ISBN 9780358274285 (hardcover)
| ISBN 9780358041535 (ebook) | ISBN 9780358310396 (ebook) |
ISBN 9780358310310 (ebook)
Classification: LCC PS3611.A82325 H68 2020 (print) | LCC PS3611.A82325
(ebook) | DDC 813/.6 — dc23
LC record available at https://lccn.loc.gov/2019026087
LC ebook record available at https://lccn.loc.gov/2019026088

Book design by Chloe Foster

Printed in the United States of America
DOC 10 9 8 7 6 5 4 3 2 1

In loving memory of my grandmothers,
Mary & Evelyn

The possibilities of pleasure seemed that morning so enormous and so various that to have only a moth's part in life, and a day moth's at that, appeared a hard fate, and his zest in enjoying his meagre opportunities to the full, pathetic. He flew vigorously to one corner of his compartment, and, after waiting there a second, flew across to the other. What remained for him but to fly to a third corner and then to a fourth? That was all he could do, in spite of the size of the downs, the width of the sky, the far-off smoke of houses, and the romantic voice, now and then, of a steamer out at sea. What he could do he did.

—VIRGINIA WOOLF, "Street Haunting"

Two decades have passed since the summer my family drove through many miles of remote marshland to reach Fripp Island. Land that smelled of wet dog and wet duffel bag, air as thick and hot as wool. Pro-life billboards with magnified ultrasounds and 1-800 numbers in blood-spatter red. Spanish moss that hung in oversized shrouds from every limb of every giant Southern live oak and bald cypress and swayed in the breeze like gangling drunken dancers. Silent and forsaken land. We went twenty miles without seeing another car on the highway.

We crossed a bridge to enter Fripp Island, a luscious, jungled little thumbprint of land that contains every shade of green you could imagine, from almost-yellow to almost-black. We had to stop the car because an alligator was in the road before us. It was the first alligator I had ever seen and much uglier than I would have expected, its hide dull, dark, and textured, as warty as a toad. Fat thighs. It sauntered across the road like it owned the island. The birds there didn't really sing, I noticed. They clicked and buzzed and occasionally they screamed.

Several days later, I was dead.

My body was recovered by a young surfer named Blade Caldwell and two of his friends. The coroner officially ruled it Death by

Accidental Drowning. My family acknowledged that I was not a strong swimmer and there was a powerful riptide, so no one had reason to suspect that the coroner was wrong. Everyone cried and spoke loving sentiments about me.

In the moment before I passed through the screen that separates the living from the dead, I can recall that something like giddy, euphoric laughter fluttered briefly within me, because the idea of being killed—being murdered, that is—struck me as so bizarre that it was downright comical. Then water entered my lungs as hard and fast as a ninety-mile-an-hour fastball to the chest, and I was enraged by the circumstances that had brought me to this place. But before I could linger on that, oopsie-daisy now, here I go. My mind loosened and skittered across a few beautiful memories that touched me and surprised me, and then it was over. No bright white light. Just a painless little snap as I penetrated the screen.

Twenty years later, I'm still skimming through and around and around the same old places, sniffing about, watching from behind the screen that separates the living from the dead. The dead don't care much for one another, I can assure you of that, we're just a sort of sleazy and unappealing reflection of each other; no fun to be had between us, no comfort to be shared. And to the living, of course, we are formless and imperceptible. Our touch has no imprint and our presence cannot be detected, no matter how relentlessly or lovingly we might stalk a living person and attempt to foist our dead self upon them. We can actually slip into a living body, did you know that?, be swept up by its movements and carry along with it, feel the banging of that heart as though it were our own. But even still, even then, the living will carry on, oblivious to our habitation. So around and around I go, taking up temporary residence within the people I once knew and attempting to recall the facts and feelings of life.

THE HOUSE ON FRIPP ISLAND

1

HOURS BEFORE THE GUESTS were scheduled to arrive, the banquet staff vacuumed up olive pits and croutons smashed into the burgundy carpet of the executive ballroom. They flattened starchy white cloths over tables, assembled the chocolate fountain, and did a test run to make sure all eight tiers were properly attached. They distributed garland and potted poinsettias throughout the room, polished glassware, and folded napkins into stars. When the room was finally ready for service, they slipped outside and stood behind the dumpster, smoking cigarettes in the snow. The dumpster steamed with fresh garbage from the kitchen: coffee grounds and shrimp shells. They passed around a tube of wintergreen Life Savers and watched as the first guests pulled up to the valet station. The driver was wearing a stupid-looking oversized elf hat, and he tossed the contents of a red Solo cup into the snow before passing his keys to the valet.

The Raslowe & Associates employee Christmas party was in full swing by seven o'clock that evening. Open bar. It had been a good year.

Midway through the festivities, Scott Daly was named the winner of the big-ticket raffle, and he dragged his wife, Lisa, onstage with him to accept the award. She was several inches taller than him. He wore a navy blazer, expensive-looking jeans with artificial fading, and Italian loafers. His thick, wavy hair was skunk-like, mostly black with a dramatic white chunk shooting out right at the part; his face was jammed full of teeth. Lisa's dyed red hair gleamed a bit oddly under the fluorescent lighting.

Scott had an arm around Lisa's waist when he reached the stage to retrieve the envelope from the head of HR, who had announced all the raffle winners. Scott took the envelope, then raised and tipped his gin and tonic to the crowd. He was met with blank faces, bored, disapproving, disappointed faces, and some lifeless applause. "Whatever," he murmured. Lisa's pale face shimmered with sad exhilaration.

As the two of them made their way back to their table, the CEO of the company took over the mic to offer a robust little spiel about how well the company had performed that year.

At their table, Lisa didn't hear a word of the speech. She was looking over the contents of the envelope her husband had just received. A small embossed card read: *All Expenses Paid. Four days and nights at Fripp Island Resort. Redeemable through the next calendar year.* A brochure accompanied the card and featured many photographs of the island, as well as a map. The island was situated just off the coast of South Carolina, midway between Charleston and Savannah. A golf course occupied a portion of the island, which was three miles from end to end. Several bars and restaurants and crab shacks were advertised in the brochure. Photographs showed bright blue birds with yellow heads, palmettos, a fawn drinking from a fountain on the golf course, an expansive white beach, a footprint in sand.

Scott leaned toward Lisa. "Place looks neat, doesn't it? Figured we'd invite the Ramones."

Lisa's upper lip curled, an involuntary flicker of objection.

Scott whispered, "I know you and Shirley aren't close, but there's nothing wrong with her. And JP's always a great time, loves golf. And the kids actually get along."

That was true. The Ramone kids shared interests with and were close in age to Scott and Lisa's fourteen-year-old Rae and eleven-year-old Kimmy. And Scott was right, there was nothing so very *wrong* with Shirley, it was just . . . nothing was quite *right* about her either.

"Mm." Lisa grunted querulously as she looked back at the brochure. She slowly emitted a soundless burp and adjusted her posture. She was no longer comfortable in her dress. Beside her, Scott resumed the joke he had been telling several minutes ago, just before his name was announced as the raffle winner. He waggled his head around to make sure he had the attention of everyone at the table before delivering the punch line. "Get it?" He snorted wetly, eyes circling the table for confirmation. "You get it?"

Lisa patted the top of Scott's hand, a gesture intended to reassure him of the joke's success and discourage him from telling any more. As she paged through the brochure for Fripp Island a second time, she felt a fresh wave of agitation that Scott had already decided who would accompany them on this vacation without consulting her. Furthermore, it occurred to her, she hadn't a clue how many raffle tickets Scott had purchased for that drawing. For all Lisa knew, he might've spent more on raffle tickets than they would've put toward an actual vacation. It would be like him to do such a thing, honestly, scoop up all the tickets, any opportunity to win. Oh well, this really wasn't her concern. Scott had provided Lisa with a very comfortable life — she hadn't held a job since she was nineteen years old, for crying out loud — and he rarely griped about the way she spent money. Lisa sipped her martini and drew an olive from the stainless-steel cocktail skewer with her lips. She'd be a good sport, she decided. It was only four days, after all.

Fortunately for Lisa, though, the Ramones had already solidified their vacation plans for the entire year and didn't have a day to spare. This was also the case with Scott's sister Nan and her husband, whom they asked next. Lisa's cousin Frank and his wife had a newborn, so they didn't want to fly, and they lived too far away to drive. Scott's friend Liam's wife was going through some weird anxiety stuff, so they couldn't commit. Lisa and Scott were on good terms with his parents but couldn't quite see their way to spending that much time with them under one roof. Lisa's mother was recovering from surgery to remove a tumor from her throat, so she was in no condition to travel. They considered going with just their kids, but Scott pointed out that "all expenses paid" included alcohol, and the house had five bedrooms, so it would be a terrible waste not to find others to accompany them.

Lisa was the one who eventually suggested her best friend from childhood, Poppy, and her family. Poppy and her husband, John, lived outside Wheeling, West Virginia, where the two had grown up and where Lisa's mother, Carol, still lived.

Next-door neighbors and both only children, Lisa and Poppy had become fast friends at an early age. Both families' homes had an open-door policy to the other, and it wasn't uncommon for them to have sleepovers several nights of the week. They shared adventures, secrets, wardrobes, gossip, homework, inside jokes, broken hearts — years upon years of life. Shortly after graduating from high school, Lisa left the area and she and Poppy kept in touch, but not closely, seeing each other only once every year or two when Lisa's family was in Wheeling to visit her mother. On these visits with the whole families, there were always other dynamics to manage, and the time together was hurried and high-strung. Between visits, Lisa and Poppy managed to speak on the phone every few months, but these calls were always interrupted prematurely by a kid in crisis or someone at the door. They never seemed to get to the stuff that mattered. There was shared history and love between them, and they could still laugh at the same stupid shit, but it was impossible to feel as close as they once had, now that they only conversed in fragments and could rarely complete a thought, much less bare a soul.

In the past year, however, the two had reconnected powerfully following Lisa's mother's diagnosis. Poppy still considered Carol a dear family friend, given all the time spent and meals consumed in her home as a child. So when Poppy received word of Carol's illness, she took on the role of surrogate daughter, since she was local and Lisa was not: transporting and accompanying Carol to appointments, taking notes on the results of her scans, arranging her medications in the weekly pill case, delivering quiches and cakes. During these months, Lisa and Poppy spoke often. Lisa was deeply appreciative and touched by Poppy's help with her mother's care. Poppy insisted it was no trouble — she welcomed the opportunity to help and wouldn't accept a dime from Lisa for the gas, meals, or time.

Scott was at the kitchen table, typing something on his laptop, when Lisa suggested inviting Poppy and her family to Fripp Island as a gesture of gratitude. He didn't look up from his computer when he said, "The Fords?," as though they knew more than one Poppy.

Lisa said, "It's the least I can offer after everything Poppy's done for Mom. And anyhow, I'd love to be able to connect with their family, I've been saying so for years. The kids would get along fine, they always have in the past. Alexis is the same age as Kimmy, remember? And Ryan's got to be seventeen, headed to college in the fall. Who knows if he'd even want to come. Rae will obviously be fine with or without a buddy. She'll spend the whole week with her nose in a book either way."

Lisa could see in Scott's face that he was already trying to work up some reason to shoot down the idea. She repeated, "I've always wanted our two families to connect."

"We've tried," Scott pointed out. "You've invited them to things before."

Lisa lowered her voice, even though there was no one else in the kitchen. "That's because they can't afford the things we do. Poppy's too proud to admit it, she'll always come up with some other sort of excuse, but I know that's why she didn't take us up on the cruise or the Disneyland weekend or Toronto. But a trip like this, all expenses paid, plenty of time in advance to ask for the time off . . . I think they might actually be in a position to accept the invitation. Anyway, Poppy's been my friend since I was five years old," she said. "We barely get any time together anymore."

"You talk on the phone all the time since your mom got sick," Scott said. "You talk to Poppy twice as much as you talk to me."

Lisa wondered if this was true. It was possible. Well, Lisa enjoyed talking to Poppy twice as much as she enjoyed talking to Scott, it was as simple as that.

Scott said, "I know Poppy's your oldest friend and she's done a lot for your mom, but staying in the same house with her for four days? Poppy can be . . . a lot."

"Sure," Lisa conceded. Poppy *was* a lot. She had strong opinions on absolutely everything, and she could be moody and unpredictable. She never asked before touching dogs, or babies.

Scott fingered his goatee. "And his drinking can get a little out of hand. Right? Do you remember the year we went over the day after Christmas? You remember. John had a few too many, and with all the kids around."

Lisa exhaled through her nose. Amazing how quickly a good idea or a good mood could be deflated these days. It could happen in the space between an inhale and an exhale. She ran a hand over the marble-topped island before her to check for dust; there was none. She gazed at a pattern of black veins in the marble that resembled gorges on a map, and felt that familiar murky and listless melancholy surging inside, threatening to overtake her.

Scott said, "Anyhow," and Lisa waited for more, but that was it, he was back to his computer.

Eventually, Lisa said, "If you don't want to invite them, I won't. But I'd prefer if you didn't try to come up with all these excuses, like *they're* to blame. Don't make it like you're all of a sudden . . . well, concerned about John's drinking, for example."

"You're not? I've heard some of the conversations you've had with Poppy." Scott's black, triangular eyebrows arched high.

Lisa blinked, surprised by this. "So you eavesdrop while I'm on the phone with my friend and use our private conversations as ammunition not to spend time with her family? That's nice of you." Lisa wound a thick chunk of her red hair into a rope and tossed it back over her shoulder. "But since you brought it up, it's not alcohol Poppy's worried about. John had surgery on his back a year or two ago and still has a lot of pain. They're trying to work out the right medications to keep it at bay. It's under the close watch of his doctor and they're trying to work it out. But thank you for your concern. Well meaning as ever."

"You always assume the worst of me." Scott looked directly at her as he said this, and it occurred to Lisa that this was the first time their eyes had actually met during this entire conversation, perhaps the first time today. This entire week. She couldn't decide which of his eyes to look at. God, they were out of sync. Things had gotten worse and worse between them over the past few years, and now they were worse than bad—they were complicated. Inscrutable. She looked away, and he looked back at his laptop.

Lisa went to the refrigerator, deciding that she really didn't give two hoots about this vacation anymore, didn't even care if *she* was invited, when over her shoulder Scott said, "Oh, hell with it. Run it by Poppy, then."

Lisa closed the refrigerator and spun to face him, carton of cranberry juice in hand. "Really?" she said. She felt something hopeful spike within her chest.

Scott, staring at his laptop once again, seemingly uninterested in further talk of vacation, looked suddenly enthused by something completely unrelated.

She said, "Scott?"

He looked up, his eyes wide but unfocused on her, empty as poached eggs. "Huh?" he said.

"Did you say I can invite them?"

"Oh," Scott looked back down at his computer. "Whatever makes you happy."

2

AS THE FORDS waited in a long line of cars to cross the bridge onto Fripp Island, Poppy observed others coming and going from the island in their BMWs, Suburbans, and Audis. She and John and the kids were in their '81 Dodge Omni with rusted-out wheel wells, and the car released a supersonic squeal from below the hood every time they made a sharp left turn.

Poppy pulled down the passenger's visor to look at herself in its tiny, smeared mirror. Her shoulder-length black hair seemed to double in size in the humidity of coastal South Carolina. Her face was deeply tanned from long days in the sun. She worked for an entertainment company based out of Wheeling that provided bounce houses, inflatable pools, photo booths, and other props and costumed characters for special events. Poppy managed the delivery, assembly, and teardown of the bounce houses, dealt with damaged equipment, and handled all the waivers and consent forms. In the off-season, she helped contract out Grim Reapers, Santa Clauses, princesses, and Big Birds. Occasionally, she had to suit up and play Mrs. Claus or Jasmine if somebody called in sick at the last minute. It was ridiculous work, and she had to deal with more than her fair share of brats and meth-addicted freelance clowns, but it beat waiting tables, which is what she had done from the time she was fifteen until she was almost thirty.

In the mirror, Poppy poked at her symmetrical acne scars, which could almost be mistaken for dimples at this stage of life. Her dark eyes were bloodshot; they had left Wheeling at four a.m. and she was low on sleep, even though John had done a lot of the driving. Her nose looked greasy, so she took a napkin from the glove compartment and rubbed it.

When she looked out her window, she saw some elegant blond people in a Lexus in the next lane over, giggling into fists as they gawked at the Omni. Poppy could feel a familiar and deeply unpleasant volatility stirring inside her. Being around rich people made her feel small and precarious. It made her want to be mean.

She glanced backwards over her shoulder to make sure both Ryan and Alex were still asleep, and they were. She said to John, "Did you see those people staring? Looking at us like we're from the goddamn moon."

"What people?"

"In the Lexus."

John said, "Who cares?"

Poppy gazed out her window. She was sweating. On full blast, the AC offered only an abysmal lukewarm breeze that smelled weird. She opened her window a few inches to see if she could catch some fresh air. The Omni buzzed while idling and sounded more like a lawnmower than any sort of vehicle for transportation.

"I just find rich people so . . . useless and predictable," she said.

John chuckled. He was a big bear of a man, six foot six and three hundred pounds, and when he laughed, his belly jerked around beneath his shirt like it was trying to make a break for it. He said, "We talked about this, though, Pop. *You're* the one convinced *me* this would be a good time."

"I know, I know, I know," she muttered. "I'll be fine once we get ourselves settled. I'm just in a mood. How's your back?"

"It's fine," John said, shifting in his seat, far too big for this car, arching his shoulders in a stretch. The muscles of his neck bulged. "I'll be ready for a pill soon as we get there."

Poppy looked at the digital clock. "I'm glad the higher dose isn't messing with your stomach."

John said, "I swear they're doin' something to my sense of smell, though. Ever since they started me on these ones, coffee don't smell like coffee. And my short-term memory's for shit. Speaking of, what's their older one's name again?"

"Rae," said Poppy. She reached for her purse at her feet, pulled out a piece of Big Red. "She starts high school this fall."

"And the younger one is Kimmy, right?"

Poppy nodded. She folded the gum into thirds on her tongue, balled up the foil wrapper, and set it loose, hippety-hopping across the dashboard. "Kimmy's just a few months older than Alex," she said. "And I did warn Lisa about Alex, by the way, just so there's no . . . confusion."

The two of them shared a smile, and Poppy glanced over

her shoulder again to make sure both kids were still sleeping.

John said, "What did Lisa say?"

"She said, 'You know, there's a transgendered in Rae's class.'"

John made a face like he'd walked into a spider web.

Just a few months earlier, Alex had announced that she wanted to go by "Alex" instead of "Alexis." Several days later, she had cut off her foot-long black ponytail, then asked Poppy to finish it off with electric clippers, a buzz cut, like she had seen Poppy do for Ryan many times. There had been no talk of changing pronouns, using the boys' restroom, or switching from the softball team to the baseball team. Nothing like that. But Alex was reveling in her new look, that much was clear, asking for a fresh buzz cut every week or so since the first.

John said, "Crying out loud. She's eleven years old."

Poppy snapped her gum. "I just told her, you know, 'Alex can be whoever the hell Alex wants to be.'"

John grunted. "And she's got plenty of time to decide that on her own, without a bunch of grown-ups slappin' labels."

He glanced at his daughter in the rearview mirror. Alex slept peacefully, mouth sagged open, a tiny thread of drool connecting her lip to her Cincinnati Bengals T-shirt.

Alex and her father shared a special bond. Ever since she was small, she loved helping John change the oil in their vehicles, stack firewood, and clean out the gutters, and she begged to accompany him on trips to the lumberyard, the shooting range, and Ace Hardware. Alex's most coveted possession was her BB gun, and she and John spent countless hours doing target practice on Coke cans in the backyard. Alex would mimic everything John did: wear her cap backwards, roll a toothpick back and forth across her lips, sniff defiantly as though someone had changed the rules every time she missed the can altogether. When she was a toddler, she'd sit on the bathroom counter and watch her father shave, then ask to have shaving cream put on her own chin, which she would remove with a comb in the same long, measured strokes that John used with his razor.

Alex's idolizing of John flattered him, especially since Ryan had never shown an ounce of interest in his father's hobbies. Furthermore, in the last year or two, Ryan had become downright judgmental about John's love of hunting and fishing. One of Ryan's high school teachers had taken the kids on a trip to the Shenandoah River, done a bunch of tests on the plants and the water, photographed the animals they saw, and picked up litter, which got Ryan all wound up about the ecosystem. Even before this, Ryan had always been happier reading books about anything from aliens to Antarctica to forensic psychology, or going on long bike rides by himself, rather than accompanying his father on tasks and excursions. Lately, Ryan's solitary bike rides had gotten longer and longer, but John didn't ask questions.

Ryan was a much better student and just plain much smarter kid than either John or Poppy had been. Fast reader.

Great memory for facts, whiz at math. Hard for John to imagine he shared any DNA with the kid whatsoever. Several months ago, Ryan had been admitted to the West Virginia University on a full scholarship and would start there this coming fall.

John couldn't believe how lucky he had gotten with Ryan and Alex. He had friends with kids who had problems John could hardly fathom. One of his buddies had a kid who had overdosed on heroin and was found dead on the floor of the bathroom at Shoney's. Fifteen years old. Another one had a twelve-year-old who was sitting in Juvie for stabbing his grandma after she unplugged his Nintendo in the middle of a game. So John knew not to take anything for granted —Ryan and Alex were great kids, easy kids, the best a parent could hope for. Even if Ryan could be a smug little shit about fishing sustainably. Even if Alex and her shaved head invited some questions.

The Dalys had arrived at the house a few minutes earlier and were bringing their bags inside, settling into bedrooms and snacking on fruit. The house was painted a pretty seafoam green, the front door grand and glass-paneled, the shutters white. On the beachfront, it had a narrow wooden walkway that passed over a small marshy patch on the way down to the water. Inside, the house was big and bright, high-ceilinged, with bland, nautical-themed art on all its walls. Everything was blue and white, clean and smelling of artificial lemon.

Poppy ran to Lisa and hugged her. "Thanks for letting us crash your vacation," she said. "I'll try to behave like a dignified person."

Lisa laughed. "You're a saint, looking after my mom like you have. This is the least we can do. I'm so glad it worked out."

Poppy opened and closed her arms like hinges, airing out. "That was one hell of a drive," she said. "How was yours?"

"Fine," Lisa said, "when Scott wasn't driving like a total maniac. That straightaway beyond Yemassee? He was pushing ninety. It's a miracle we lived."

"Oh, for God's sakes," Scott said, turning to John. His expression made it clear he expected an instant ally in his guest.

"Poppy's a speed demon too," John offered.

"Am not," Poppy said. "How would you know anyway? The Omni maxes out at sixty."

Alex piped up, "Mom, you were going seventy in a fifty-five this morning, I saw it."

"I would never," Poppy said. "You must have dreamed it."

Kimmy stared at Alex's shaved head but did not comment on it. Instead, she announced, "We saw a gator on the way in. It was right in the middle of the road. Daddy almost ran it over."

Alex said, "That happened to us too."

"The other thing we saw," Kimmy said, addressing the whole group now, "was we were behind this car back in North Carolina, and the lady in the passenger seat reached over and picked something out of the driver man's ear and she *ate it,* just like a chimp!" She demonstrated this, reaching over to Rae's head and withdrawing something invisible from her ear.

Rae swatted her little sister's hand away. She said, "You're making that up." Sourly, to the others, "She's making that up."

Ryan lifted his hand in a shy greeting to the Dalys. He had Poppy's wild black curls, and they were stuffed under a baseball cap. He was tall and tanned and broad-shouldered like his father but not yet sporting John's round gut. His eyes were dark and lovely, gentle and long-lashed like a deer's.

Lisa said to him, "God, you've grown. Are you six feet?" As soon as this came out, Lisa saw Scott's posture go hard in her peripheral vision—he was self-conscious about his own height—and she couldn't help feeling amused by the success of her unintended jab. She clapped her hands together brightly, eyes still on Ryan. "And congratulations on university. You start in the fall, right? Studying science something or other?"

Ryan nodded. "Ecology."

Poppy turned to Rae. "And *you* start high school in the fall, right?"

Rae nodded. She was very pale and pretty and green-eyed, her light copper-colored hair cut straight around at her chin, big hoop earrings. Kimmy looked like a miniature version of her older sister, same complexion, same eyes. Similar haircut, although the hairdresser had gone a bit too short with Kimmy's bangs, giving her the look of someone in a state of perpetual shock. And Kimmy's permanent teeth were huge in her tiny head, her smile was rabbity and severe.

Lisa said, "Anyhow, we thought you two," nodding toward Poppy and John, "could do the bedroom right up these stairs—it has a wonderful deck, queen-size bed—and *you* two," pointing at Alex and Kimmy, "can take the bunk room in the basement. That leaves the two rooms with the double beds, one for Rae and one for Ryan—they're both in the wing off the master." She pointed down the hall.

Rae said to Ryan, "I already looked at the rooms, they're both nice, you can decide." She couldn't quite bring herself to meet his eyes. He was so much more handsome than she remembered. And she loved boys so much. God, Rae could hardly stand how much she loved boys these days. She could think of little else. Her brain went haywire every time she spoke to one; words became weird and soft and dry in her mouth.

Ryan said, "Doesn't make any difference to me." His voice was deep and full, not like the boys her age, who had voices that were still either as high and singsong as her own or croaked between octaves like a broken clarinet.

They all walked through the house together and Poppy tried to conceal her awe, which quickly gave way to discomfort. She had never set foot in a place like this. She'd only seen homes this nice on those TV shows that featured the houses of athletes and pop stars. It had to be worth many millions. Lisa breezed through the place looking perfectly at ease in her white linen dress, grazing her fingers elegantly over this piece of furniture and that piece of art. Scott sniffed things up close and picked at several imperfections throughout the house: a scratch on the coffee table, a stain on the bathmat. It occurred to Poppy that Lisa and Scott probably vacationed in places like this all the time. Probably even nicer. They didn't exactly seem thrilled with the house.

Lisa said, "Careful for splinters going barefoot on the deck, looks like it's been a while since it was refinished," and, "The only clothing steamer I've seen is in our bedroom, so if anyone needs it, just ask."

Poppy said, *"Clothing steamer?"*

"Like an iron but does a better job," Lisa explained. "Less direct heat."

Kimmy said, "It *is* hot, though. I burned my thumb on ours at home when I touched my communion dress before it cooled down. I even have a scar." She shoved her thumb into the air at Poppy's nose.

Poppy searched for the scar but gave up after a few seconds.

Next, Lisa pointed out the juicer and SodaStream water carbonator in the kitchen.

It came as a strange realization for Poppy to consider that there were many parts of Lisa's home life and daily routine that were completely foreign to her, objects that seemed senseless and redundant, whereas Lisa would be all too familiar with the things in Poppy's home. The duct tape that held the screen door together and kept the batteries in the remote, the stockpot that lived under the leak in the garage. Coupons and buy-one-get-ones. Lisa knew Poppy's life inside out because she had once lived it, but Poppy would only ever have these curious glimpses into Lisa's daily existence.

As they continued through the house, it pleased Poppy to notice that her children seemed either unintimidated by or completely oblivious to the wealth on display. Ryan and Alex made polite comments about the accommodations but seemed keener to get down to the beach than continue gawking at the house.

After the tour, all four kids changed into their swimsuits, and before they headed down to the water, Lisa gave strict instructions for Rae and Ryan to keep a close eye on Alex and Kimmy.

"It's low tide and not much in the way of waves," she said, "but make sure you've got eyes on whoever's in the water." She looked at Rae for a moment. "What've you got those for?"

Rae was sporting a pair of binoculars on a black leather strap around her neck. They bounced against her navel, a shallow and demure innie.

A bright flush appeared on Rae's cheeks when all eyes in the room turned to her. She shifted her weight, popped her hip to the side. "For watching birds, Mom. *God.*"

Lisa put her hands in the air, a sign of retreat. "Forgive me," she said. "I did not know you were into birds." Lisa turned to the others. "They're nice binoculars, though. I got them for Rae before the Keswick Horse Show last spring because our seats were so far away. If anyone else wants to watch the birds . . ."

Poppy said, "I'm gonna use them to spy on our neighbors."

Kimmy stared at Poppy in wonder, lips back, teeth prominent. "Are you really going to do that?"

"Yes."

Ryan carried towels and his snorkel gear, Rae took a book and her binoculars, and Alex and Kimmy took plastic buckets and shovels and goggles and a boogie board.

All four adults settled in the kitchen, where they could easily see the children through the glass doors that led to the patio and, beyond it, the beach.

Lisa stirred up a pitcher of sangria. She sliced apples and dumped them in, along with a can of mandarin oranges.

They sat on barstools and sipped their sangria.

Poppy said to Scott, "I like your thingie," touching her own chin.

He turned to Lisa. "Told you so," he said, then turned back to Poppy. "She thinks goatees are sleazy."

Poppy said, "I think it suits you."

Lisa said to John, "Poppy says work has been busy for you?"

"Can't complain," John said, shifting his posture. The legs of the slender barstool looked like matchsticks beneath his big bottom. "Couple months ago our company landed a huge student housing development, so we're locked into full-time work for the next five years." John worked for a contractor in Wheeling specializing in interior painting and trim. After decades of spotty work and short-term contracts, news of this project had come as a big relief.

Lisa reached across the counter for her purse and withdrew a disposable camera. She handed it to John, draped an arm over Poppy's shoulders, and said, "Before I forget, grab a picture of us, would you? I want to fill up the film by the time we leave."

Poppy wormed out from Lisa's arm. "I don't want my picture taken. You have to get my consent first, don't you? In writing? I'll sue."

John quickly snapped a picture before Poppy could move outside its frame.

Poppy glared at him, then at Lisa. "I'm unphotogenic to begin with, and put me next to you . . ."

Lisa said, "I've always thought you photograph really well, Pop."

"That's even worse," Poppy whined. "That means I'm ugly *and* delusional. Just fill that film up with pictures of the kids, why don't you. Leave me out of it."

John asked Scott about his work.

"Just coming off a great quarter," Scott said. "Record profitability for the firm. So."

"You still working for that big law firm?" John asked.

Scott nodded.

"*Well,*" Lisa interjected, "not exactly."

Scott's face darkened.

"It's a debt collection firm," Lisa explained. "He's in the legal department."

Poppy said, "Po-tay-to, po-tah-to," attempting to mitigate things. She glanced anxiously at Lisa.

"Exactly." Scott grinned fixedly and tipped his glass in Poppy's direction. "That's what I say."

Lisa explained to John, "Basically, Scott files lawsuits, small civil claims, against people who owe somebody else money. People whose credit cards were charged off, or people with, you know, outstanding debt to a hospital or a utility company, stuff like that. Lenders sell the bad debt to Scott's firm, then he goes after the borrowers for that money. Sues them."

John considered this for a moment. "But if these people couldn't pay off their credit card or whatever, how are they gonna have money to pay for a lawyer if they're getting sued?"

Scott's eyes darted nervously around the room as he said, "Well, usually they don't show up to court, so we win a default judgment."

"Gotcha." John sipped his sangria. He didn't particularly want to know what happened next in this scenario.

"So *then*," Lisa continued, "when the people can't pay up, Raslowe and Associates garnishees their wages. That's basically how they make their money, in a nutshell."

John stared at her. "Is that when they take money right out of your paycheck?"

Lisa nodded. "Scott processes the highest volume of these lawsuits in the company. He bangs out paperwork for, you know, dozens of these cases a day. That many lawsuits in a single day. Can you imagine?"

Scott said, "Babe, you make me sound like the friggin' Antichrist."

"It's *your* job," Lisa said.

Poppy was uncomfortable, so she laughed. Lisa had to know that explaining Scott's work to the sort of people who would max out a credit card on groceries would make Scott feel like a real piece of shit. And Poppy had never been a big fan of Scott's—she'd always found him insufferably arrogant—but she was not yet drunk enough to enjoy watching him squirm.

John was not enjoying this moment either. He still owed the hospital six thousand dollars from the procedure on his back. Insurance had covered a portion of the surgery, but not nearly the whole thing. He had worked out a payment plan with the hospital but had missed a few payments over time and was now considering the possibility that the hospital would sell the debt to Raslowe & Associates, that he would get sued and start having to turn over a portion of his paychecks to guys like Scott. John quickly drank two-thirds of his glass of sangria. He was allowed to drink with the medication they had him on, but not much, and they advised against operating heavy machinery. He stole a glance at Scott, who looked utterly miserable. John thought it was likely that he and Poppy reminded Scott of all the stressed-out rednecks he sued, who couldn't quite make ends meet, and Scott was obviously not accustomed to sharing a pitcher of sangria with their kind.

Poppy abruptly pointed out the window at a bird that circled above the kids on the beach. "That thing's massive!" she remarked. "What is it?"

"Osprey, I'd guess," Lisa said. She squinted toward the sand. "Is that Ryan with the snorkel gear?"

Poppy nodded. "He'll be at that all week."

Ryan was loping, shoulders hunched, along the water's edge with his snorkel gear fully in place, looking like some disoriented extraterrestrial.

Poppy said, "Kid's got some interesting interests. On the drive down, he was going on about how the moon might not actually exist."

Scott grunted a bit of laughter through his nose. "Kids and conspiracies, man."

Lisa said, "If the moon doesn't exist, what are we looking at up there every night?"

Poppy said, "A hologram, so he says. The real moon has been eaten away by pollution or inhabited by aliens or something, so now the government projects a false image. You'd have to ask Ryan for more details. Don't look at me like that! Those are his words, not mine."

John added, "It's hard to keep up with the kid. Last week he was talking about brainwashing people with fluoride the government's putting in the water."

"Least he's got imagination and asks questions," Lisa said. "It's groupthink that scares me more than any conspiracy theory. Better to have some radicals out there shaking us all up. Better if we're not all sheep. *Bahhhhhh,*" she bleated.

Scott gazed at his wife. "I've never heard you say something like that," he said with what sounded like a hint of annoyance or disapproval. "Sheep and radicals." Then he muttered to himself, "Fake moon."

Lisa faced him. "Never heard me say something like what?"

"Never heard you say anything about conspiracies, period."

"You've never asked what I thought about them."

"Well, you've never shown an iota of interest, so why should I ask?"

Lisa offered a brief and unconvincingly apologetic look to John and Poppy, then turned back to Scott. "Some men ask their wives about things other than whether or not the dry-cleaning's been picked up, ya know."

Poppy *ooohed* tremulously and dipped her fingers into her sangria to draw out an ice cube, which she held to her forehead. "Let's not fight," she said.

Watching the drama unfold between Scott and Lisa this early in the vacation was making Poppy feel claustrophobic and unsettled. She couldn't look away, but she didn't like what she saw and certainly didn't want to know it this intimately—it was like sharing sustained eye contact with a shitting animal.

"Let's not," Scott agreed. He polished off his glass of sangria, crunched on ice, and rose from his barstool. He slapped John on the back. "What do you say we get a round in this afternoon?"

John said, "I hope Poppy relayed that I'm not much of a golfer."

Scott said, "I bet you'll be a natural with those shoulders. Whaddaya say? Let the ladies get settled in, be back for dinner around five?" Irritated as he was with Lisa, Scott glanced briefly at her to confirm this plan.

Lisa said, "Sure, let's grill tonight, plan on five."

Scott said, "I've got clubs for both of us, and do you need golf shoes? We passed a rental place on the way in."

"Sorry to say I'm stuck in these," John said, pointing down at the ergonomic Brooks sneakers he wore. Last week, John had asked his doctor about golf, half hoping his doctor would forbid it so he would have a good excuse to avoid one-on-one time with Scott. But the doctor said golf would be fine as long as John did some stretching beforehand, didn't get overzealous, and wore those Brooks sneakers rather than something with less support.

"Doctor's orders," John explained to Scott, and he offered a small, shy smile.

John had two dead teeth on the top left side of his mouth and a pinched-off smile that was trained to conceal them. Only when he and Poppy were alone did he laugh fully, allowing the muscles around his lips to relax, exposing those two brownish half-teeth without shame. Poppy had noticed over the years that the more comfortable John was with a person, the wider and more natural his smile became. Watching John now as he offered Scott and Lisa the grimmest, tightest smile she'd seen in years, Poppy was overcome by a swell of love for him that hit so hard, air locked in her throat for a moment. She gazed at John's hands, large and red and textured with calluses, awkwardly clutching that small glass of sangria. She wished he'd talked her out of this vacation. She wished they were back at home.

Once the men had left for the golf course, the high energy of reuniting with one another, exploring the house, and getting superficially settled into the place gave way to a familiar and comfortable connection between Lisa and Poppy.

Their frequent phone calls over the past months kept them up to date on major goings-on with each other, so there was no need to refresh on the basics of Lisa's mother's health, the kids, or the husbands.

Poppy gestured toward Lisa's breasts. "Are they real?"

Lisa laughed. "It's just this bra. You look great too, Pops. Are you still doing those videotapes?"

Poppy nodded. She was barely five feet tall, eight inches shorter than Lisa and much curvier in the hips, but she was managing to keep her waist tight with Cindy Crawford's at-home workout tapes. "I've been slacking," she said. "That's why my butt's the way it is." Poppy reached out to tug on Lisa's long red ponytail. "And is *this* real?"

Lisa swatted her hand away. "The color? Of course not, you know that."

"I meant, it's not one of those ponytail wigs? They're all the rage in Wheeling. Eighty-five-year-old women sporting ponytails like this. They Scotch-tape them to the back of their bald little heads."

"*Ew.*" Lisa stirred up another pitcher of sangria, and she

and Poppy took it out to the deck that overlooked the beach. Lisa pulled the door shut behind her.

The hot air that met their faces felt as dense as a velvet curtain. Lisa's pink lipstick liquefied and seeped beyond the edges of her lips. Poppy's curls seized up.

"I think the fridge is broken," Lisa said, settling into a deck chair, wiping her lips on the back of her hand and examining this slick residue in the sunlight. "When we got here it was on the coldest setting and barely had the slightest chill."

"You want me to look at it? Or John when he gets back? He's a whiz when it comes to appliances, though I imagine this fridge is way more high-tech than what he's used to."

"I called over to the property manager already," Lisa said. "He's sending his maintenance guy, said he'd be here in the next hour or two."

Poppy chewed on a fingernail and spat a little shard from the corner of her mouth. "Probably warms up when the guests checking out are cleaning their stuff out. Might fix itself if you leave it be for a while."

"Might."

Poppy gazed out toward the water. Whitecaps rose and fell and tumbled and played along the surface of the giant rolling turquoise sheet of the ocean. A man making his way slowly down the shore was bobbing and churning and extending his arms to expertly fly a bald-eagle kite. It bounced and dipped and soared. No child in sight, just a grown man and his bird on a string. Thin, ribbed clouds drifted overhead.

It was quiet for a bit, then Lisa said, "Sorry I made it awkward just there with Scott. Sometimes I'm convinced I'm a real bitch."

"What makes you say that?" Poppy said.

"Mainly the fact that I behave like one."

Poppy laughed.

Lisa said, "The way he talks about his job has really started to bug me. Drives me up a wall how he'll skirt around the truth of it. He's very good at that, you know, dodging the truth of things. I used to be the same when it came to his job. You remember, I'm sure. I didn't want anyone to know and judge. Took me forever to fess up to you that he worked for a debt collection firm, not law. But I just don't care anymore what people think of him and what he does for work. I'm sick of the charade." Lisa paused and combed her fingers through her ponytail. "Not sick of the money, though. There's always that to consider." She lifted one shoulder in a slight shrug. The pretty features of her face were hard, as if they'd been set in a mold. "We had to take our names out of the phone book. Did I tell you that?"

Poppy shook her head. "How come?"

"People Scott was filing suit against would get his name off the paperwork and look him up. Then they would leave these messages on the machine, begging him to drop the suit. Sometimes crying, sometimes hollering, threatening him and the family. Desperate people. Who could blame them? God, what a mess."

Poppy frowned. "Did you feel unsafe?"

"Not really. We had that ADT mumbo jumbo installed.

Nothing ever came of any of it, and we don't get the calls anymore, ever since we got an unlisted number. But . . . well, anyhow." Lisa released a heavy sigh and drank an inch of sangria in one sip. "You know how things are with Scott. I don't need to go too far down that road at two o'clock in the afternoon."

Lisa was deeply unhappy in her marriage, but that was old, old news to Poppy.

Poppy fingered the stem of her sangria glass and said, "Why's this thing so small? Am I supposed to stick my pinkie out like this? Is that how the rich do?"

Lisa laughed but was finding herself slightly irritated by Poppy's constant references to the expense of things around the house and her commentary on how out-of-place she felt there. It reminded Lisa of how uncomfortable her own mother was in her and Scott's home. Though they had been living there for twenty years, Carol still tiptoed around the place like she was in a museum. One time she had spilled red wine on a cream-colored loveseat and almost cried, even after Scott and Lisa assured her again and again that it didn't matter. Carol refused to wear shoes in their house, despite the fact that everyone else did. It was obvious to Lisa that regardless of what measures she took as a host, her mother would never, ever be at ease in her home, and now it appeared that would be the case here at the beach house with Poppy, too. It bothered Lisa that people without money seemed to think they could squawk on and on about people with money, all the ways their lives seemed so different and strange, whereas Lisa would never dream of breathing a word about their lives or homes.

"Anyway," Poppy said, chomping on an apple slice from her sangria, "why don't you just have an affair? Or move back to Wheeling, find you a good ol' boy."

Lisa laughed. She spread her polished nails over the table to examine them. "You joke," she said. "But I'm pretty sure Scott is actually having an affair by now. Been going on for quite some time, too, if I had to guess."

"Really?" Poppy stared at her. "You're kidding."

Lisa said, "I thought about telling you before now, but then decided it could wait till I saw you in person. There've been a couple times I caught him in lies but never could quite prove it."

"Like what?"

"Being in the wrong place at the wrong time." Lisa picked at her nail polish, blew away a stray fleck. "He'll say a happy hour with his buddy Jordan kept him out all evening, but then the next time I see Jordan, he won't know anything about it. Or one time I was trying to reach him at his office and he wasn't picking up his office phone, so I called the secretary at the front desk, and she said he hadn't been at work all day. That evening I told him I'd been trying to reach him, and he said, 'Oh, my office phone must've got unplugged again.' Then, when I told him I'd gotten through to the secretary, he got all flustered and said she must be mistaken. Swore up and down he'd been there. I mean, *come on.*" Lisa rolled her eyes and laughed harshly without smiling. "But even if it weren't for the lies, it's obvious in other ways."

"How so?"

"He's just different. Distracted. Jumpy. Mind always somewhere else. And he was hounding me for sex *all the time* when we were younger. Even after the girls came, he was still pushing for, you know, at least a few times a week. But it dropped off suddenly a few years back," Lisa said. "And nowadays, I mean, it's like . . ." She paused and lowered her voice to a whisper. *"Never."*

"How long's it been?" Poppy said, pushing black curls from her eyes.

Lisa thought. "Before Christmas was the last," she said.

"Jesus." Poppy drank the last of her sangria and crunched into an ice cube. She caught a chunk of cheek between her molars and warm iron flooded her tongue. She winced, then offered Lisa a grotesque, bloody grimace.

Lisa recoiled. "Did you just lose a tooth?"

Poppy laughed, wiping blood on the back of her wrist. "Doesn't Scott fancy himself some kind of a saint? Dragging you and the girls to mass every Sunday, and that creepy crucifix around his neck? Isn't he supposed to either behave right or shrivel up and die from guilt?"

"Seems like he manages to avoid that guilt part altogether," Lisa said. "As far as I can tell, in his view if he wears that crucifix and hits communion once a week, he's pure as a lamb." Lisa was quiet for a bit. Her green eyes swirled bright with the reflection of blue sky. "When I think of him with another woman, though," she said, "it's like I almost . . . Put it this way, if there *is* another woman, part of me almost feels grateful to her, because he requires so little of me. He's clearly getting what he needs somewhere else, so I'm off the hook. Know what I mean? In my heart of hearts," Lisa said, pinching her nostrils, then releasing them, "if he's having an affair, I don't think I give a shit."

Poppy's chin jerked into her neck. "Really? In *my* heart of hearts I think, if he's cheating on you, he's an imbecile." She paused. "But if you're OK with it . . . I guess it could be a lot worse then."

"I wouldn't leave him now, I don't think. Probably not until the girls are out of school. I don't want to shake up their lives. He's a great dad, much as it pains me to give him even that. But credit where it's due. I mean, he's got way more patience with Kimmy than I do. He can listen to her stories the whole way through and pretend he's interested in every word. He's almost always the one that helps her with homework. He makes up dumb little jokes that just thrill her . . . Anyway, like I said, I don't want to take away from who he is as a parent. I'll give him that. And for the most part, he and I stay out of each other's business these days." A stray red hair had caught on Lisa's sticky lipstick, and she drew it away with a pinkie. "Besides," she said, "dating seems awful, doesn't it? Especially at this age. I wouldn't want to be alone, but I'm also not too eager to try and meet somebody at this stage of life. Did I tell you about my friend Karen?"

"I don't think so."

"We're in book club together," Lisa said. "She caught her

husband cheating about five years ago and divorced him straightaway. She thought she'd have some fun with some young guys, get her groove back, then settle down with someone else. But it's been nothing but trouble for her since leaving her husband."

"In what way?" Poppy asked.

"These *men* she dates."

"Does she have bad taste?"

"Sure, that's part of it," Lisa said. "But also, things aren't like they used to be in the dating scene. It's a different world out there these days, Pop. You can't know what you're getting into with a guy who's single at a certain age."

"That's awfully old-fashioned of you."

"First guy Karen went out with was a meth addict who stole all the cash from her purse when she got up to use the restroom."

Poppy scoffed. "Well, where'd she meet this guy? In a cardboard box on the street?"

"In the *library*," Lisa said.

"Go on."

"Another guy she met at a bar. Musician, I believe, taught guitar. She said he was really good-lookin'. Long blond ponytail. They went on a few dates, eventually he invited her back to his place. Turned out he lived in his parents' basement. Walls of his bedroom were covered in Santana posters. Fritos crumbs in the bed. Hamster in a cage. Guy was forty years old."

"Come on."

Lisa added, "By this point Karen was so hard-up she did

sleep with the guy, but just the once. And she said the hamster watched the whole time."

Poppy howled.

"I have one more," Lisa said. "But you're not gonna like it." She gathered her hair over one shoulder and twisted it. "So finally Karen went out with a professor who a friend set her up with. She thought she couldn't go wrong with a friend of a friend. And she was really into the guy, seemed like it was heading in the right direction. He was smart, polite, funny, had a good job, spoke nice about his folks but didn't live in their basement . . . So the two of them started spending some nights together. And then, out of the blue, one night while they're in the middle of doing it, the guy asks if she wants him to hit her. You know, during sex."

Poppy pitched back, terrorized.

Lisa continued. "Karen said, 'Uh, not really,' and he did it anyway. Kept at it, too. Put his hands around her neck and squeezed. Said it really turned him on and all the other women he'd dated were OK with it. She tried to talk herself into being OK with it, thought maybe she was being a square. And *then,* amidst all this, she found out the guy was sleeping with half his students. So . . . yeah. That last one really messed her up in the head. I don't think she's been on a date since."

"I should think not! Who are these people? And we're supposed to raise daughters in this world?"

"It's rough out there," Lisa said. "How'd I get into this anyway? Oh, right. What I'm trying to say is that Karen might not admit it, but I think she would *gladly* take her husband back at this point, affair and all." Lisa picked at a knot on the armrest of her chair. "I think she'd be better off if she'd stuck it out in the first place, though at the time everything inside her was telling her to run."

"I don't know," Poppy said. "I think she was right to follow her heart. I think people usually are." She rubbed her eyes. The sun felt like a weight on the world. "If you can't trust your own heart, what can you trust?"

Lisa was quiet for a while, then she said, "I think things aren't always as they seem."

"Even your own heart?"

The melancholy changed shape and moved around inside Lisa, oozing and shifting like oil in a lava lamp.

"Well, anyway." Poppy released a heavy sigh. "You've depressed me."

"Me too. Sorry." Lisa patted Poppy's hand, then reached up to brush a few curls away from Poppy's bright sweating cheek. "Still," Lisa said softly, "sometimes I wonder what it would've been like."

"If you'd married Rex Wright?"

"Hah!"

Poppy knew this would get a laugh. Rex Wright was the dishwasher at Luigi's, the restaurant where Poppy and Lisa had worked together in high school. He kept his hair shaved clean and shiny to the skull and had a drawn-to-scale lightbulb tattooed on the back of his head. He had spent his twenties in jail for armed robbery. Management was too scared to fire him, though they knew he was snorting amphetamines in the employee restroom during his shift. Rex had been hopelessly in love with Lisa when she worked at the restaurant and gave her a stuffed koala bear that smelled powerfully of cigarettes and old perfume.

"No," Lisa said, "I wonder what it would've been like if I'd stayed in Wheeling."

"Oh," Poppy said. "Sounds like a dangerous game."

Lisa sipped her sangria. "Do you ever play it? Wonder what your life would be, in another life?"

"Nah," Poppy said. "I don't have the time or the imagination."

"So things are good with John?"

Poppy nodded with such easy assurance that Lisa felt a twinge. She looked away and stared out at the water. She didn't want to feel spiteful. *Of course things were good, things were always good with John,* Lisa thought, *even when things were bad with John, things were fine with John.*

Envy could zoom up through Lisa as quick as a puff of air, and then it might disappear just as quickly, or it might twist around like a snake in her stomach for days. Lisa had never been attracted to John—he was a kind man, a handsome enough man, a *manly* man who knew how to use tools and fix problems—but still, there was nothing even resembling attraction there. So it wasn't that Lisa wanted to be Poppy, or to have Poppy's husband. But seeing what Poppy and John had, what they shared, and the simple awareness that her best friend had *another* best friend in her spouse, was not painless or uncomplicated.

The smell of charred burger fat wafted over from a barbecue next door.

Down at the beach, they could see that Ryan was in the water, Rae was in her chair, and Alex was using a plastic shovel to bury Kimmy in sand, up to her chin.

Abruptly breaking the silence, the doorbell's pleasant electronic melody sang through the house and reached Lisa and Poppy on the deck.

Lisa said, "That'll be the maintenance guy, for the fridge," and she got up to let him in.

Poppy followed a minute later, carrying the half-full pitcher of sangria inside to replenish the ice, and she found that Lisa was not in the kitchen but still at the front door, where the maintenance man stood before her. Poppy gazed down from the top of the stairway. The maintenance guy looked to be in his mid-twenties, clean-shaven, dirty blond hair, bright cheeks, lean, muscular build, wearing khaki shorts and a Dickies work shirt. Really cute guy. In swirling white cursive embroidery, his breast pocket read *Keats*. He held out a clipboard to Lisa, awaiting her signed approval for the work he intended to do.

Poppy hesitated before approaching the entrance and caught only the tail end of what Lisa was telling the man.

". . . just fine," Lisa was saying, her voice at a bizarre, nervous pitch that Poppy did not recognize. She did not take the clipboard from him but instead took a step backward.

"Sorry for the trouble," Lisa said. "We won't be needing your help after all."

A strange look passed briefly over Keats's face, and his natural flush spread. He lowered the clipboard and tapped it against his thigh, eyes low, then turned and left the house.

Lisa closed the door quickly behind him and locked it. She paused, then locked the deadbolt too.

Poppy said, "What the hell was *that* all about?"

Lisa spun, startled to find that Poppy had followed her back inside and witnessed the interaction.

"Nothing." Lisa flapped a hand in the air.

Poppy dipped her chin. "Don't lie to me, liar."

Lisa said, "I need another drink." But before making a move for the kitchen, she turned and stared out front to make sure he was actually leaving, then actually gone.

3

OUT ON THE golf course, they were only on the fifth hole, but Scott was already pleasantly drunk. He had brought a handle of Scotch with him, and they were drinking out of little wax paper cups. John had a surprisingly good midrange swing and was a decently skilled putter as well. Scott was tempted to try and twist John's arm into playing for money, something small, a buck a hole, anything to raise the stakes, but he didn't think John would go for that, even if Scott worked up some sort of handicap for himself to even things out. Nah, John didn't seem the betting type. And Poppy would probably blow a gasket if John lost a single dime out on the golf course. Poppy was such a tyrant, she probably counted the cash in John's wallet every time he came and went from the house. Probably counted the bills *and* the change. Scott chuckled to himself at the thought of this.

John was driving the golf cart across the range now, up and over the smooth manicured hills. A sweet sea breeze wafted through and seagulls soared overhead. The fairways were surrounded by thick, lush woods. Insects hissed and rasped, and woodpeckers hammered at the trees, which creaked in the wind like rusty hinges. These strange frequencies echoed over the course and gave the impression that a very different and wild world lay just beyond its borders.

John lifted his finger from the steering wheel to acknowledge another pair of men tooting by in a golf cart. Like Scott, both of them were wearing white linen shirts, pastel shorts, and aviator sunglasses. John was trying hard not to feel self-conscious about his tennis shoes and his second-hand polo shirt. Poppy had done some shopping for both of them at the Goodwill in Wheeling in anticipation of this trip, but John felt itchy and weird in this blue polo that was too tight around the neck and smelled of another man's life.

Scott was also wearing a sharp white leather golf glove on his left hand. He fussed with it constantly, doing and undoing the Velcro strap over his wrist like it was a tic, stretching his fingers out to admire the glove, balling them into a fist to examine his knuckles.

Scott said, "Lisa reminded me you two celebrate your twentieth anniversary in a few weeks."

John nodded. "Planning to get away for a night, go down to the Luray Caverns and have dinner at a Mexican joint. I guess that means your twentieth is coming up too, what, this fall?"

"September," Scott said. "If we make it that long." He laughed.

John didn't know what to say, so he laughed too. He'd heard from Poppy that things were not great between Scott and Lisa, but he didn't know all of the details and didn't particularly want to.

Scott sipped his Scotch and ran his gloved hand through

his hair. He was feeling chatty and generous and open to being vulnerable. "Man to man," he said to John, "you're still in love with Pop, then, are you? Twenty years later?"

"In love with her?" John said. He too was getting pleasantly drunk. It occurred to him that he probably shouldn't be driving the golf cart, since he'd had a few drinks after taking his pill, but he felt perfectly competent and judged that he was a good deal less sauced than Scott at this point.

"In love?" John repeated. "I don't reckon I know what that even means anymore. Can't remember. I guess I'd say . . . I can't imagine my life without her. Whether that means I'm still in love with her or just that I've got no imagination . . . hard to say."

This made Scott laugh very hard, and he clapped John on the back. He took off his sunglasses to adjust the little rubber feet, fitted them back over his nose, took them off to adjust them again.

Scott said, "Your boy do any golfing?"

"Ryan? Nah," John said. "He's never been much into sports."

"Shame," Scott said, squinting. "He's built for it."

"I suppose."

"Your younger one's got some balls, shaving her head like that," Scott remarked, then he screwed his face up, appearing to regret his choice of words. "I didn't mean she's actually *got balls*. Not that there'd be anything wrong with that. What I meant was that I think it's cool."

John laughed. "I think it's cool too. Alex is her own bird. Always has been."

Scott wiped a dead insect from the dashboard of the golf cart. "Man, you're lucky, ya know," he said. "I love my girls, honest to God I love them more than anything, but sometimes I feel like I'm living with three of my wives. If you can imagine what *that's* like."

"How's that?"

"Oh, Rae and Kimmy are both Lisa's little Mini-Me," Scott said. "Always harpin' on me, all three of them. Wears me out. Enough to drive a guy mad." Scott was looking down at their scorecard, tapping it with the three-inch-long pencil. He said, "You ever cheat?"

John glanced over at him. "Nah. This is pretty much my first time, like I said, except for putt-putt, and that's always with the kids."

Scott made a face indicating that he found this answer boring or disagreeable, and John realized that Scott might not have been referring to golf.

It seemed that the easy banter John and Scott had established in the past hour might already be running dry.

They were coming up on the putting green. John parked the cart and wiped sweat from his brow. The sun spread across the baked grass. Scott downed the rest of his Scotch in a single swallow and swayed a bit as he got out of the cart. John pointed out a gator just up the way, sunning itself next to a small pond.

Scott pulled out his putter and did a little dance, using the putter as a prop. He wobbled ignominiously. Then he stared at the gator. He said, "Whaddaya think that fellow would do if I gave him a poke?"

John looked at Scott, then at the golf club. "With that thing?"

Scott nodded. "You think he'd bite my dick off?"

"He might," John said.

Kimmy and Ryan were in the water, Alex had just gone up to the house for something to drink, and Rae was seated on a lawn chair under the shade of a large canvas umbrella. She wore a black bikini and large plastic sunglasses. She was alternating between observing Ryan and her sister out in the surf through her binoculars and rereading the same passage of her book that she had read a hundred times before.

Of course, Rae didn't give two hoots about birds. She had brought the binoculars along on vacation because they made her look chic and sophisticated. As it turned out, the bird-watching lie, though unplanned, had panned out quite well. Indeed, the binoculars were not only a cool accessory, but they also provided prime cover for staring at people, and staring at people was one of Rae's favorite things to do.

Ryan had been snorkeling for a while but was now wading casually around a sandbar in turquoise water that reached his waist. The water was calm, and Kimmy had joined him at the sandbar for handstands. Now the two of them were chatting.

Kimmy wore a silver one-piece, and she bounced and paddled and floated around, looking as happy and sleek and at home out there as a little fish. Ryan pointed at something in the water and Kimmy listened intently. Then she was laughing, all big and cute and shaking out her hair, pulling and snapping the straps of her silver swimsuit, obviously thinking she was hot shit. Rae adjusted the focus on the binoculars. Kimmy was chattering, face lit up and wildly expressive. She was probably humiliating herself per usual, Rae thought, with incredibly boring and detailed stories that lacked a satisfying conclusion.

Rae's grumpiness was compounding. She found her younger sister incredibly annoying lately. It was just in the past few months that Kimmy had become interested in mascara and brand names and boys. Rae resented her little sister for a thousand things; at this moment it was for the way Kimmy was splashing carelessly and confidently around in the water with Ryan. He was seventeen, so of course nothing would ever happen between the two of them, but it was still really annoying and unsettling. What on earth could they be talking about out there all this time anyway? What could they possibly have in common?

See, Rae had real, actual adult interests that Ryan would probably want to hear about, if Kimmy would stop demanding all his attention. Rae enjoyed literature and movies and other grown-up things. She'd had wine and whiskey and other adult beverages before, and she liked them. She had started horseback-riding lessons several years ago at a stable ten miles from home. Her parents had said they would buy her a horse if she stuck with lessons for one more year. Rae could explain to Ryan the difference between English- and western-style riding, and why she preferred English, and all the different components of a saddle. She could tell Ryan that the horse she rode, Casper, was a beautiful Arabian, and he competed in dressage. (Rae could say this word with the proper intonation, because she had taken a semester of French in eighth grade and was well versed in French culture.) See, Rae was refined and interesting and elegant, whereas Kimmy—Rae stared at her sister—whereas, *God,* Kimmy was like a cheap mechanical toy that had been too tightly wound.

Rae wiped sweat from her upper lip and stared down into her book with a frothy, unsettling feeling in her groin. She wanted so much more out of this world.

Out in the water, Kimmy was creating bubbles in her palm and releasing them one at a time to the surface. She said to Ryan, "Does your sister like boys or girls?"

"What?"

"Because there's a boy at my school who grew his hair out long and it's because he likes boys. He's gay, that's why he wants to have long hair and look like a girl, because he likes boys. I just wondered, with Alex doing that with her hair, I wondered if she likes boys or girls."

Ryan looked at Kimmy. "Neither," he said.

Kimmy laughed. "Really?"

Ryan laughed too, then he went underwater for a moment, and when he came up he had a small shell in his hand.

Kimmy said, "I like Alex. I don't care if she likes boys or girls. I was just curious. But I really don't care one way or the other."

Ryan said, "Me either."

He held the shell out to Kimmy. It was beautiful, the outer cone brown and grayish, soft pink on the inside vortex. He said, "This is a hawk-wing conch."

Kimmy said, "Hawk-wing conch."

"Doesn't look like there's a little guy in there now, but these shells house marine gastropods."

"Gas—what?"

"Sea snails," Ryan said.

Kimmy examined the shell. "I want to put it on a necklace. Could you keep it in your pocket for me?"

Ryan put the shell in the zippered pocket of his swim trunks. He wiped salt water from his eyes and dug his toes deep into the sand.

Kimmy did a headstand, then came up and said, "I heard that in West Virginia the kids get a day off school to go hunting. Is that true? Like a day off, like a holiday? That is *so weird!*"

Ryan nodded.

Kimmy said, "Do you do it?"

"I don't like hunting myself, but a lot of my friends go with their dads on Hunting Day."

"Is West Virginia full of hicks? It must be, if you get a day off school to go shoot animals in the woods."

Ryan ran a hand through his wet hair. "Some people there rely on hunting to eat. They haul in a buck, that's fifty pounds of meat they can freeze and eat all winter long, when they might not be able to afford to buy that much meat from the grocery."

Kimmy's easy smile and happy mood vanished immediately. She felt something bad and hard inside and said, "I'm sorry."

Ryan laughed generously and dropped low into the water and kicked back so that he was floating. "Don't be. I'm sorry I made you feel bad. That's just life where I'm from. I know it's different where you're from." He remained afloat on his back without moving a single muscle. He said, "Can you float?"

Kimmy said, "How do you mean?"

"Can you keep afloat on your back like this without paddling or moving at all?"

"Well, I don't know. I'm not really a good swimmer."

"I'm not either. Just a good floater."

Kimmy kicked up her feet. Her silver one-piece filled with water and bubbled up over her belly and chest.

Ryan said, "It's easier if you get a big lungful of air."

Kimmy did this and found that she was able to float if she kept the slightest current going with her fingers.

Ryan said, "That's good. But now you can't laugh. If you laugh, you'll let all that good air out and your muscles will tense up and you'll sink right away. *Don't laugh,* OK?"

When Kimmy looked over at him, he was making a ridiculous face, eyes crossed, lips in a snarl, and tongue sagged out to the side, and she could not help laughing. She sank right away, then she stood up, laughed more, and splashed water at him. "Funny, funny, funny!" she said. She dove under and did a somersault while Ryan continued to float easily on his back. Kimmy came up, shook out her hair, and said, "Do you believe in ghosts?"

Ryan maintained his position, flat on his back, chin to the air, and he didn't turn to face her. "Why do you ask?"

"I asked my teacher in catechism a few weeks ago if ghosts were real, and he said it was unrighteous and ungodly to believe in ghosts except for the Holy Ghost, and so then I had to go to confession, and the priest made me do one Hail Mary."

"Did that make you stop believing in ghosts?"

"No." Kimmy drew small circles in the water with her index fingers. "I wanted it to, but it didn't. There are lots of times when I want to stop thinking a thought and I can't seem to."

"Mm."

"Well, anyway," Kimmy continued, "my friend Marti lives in a creepy old house where a little girl died a long time ago, and sometimes Marti sees a little girl in the hallway at night, and she doesn't have a sister, so it could only be a ghost."

"Do you believe her?"

Kimmy nodded very seriously. "Marti doesn't lie. So even though I want to stop believing in ghosts, I can't seem to make myself. It's weird."

Ryan said, "I guess I wonder . . . if ghosts are real, why do they spend so much time sulking around the old houses where they died?"

"What do you mean?"

"You always hear about people seeing ghosts in creepy old houses where they died. Like your friend Marti's ghost. Wouldn't you think, if you were a ghost, that you'd want to go zooming around to all the places you didn't get to see when you were alive? Instead of walking up and down the same old hallways like some broken toy?" Ryan did a zombie imitation and Kimmy giggled.

She was quiet for a bit, then said, "My grandma's got cancer, bad. So we'll probably be coming to Wheeling for more visits soon. I like going to the train museum."

"If you like trains, the next time you guys come visit your grandma, you should go to the depot," Ryan said.

Kimmy squinted at the sun, then at Ryan. "You didn't answer, though, if you believe in ghosts."

Ryan tapped his fingers over the water before him, like it was a table. "I don't wanna put something in your head that's gonna get you in trouble with your priest, have you saying Hail Marys for the next ten years."

"I don't always tell him *every*thing I'm thinking," Kimmy ventured.

"I think believing in ghosts is a self-fulfilling prophecy," Ryan said. "Same with believing in anything that can't be proven. Like God. Or karma. Anything that's a feeling, not a fact."

"You think those things are feelings, not facts?"

Ryan raised one shoulder indifferently.

Kimmy said, "What's a self-fulfilling prophecy?"

"It means once you've decided you do or don't believe in something, everything you see is just going to reinforce your decision."

Kimmy considered this, then she said, "Wait, so do you think ghosts are real or not?"

"I think there's a strong possibility." Ryan slapped at some fish that had bonked up against his back underwater.

Kimmy gazed toward the beach and waved at her sister. Rae did not wave back. "I can't ever tell if she's ignoring me," Kimmy said, "or if she's just not seeing me."

Lisa and Poppy stood together in the kitchen as Lisa stirred her sangria with a butter knife. The pale skin of her cheeks was a patchwork of delicate ruddy veins, and Poppy didn't know if this was from twenty minutes of midday sun or whatever it was that she had just witnessed at the front door.

Lisa said, "Have you heard of Megan's Law?"

Poppy nodded. "Girl was abducted by her neighbor a couple years back, right? The guy killed her."

"That's right," Lisa said. "The guy was living right across the street from Megan's family for years and had some prior convictions, sexual offenses, served his time. The parents didn't have a clue. After she was killed, they advocated to change the law on making that information public, so parents can know if they're living next to somebody with a record."

"Sure," Poppy said. "I remember reading about that."

"The story hit close to home for me because Kimmy was about the same age as Megan back when it happened. And the idea that that guy was living so close to her family, right there the whole time, and those poor parents didn't have a clue . . ."

"Why've you got something like that on your mind?"

Poppy said. "You watching too much late-night *Forensic Files*?"

Lisa said, "I know this sounds like total paranoia, but ever since then I'm in the habit of getting names off the registry."

"How's that?"

"The sex offenders registry. Any local police department will give you a list of names and addresses if you ask."

Poppy stared at her. "And?"

"There's no one in our neighborhood at home," Lisa said, "no one near the girls' schools. But"—a chill shook through her shoulders—"I always get the list for any place we're vacationing, too. It's total paranoia," she said again, "but I want to know. Not that I'd do anything or say anything, but I'd just want to know."

"Sure," Poppy said, feeling a tense energy rise within her.

"Anyway, there was one name on the registry for Fripp Island, and I remembered it because it's so unusual," Lisa said quietly. "Keats Firestone. You don't forget a name like that. And when I went to sign for the work on the fridge, there it was, printed on that paper staring right up at me."

"He's on the list," Poppy said.

Lisa nodded. Hot sangria breath puffed out of her.

"I don't reckon we'll need to make any more maintenance calls this week," Poppy said.

"This island is only three miles long, though, Pop. It's not like he's on the other side of the world. He probably lives here. I'm sure he's *around*. You know?"

Poppy considered this. "Did you say they give out the addresses of these guys?"

Lisa nodded. "It's on the paper in my purse."

She returned a moment later with a handwritten list on yellow legal paper and a map of the island. Together they approximated the location of their beach house on the map and then that of the address listed for Keats Firestone.

Poppy breathed, "Well, shit," realizing that he lived about a quarter of a mile up the beach. "How's a guy working maintenance afford to live in a beachfront house?"

Lisa said, "Oftentimes a property owner will rent a tiny apartment in the basement or above a garage for their maintenance guys so they can get to all the rentals in a flash." She stared out the window, down the beach in the direction of Keats Firestone's house. "Do you think the property manager knows?" Her eyes flashed. "The property manager who *sent this guy to our house?*"

"No way," Poppy said. "If he knew, he definitely wouldn't be employing the guy."

"I should think not," Lisa said. "Sending him into people's homes. We should tell him."

"You think?" Poppy said.

Lisa nodded. "Definitely. Wouldn't you want to know?"

Poppy hesitated. She felt crowded by the facts of this situation. "Yeah, I would," she eventually answered. It was quiet for a bit, then she said, "He was wearing a wedding ring."

"Was he?"

Poppy nodded. "And he was a looker, wasn't he? You usually don't imagine . . ." Her voice trailed off. Poppy didn't know about Lisa, but *she* imagined that sexual predators always had weird haircuts and sunken, piggy eyes. Nothing like this Keats guy.

Lisa downed the rest of her Sangria. She loosened the braid she had put in her ponytail, brushed her chin with the tail of it. "For all the times I've done this over the years, I never put much thought into what I'd do if I actually came face-to-face with one of these guys on the list. You don't think . . . No, we shouldn't tell our guys. Right? The husbands or the kids."

"I don't want the kids to be scared to leave the house," Poppy said. "And the husbands would probably be overprotective about it. Let's keep it between us and keep a close eye on things." She nodded toward the beach. "Make sure nobody goes wandering too far unsupervised."

"I am going to tell the property manager, though," Lisa said. "I just need to decide how. And when."

Poppy glanced back out toward the children and was just noticing that there were only three instead of four out there when she heard a sudden noise from the staircase at the far end of the room.

Alex's head emerged, and she came up the stairs and into the kitchen. Towel draped over her shoulders, pink-cheeked and wet-lashed, a patch of sand on her collarbone. She wore a banana-yellow one-piece swimsuit and blue flip-flops.

Lisa said, "Hey, hon, you need something?" She smiled with teeth that were purpled by sangria.

"My tummy hurts," Alex said. "And I'm thirsty."

Poppy studied her daughter's face for a moment. "How

long were you there on the stairway?" she said. "Did you hear what we were just talking about?"

Alex shook her head, but she wore such a strange expression that Poppy was almost certain she was lying. She hadn't a clue how much of the conversation Alex would even understand, terms like "offender" and "registry."

Poppy said, "If you *did* hear anything we were talking about, it's nothing to worry about."

Lisa said, "How about a Capri Sun?"

Alex rubbed her palm over her scalp, forehead to neck, which sent a small mist of salt water into the air. "Sure."

Poppy pulled her daughter close and tickled her bare neck.

Lisa popped the yellow straw into the foil packet and handed Alex her drink.

"What's Daddy doing?" Alex said.

"They're golfing," Poppy said. "How's the beach?"

"We saw a live crab," Alex said. "And Kimmy made a drip castle. Ryan's looking at fish. I didn't know Daddy knows how to golf."

Poppy said, "He doesn't."

"When's he coming back?" Alex said.

It wasn't unlike Alex to ask after her father—she always wanted to be in on whatever John was doing—but Poppy felt quite certain now that Alex had overheard their conversation, and she understood just enough to feel unsafe without her father in the house.

"In a few hours," Poppy said. "Did you say your stomach hurt? Are you gonna yak?"

Alex shook her head and rubbed low on her belly. "I don't think so."

Poppy said, "It's probably a swim cramp. Gotta make sure you don't go out for a long swim right after eating. You wanna lay down?"

"No."

"Here," Poppy said, "let's fill up a cooler with more juice and some snacks and we'll all head down to the beach together. If you get to feeling worse, we'll come back. Capeesh?"

4

JOHN AND SCOTT sailed over a low hill in the golf cart, and Scott held his Scotch high in the air so it wouldn't spill as they thumped through a patch of swampy terrain. John's lower back suddenly shrieked with pain, and he stifled a gasp as he shifted his position and slowed the cart.

The pain was still there, and it was still bad. Unless John was asleep, one position was rarely comfortable for more than a few minutes before a dull ache would start to thrum at the base of his spine with rhythms as deep and dark as a bass drum. Often the ache became sharp and acute, a blade, metal on metal, until he shifted position. Sometimes that made it even worse, and his balls would seize up, his lungs would seize up, and when that happened John simply had to wait. Bear down, hold on, and fight the urge to blow his brains out just to end the thing.

John had made an appointment to discuss these episodes when he first started having them, about a month or two after the surgery. The doctor said it would improve. When it didn't, and when the steroid injections, over-the-counter anti-inflammatories, and weekly physical therapy weren't doing jack shit either, John brought it up again. Poppy was at that appointment. She was in tears, listening to John describe the pain. She pled with the doctor, "What do we need to do? What the hell is happening? *Help us!*"

The doctor prescribed a painkiller, recommended weight loss, and authorized an MRI scan. John cut out the dessert and quickly lost ten pounds. The pills helped him sleep at night but made his emotions bizarre and unpredictable. Crying over commercials for Bob Evans. Irritable and morose over nothing at all one moment, overcome by ripples of euphoria and world-conquering notions the next. By and large, he didn't like how the pills made him feel, so it was odd how often he found himself counting down the hours, then the minutes, until he could take the next one.

When the results of the MRI came in, the doctor identified inflammation and nerve damage, which was not necessarily a result of the surgery, but John's body wasn't healing the way a body ought to. The weight loss was promising, but unlikely to correct the underlying problem. He was glad the meds were helping John sleep but wasn't inclined to increase the dose.

When the doctor recommended a second surgery, Poppy just about lost her mind. John nearly did too. A second surgery would mean at least another four days in the hospital. Their health coverage was abysmal—they were still crawling their way out of debt from the first operation. And the doctor wasn't even able to guarantee better results; it was just his best recommendation. John had to drag Poppy out of the office that day before she hurt someone. Right before they left, the doctor had slipped John an increased prescription for the painkiller.

Back at home that evening, John and Poppy talked it over. She was still livid over the failure of the first operation but ultimately in favor of doing the second, so that he could get off the medication. John wasn't so sure. "I came out of the first one worse off than I was before," he pointed out. "And our debt's already through the roof, Pop. I go in for another one, we'll be paying it off for the next twenty years. And with no guarantee? Why don't I give it a go for a few more weeks with the new dosage, try and do better with the exercises I'm supposed to be doing, then see where we're at."

The combination of a higher dosage and renewed diligence with his exercises at home had helped. He continued to watch his diet and was shedding a pound or two a week. John still had episodes, but they were less frequent and passed more quickly. As he gained strength, he was less afraid to be active—to throw a football with his kid, to swing an ax. He was nearly back to full functionality at work.

When he was first prescribed the pills, John had vowed to himself that he would be one hundred percent honest with his doctor about his level of pain and dependence on the drug. Now he knew that if he was honest about his progress at his next appointment, which was scheduled for the week they returned from Fripp Island, the prescribed dosage would almost certainly be scaled back. He was contemplating whether he wanted to delay the appointment.

John sent fresh oxygen directly to the base of his spine as he shifted in his seat and cruised toward the next hole at a slower pace. *Gentle, gentle.* He glanced Scott's way to see if his pain had caused any alarm, but Scott was oblivious, staring vacantly out over the course and fingering the gold crucifix he wore around his neck.

John shifted again, absorbing the tension from his spine into his tailbone. *Easy does it.* He sipped his Scotch.

Their golf cart crapped out on the eleventh hole, coughing instead of moving when John hit the accelerator, then sputtering out altogether. John turned the thing off and removed the key, then tried to turn it back on, and the starter wouldn't even turn over. John gave this a few more tries, with no success. He got out of his seat in order to look at the motor and belts.

"Scott, take the keys and give her one more go while I look inside to see if it's something I can tinker with."

Scott tried to start it up while John peered in. The volatile odor of hot rubber rippled through the air.

John said, "Reckon it's either the battery or the alternator. Either way, we're not gonna get her up and going on our own again, that's for dang sure."

Scott had gone through about a third of the bottle of Scotch by this point. His speech was baggy and he was not steady on his feet. He ran a hand through his hair, which was now slick with sweat over the crown of his head, and said indifferently, "What are we gonna do?"

"Probably just need to abandon the cart and walk back to the clubhouse to let them know." John stared out over the sun-soaked fairway. It was a two-mile walk back to the clubhouse, and the temperature had to be pushing ninety. He glanced at Scott and said, "Why don't you stay here in the shade, watch the clubs, and I'll head back in."

John welcomed the thought of a break from Scott's company, even if it involved a long walk in the direct sun. In the past hour, Scott had gone from a merry, giggling drunk to a melancholic and unpredictable one. A few holes back, Scott had bungled a ten-inch putt, then smashed the head of his putter to the ground in anger and hissed something under his breath—John thought it might have been the C-word, which would have been both vile and bizarre—but he wasn't sure if he'd heard correctly and decided not to ask Scott to repeat himself or clarify.

Scott didn't object to the idea of John going for help while he sat in the shade of the cart. He tipped his glass toward John, offered a brittle laugh in response to no joke, and said, "I'll hold down the fort, then."

Lisa and Poppy settled themselves on beach chairs that faced the water. Lisa was slick as an otter, gleaming with a sheen of sunscreen. She wore a white bikini and a wide-brimmed straw hat that shaded her face. Poppy had tied her hair on top of her head and sported a distinct farmer's tan—forearms deep brown and freckled, shoulders nearly as pale as Lisa's. She wore a navy one-piece and large aviator sunglasses with reflective lenses.

Alex was napping on a towel next to them, a baseball cap over her face, and Rae was on the far side of her.

Lisa called down, "Rae, what're you reading?"

Rae didn't look up. "A book."

Lisa persisted, "What's it about?"

Rae released an annoyed exhalation and tucked her auburn hair behind her ear. "I don't know, like, this family. It's about a lot of things. OK? *God.*"

"Excuse me for showing an interest," Lisa said, and gave Poppy a nervous and apologetic smile.

Rae shifted on her towel and fiddled with a hoop earring. She was trying to maintain a nonchalant expression on her face, hoping to high heaven that her mother wouldn't ask to see the book and open it to the page that Rae had been reading and rereading for the past hour.

Rae spent several hours in their local library each week. Her top quest was to find books in the Adult Literary Fiction section that contained graphic sex scenes, but had benign covers and synopses that her mother wouldn't question. Lisa wouldn't let Rae check out erotica or any other sort of genre fiction with a trashy cover, and Rae had already exhausted the YA section for sexually explicit material—Judy Blume was about as racy as it got. So nowadays, library visits consisted of Rae feverishly skimming adult literary novels with an eye for words like "naked," "throb," and "breast." In her current pick, Rae was reading again and again the scene in which a young woman seduced her father's best friend.

The young woman knew it was a terrible idea, but she did it anyway, and they became secret lovers. As Rae devoured the description of the seduction, a foamy sweetness curled up through her.

Rae looked up from her book when she saw that Ryan and Kimmy were making their way in from the ocean. Ryan's black hair was dripping, blue swim trunks tight around his muscular thighs. Rae kept her chin low, her eyes hidden behind sunglasses. Kimmy spread out her towel next to her sister, and Rae emitted a small groan, as though Kimmy's very existence on the beach made it a less pleasant place. Ryan shook out his snorkel gear and set it on the ground next to Poppy. In his hand he cradled a tiny dead crab, its body dime-sized, legs white and delicate as a snowflake.

Poppy said, "Whatcha got there?"

"He's got a fungus on him," Ryan said. He held the crab closer to Poppy's face, and she pinched her nose.

Ryan pointed out patches of gray-green fuzz on the crab.

Poppy said, "What is it?"

"I don't know," Ryan said. "Doesn't quite look like *Lagenidium callinectes*."

"What?"

"A fungus that grows on crustaceans sometimes, but I don't think that's what this is. I'm gonna try and figure it out. I brought some books along and some litmus paper and stuff."

Poppy said, "I hope you're not planning to take that thing into the house. It stinks."

Ryan glanced at Lisa, as though she would have the final say in this.

Lisa waved a hand in the air. "Do whatever you want with that thing. Stick it in a martini glass in the fridge for all I care."

Poppy shrugged, then said to Ryan, "If you're going inside, put on some more sunscreen and bring me a string cheese, would you? They're in my purse."

Lisa said, "Cheese in your purse?"

"String cheese never goes bad."

Ryan said, "I think you're wrong about that. String cheese is still cheese. I think."

Lisa said, "Yeah, Pop, that's gross. We stocked up on real cheese and charcuterie anyway, it's in the fridge. Bunch of different kinds." She turned to Ryan. "Grab some of that instead," she said.

Poppy whined, "I like my string cheese."

Ryan draped his towel over his shoulders and headed in to the house, crab in hand. Lean brown muscles swelled in his calves as he made his way up the beach.

Poppy settled back to lie on her towel, and shortly she slipped into a sun-struck daydream, her thoughts going as loose and bland as old Jell-O.

This pleasant haze was interrupted a few minutes later when Lisa's sharp intake of breath woke her. Poppy sat upright. Lisa was gazing down the beach. She didn't lift her hand to point, but dipped her chin in the direction of a nicely built young man in swim trunks and a white T-shirt, walking a handsome chocolate Lab with a bright red collar along the water's edge.

She said to Poppy in a low voice, "Is that him?"

Poppy stared at the man. "Keats Firestone?"

"Mm."

It was hard to tell for sure from this distance and because he was in swim trunks versus the work clothes he had worn half an hour earlier, but that handsome, boyish face and something in the posture . . . "I think so."

Lisa grabbed Rae's binoculars, which were sitting on top of the cooler, looked through them, and whispered, "It's like he's rubbing it in our faces."

"What, the fact that he exists?"

"The fact that he lives a ten-minute walk up the beach."

Poppy said, "*Chill*. Put those binoculars away. Don't make like we're watching him. He hasn't noticed you."

Lisa ignored her and adjusted the focus on the binoculars. "You're right, he is wearing a wedding ring." She was silent for a bit, then whispered, "Do you think his wife knows?"

"How could you not?" Poppy said, then reconsidered. "Well, I guess it's possible you wouldn't know."

Lisa said, "I think it's more likely she *doesn't* know than she does, don't you think? Because what kind of a woman would stay with a man if they had any sort of —"

Lisa cut herself off abruptly when Alex rose from her nap on the other side of Poppy and pulled the baseball cap from her face. She rubbed her eyes, gathered her knees to her chest, brushed sand from herself, and gazed at the tide line, where Keats and his dog were now passing directly in front of them.

Poppy watched as Alex lifted handfuls of sand and released the grains slowly through her fingers, eyes on Keats and his dog.

A weighty thrust of sunshine made Poppy feel trapped.

Lisa coughed loudly and said, "Well, anyhow. How's the water, kids?" She looked down the row of them: Alex, Kimmy, Rae.

Kimmy said, "I'm ready to go back in." She turned to Alex. "You want to come? Out at the sandbar it's really calm, and we can do handstands and grade each other."

Lisa saw that Keats and the dog had passed and were now a ways down the beach.

Alex said, "I have to plug my nose underwater, so I don't know if I can do that one-handed."

Kimmy said, "I can hold up your legs to train you."

The two young girls headed back toward the ocean.

Lisa said, "Rae? You been in the water?"

Rae shook her head.

Lisa rose from her chair and said, "I'm going to get my feet wet. Care to join?"

Rae shook her head again.

Lisa sighed with a sweetness, her pale chest rose and fell, and she wore the slightest pout. Rae had seen her mother put on this look before, and noted that it almost always produced good results. It seemed to Rae that it wasn't very hard for Lisa to get what she wanted from people, just by being beautiful. And when that wasn't enough, it was with one of these subtle gestures — a shy smile and dip of the chin, a feminine sigh. Rae had tried some of these moves on boys in her class at school, but they seemed to go unnoticed, except for the time Erik Moyer demanded, "Why are you being weird with your eyes?" Generally speaking, the boys at Rae's school were not quite right in the head. They went crazy for video games like Mortal Kombat and movies about robots and zombies. As far as Rae could tell, some of them didn't even brush their teeth in the morning.

Lisa had certain looks she used to get what she wanted, and so did Rae. In fact, Rae had cultivated a perfect look of jaded disgust to get out of doing things with members of the family, and she wore it now.

Lisa grimaced, taken aback even though she had seen this look many times before. "Alright, then," she said. "I'll leave you to it."

Poppy said, "I'll come along."

As the two of them approached the water, Lisa said, "I try to remember what it was like, being fourteen. It was miserable, right? That's why my daughter is such a sourpuss? Well, she's never been much for swimming anyway. But it's not that my daughter is a *miserable person*. Right?"

Poppy laughed. "It's tough at that age," she said. "You think whatever you feel is how it really is. Truth. And even worse, you think that whatever you're feeling is the way you're always going to feel. You can't see a way around it."

Lisa said, "Ryan seems like he got through it just fine. Was he like that when he was fourteen?"

"Sure."

"When did he grow out of it?"

"Around sixteen," Poppy said. "He sort of . . . well, I don't know really how it happens, but things just got better. He got out of his own head, I suppose. Developed interests."

"It's not that Rae doesn't have interests," Lisa said. "She's a reader, obviously, and the riding lessons . . . But it all seems so useless. Her interests seem no more than expensive distractions. Nothing actually makes her *happy*. I might as well let her sit in her room all day, scoot sandwiches under the door. Not even bother. Know what I mean?" She swatted at a deer fly buzzing at her thigh, and her palm thudded wet and slippery against her greasy leg.

Poppy said, "Is she into boys?"

"Nah. Not yet. Is Ryan into girls? I imagine he has a hard time fending them off."

Poppy rocked her head back and forth, her lips, chapped and swollen from the sun, bunched to one side. "Hard to say. There was a girl he took on a few dates this past year, brought her over to meet us, but that didn't seem to go anywhere. I haven't heard boo about her in months. Fine by me, she seemed like a moron anyway." Poppy created a shape in the sand with her toe, then erased it. "I told you about the *Playboy* magazines I found under his mattress a few months ago, right? I think maybe that's enough to occupy him in that department. For now. I hope."

Lisa laughed.

Poppy added, "I reckon he brought one along on this trip too, based on the way he reacted when I went into his room earlier, when he was unpacking and getting settled in. Guess I caught him by surprise while he was getting his things together. He bolted across the room, trying to close his suitcase before I got a look. I realized he probably had one of those magazines tucked in there, and decided not to say anything to embarrass him. Poor guy thinks I don't already know all his dirty secrets."

The two of them had reached the water, and Lisa let her feet sink fully into the sand, creating small pools around her ankles. The water was warm. Tiny white and silver and brown shells gathered and scattered all around their feet. A seagull dipped into the water a few yards out, then came to rest on it, settling its wings and bobbing gently over the waves. Lisa could see through the water to its black webbed feet, which swung lazily with the current.

Farther out at the sandbar, Alex and Kimmy were splashing around at handstands and somersaults, their voices carrying smoothly over the water's surface.

Poppy said, "Lately, though, Ryan is more . . . 'withdrawn' isn't quite the word. He's a little more private, maybe. Happier than ever to spend tons of time by himself. The science stuff, seems like he's always got something going with that, like that crab he found. Always got some sort of project going. And long bike rides, always by himself. Anyway, it doesn't really concern me, it's just something new."

Lisa said, "Maybe he's subconsciously preparing himself for college, pulling away a bit, knowing things will be different soon. Creating some distance."

Poppy said, "That hadn't occurred to me."

Lisa was quiet for a while, then she said, "You don't think Alex heard us, do you? Talking about the registry stuff? The way she sat up when we were talking again just there . . . I should have been more careful."

"Nah. I think she'd speak up and be asking questions if she heard anything that upset her."

"It's funny, isn't it," Lisa said, "how kids have such a fascination with strangers. Especially when it's their parents interacting with strangers."

"How do you mean?" Poppy said.

"Well, I guess I'm thinking how my girls, especially Kimmy, always ask, 'Mommy, who was that? What did that man say to you? And what did you say to him? And what did that mean?' And it's rarely anything at all. You know, I'll be like, 'He asked if we want our groceries packed in paper or plastic.' But even when it's nothing, they think they *must* know everything about it."

The two women watched in silence as their daughters played happily together by the sandbar, while both of their minds thrashed and toiled over private concerns.

John was drowning in heat and light and sweat after a twenty-minute walk in the sun, but he had nearly made it back to the clubhouse when the air changed, suddenly becoming as thick as paste and smelling of overturned earth. The sky darkened to the color of ash, it grumbled and cracked, and then it exploded. John made his way toward shelter under the awning of the clubhouse. It occurred to him that he'd not passed anyone else on the course during his walk; others must have wisely looked at the forecast, he thought, and headed in earlier.

John could see dozens of people through the windows of the clubhouse, hobnobbing in their visors and pastels, sipping on cocktails in plastic cups while they waited out the storm. He had no interest in going in there; he was drenched already and would probably catch pneumonia if he set foot in that overly air-conditioned room.

The rain was heavy and wild and warmish, slapping against the concrete like applause. It pounded against the canvas umbrellas that covered the patio. The sky continued to growl, and it flashed in vibrations with purple-white lightning. John could not deny himself the pleasure of imagining Scott out there in the storm. The rain had come much too quickly, and Scott was much too far from any sort of shelter to possibly have found refuge. He was probably out there waving his putter at the sky, begging to get scorched.

Once the storm had passed, John waited until the clubhouse had cleared out a bit before approaching a staff member. This young lady paged a manager who paged a maintenance guy named Barry, who drove John out to the eleventh hole in an impressive four-wheel-drive cart with towing power. Their golf cart was just where John had left it, but Scott was nowhere in sight. John stared out over the fairway, and the grass was brilliantly green. The air was thinner now, clean and clear as glass. The clouds were dissolving, the temperature already rapidly increasing with the return of the sun.

Barry spat out of the side of his mouth and said, "Where'd your partner make off to?"

John said, "I don't have a clue." He looked in every direction, but no Scott. The golf clubs were there in the zippered bag, but when John peeked inside, he saw that Scott's prized putter was not among them. Scott must have taken that with him, wherever he'd gone.

Barry confirmed that the problem with their cart was the alternator and said he would tow it back in order to do the work in the shop rather than out on the course. John helped him attach the cart to the tow line.

Barry said, "I'll give you a lift back. We'll get you a new one of these rented out for the rest of the week."

John gazed out over the course again. "I guess so," he said. "Can't imagine where he went . . ."

"I'd say you've done your part," Barry said. "The island's only a few miles long. I'm sure he'll find his way back just fine."

John was not sure about this at all. "I don't know," he said. "Guy doesn't seem to have much in the way of street smarts, and he's about as tough as the Pillsbury Doughboy."

Barry laughed hard at this, and John felt like he'd made a friend.

John rode to the clubhouse with Barry, used the restroom there, and was provided a replacement golf cart. Barry wished him luck in finding Scott.

John transferred Scott's clubs to the replacement cart and

decided to circle the perimeter of the course before returning to the house.

He did this, and it ate up a good chunk of time, but there was no sign of Scott. Not far from the eleventh hole, he passed a young couple on bikes, both of them completely drenched; they too had probably gotten caught in the storm. John slowed the golf cart and said, "Y'all happen to see a guy, on the short side, 'bout five-five, hair's mostly black with a white streak? Wanderin' 'round here with a big old putter?"

The couple looked at each other, then back at John.

John said, "I just thought, he got caught in the rain too. Not too terribly far from here. Thought maybe you ended up the same place or somethin'."

The woman shook her head, her face blank.

John said, "Alright now," and the couple cycled away.

He passed another woman on the footpath. She wore skin-tight blue spandex and a white visor and was pushing a freckled baby in a stroller that looked as complex as a rocket ship. Massive mesh extension on the sun visor. Five wheels, built for speed. The woman nervously steered the baby in a far angle when John approached, so he didn't bother. *Jesus Christ,* the way these people looked at him, it was like there was a dead body strapped to the roof of the golf cart. Was it the thrift store polo? The sneakers? The haircut? Coming into this trip, John knew he would feel different from the moneyed vacationers here, but he hadn't counted on *them* feeling so different toward *him.* He supposed he had expected that they might make some effort to let him think he was blending in. That they might at least have the courtesy to pretend.

Eventually, John drove the cart back to the beach house, preparing to explain the situation to Lisa: why the two of them had become separated, and the territory he had already covered in attempting to locate Scott.

5

KEATS WAS AT home when the storm hit. His wife, Roxie, had taken the truck across the island to pick up coffee and paper towels. Keats felt bad that she was out when the weather struck its hardest, but he was relieved she had decided to drive to the Quik Mart instead of biking, as she often did.

He stood at the window as water beat against the glass and thunder vibrated through the walls. Beachgoers fled for cover, books in armpits, flip-flops in hand. The white sand, dimpled with footprints, went brown and flat in the rain, then charcoal and even flatter, as though the world were sinking before his eyes.

The dog was in the bathroom, the only windowless room in their tiny above-garage apartment. He whined and tittered pitifully, soft and high-pitched, tail thumping the linoleum.

A gust of wind screamed, the windows rattled. Lightning broke the sky into pieces. Keats felt wild, almost scared, like a kid. Storms blew through practically every day at this time of year, but rarely came on so sudden and severe.

Keats was startled by a noise at the door—he had expected Roxie would wait out the rain in the truck. As soon as the door opened, it was torn from Roxie's grasp and knocked hard on its hinges against the exterior of the garage, carried by the force of the wind. Rain pelted the floor of the entrance, there was a howl of air, an invisible force that seemed intent on drawing the outside world in. It was like an angry and insane ghost had just entered the room.

Roxie grabbed the doorknob, slammed the door shut behind her with great effort, and shuddered. Her pretty face was lively and expressive, eyes large. "Good God!" she exclaimed, squeezing a handful of water from her T-shirt. She was soaked.

She kicked off her flip-flops and left them at the door, dropped the plastic grocery bag there as well. She moved to the kitchen, where she peeled off her clothing one item at a time until she was completely naked, then she dropped the bundle of sopping-wet clothing on the counter. Keats admired his wife. Roxie's skin was deeply and evenly sun-bronzed, except for bikini triangles surrounding her nipples and pubic hair and across her bottom, where her skin seemed whiter than white.

Roxie squeezed her long, wet hair into a rope and wrung it out over the kitchen sink.

Keats grabbed a beach towel from the basket of fresh laundry next to the couch, went to her, and wrapped her in it, tight and tucked edges, a burrito. He hugged her, and her scalp smelled earthy and fresh, like a root that had just been pulled from the ground.

He said, "You didn't want to wait it out in the truck?"

Roxie sniffed and a shiver vibrated through her. "I didn't know how long it might last."

Keats smoothed wet hair back from her face. "You hungry for lunch? I can make something while you dry off."

"Maybe in a little," Roxie said. "Let's watch the storm together."

They returned to the window, where rain came in such great torrents and bursts that the glass seemed to ripple before them. Pieces of debris went skittering across the sand, some lifted and swirled in the strong wind.

Without turning to face Keats, Roxie said, "It happened again, didn't it?"

Keats nodded. "No big deal."

Roxie reached an arm out from under her towel to take her husband's hand. "How bad?"

"Not bad," Keats said. "Just one lady, she took one look at my name on the clipboard, said their fridge was fine after all." He raised one shoulder.

Thunder rumbled low. Their heads moved in tandem to follow a blue canvas beach chair that bounced and cartwheeled across the sand, down near the water.

Roxie said, "Five more months is all."

On the beach, a man was sprinting along the tide line, palming a bucket hat to his head. Going after that blue canvas chair, most likely.

Roxie said, "He's never going to catch up to it."

Keats said, "You don't think so? I bet the storm peters out before he does."

Thunder cracked like a cannon and they both jumped. From the bathroom their dog emitted a deranged sound.

"Poor Leo," Roxie said over her shoulder. "Do you think he thinks the world is ending?"

Keats laughed. "Maybe he knows something we don't."

"Maybe," Roxie said. She took his fingers and tugged them playfully. "Come on, let's go listen to the world end from bed."

Keats followed her to the bedroom, where she dropped the towel from her shoulders and started to unbutton his shirt. He glanced out over her head just as radiant white lightning illuminated the gray ocean, and the world did not end, but for an instant it looked like it had been turned entirely inside out.

6

JOHN PARKED THE golf cart and was surprised to find the front door of the house locked, so he went around the back, where Scott was sitting on the deck in a fresh and dry white linen shirt and khaki shorts, sipping a glass of white wine. Lisa and Poppy and the kids were there too, eating cheese and crackers, all seven of them looking freshly showered and relaxed.

Poppy caught sight of John first, and she called out, "Look what the cat dragged in!"

Kimmy sang the tune from a Meow Mix commercial.

John made his way up the wooden stairs, unspeakably weary. His clothing was stiff and damp, having at one point been soaked with sweat, then with rainwater, now partially sun-dried, with some fresh sweat added to the mix. His hair was matted and his sneakers were soaked. He wheezed with every step.

Lisa said, "You poor thing!"

Kimmy said, "Daddy was telling us how the cart broke down."

Scott nodded animatedly, evidently both revived and re-stored to good spirits by however he had spent the past two hours. He said, "I was just telling them we figured it was either the battery or the alternator."

John blinked.

Scott said, "So? Which was it?"

"Alternator," John said dully.

"I had a feeling," Scott said. "Anyway, after you headed off to the clubhouse, a couple guys came by in their cart, saw me stranded out there. They'd seen the forecast and offered to take me back to their condo for cover, by the north end of the course. I had a cocktail at their place. Missed that storm by the skin of our teeth; rain started up the second we got to the condo. Anyway, we hung out for a while, then they ran me over here."

"I see," John said.

Alex said, "Daddy, did you get caught in the storm?" She was wearing a backwards baseball cap and stacking cheese cubes on a toothpick.

John said, "No, I made it to the clubhouse."

"Good," Scott said. "I'm relieved to hear it. Once those guys came for me, I thought about having them come for you too, in case you hadn't made it back, but figured you *had* to be close, you'd been gone so long, and I figured you were gonna wait out the storm in the clubhouse. I just hoped that *you* weren't worrying about *me*."

John said, "Not really."

Alex said, "We didn't get caught in the storm down at the beach, but it was close. We saw it coming and brought everything in like a split second before it started to lightning." She gripped a cheese cube with her lips.

John said, "Reckon I could use a shower," and he went in the direction of the door. He passed the grill, where many pieces of raw chicken coated with an orange dry rub were laid out in neat rows.

From his seat, Scott said, "We've got dinner under control, don't worry about a thing. I just put the chicken on. It'll be ready"—he paused and turned to Lisa—"whaddaya think, hon? 'Bout ten minutes?"

Lisa was replenishing the cheese plate for the children. Her eyes darted to Scott with a look of annoyance. "The coals are barely even warm yet. I don't know why you wanted to put it on already. It's gonna be at least an hour."

"Alrighty, then." Scott shrugged helplessly.

Kimmy said, "Daddy, you're stupid!"

This made Rae laugh, and Kimmy was so pleased by this slight affirmation from her older sister that she said it again: "Daddy, you are stupid!"

Ryan and Alex shared a nervous glance, unfamiliar with the Daly family dynamic and what sort of consequences might result from Kimmy's teasing. But Scott appeared to be completely accustomed to this sort. He turned to John and said, "What did I tell you?," as though they had spent all afternoon commiserating about the abuses of their children.

Kimmy looked like she desperately wanted to say it a third time, but she managed to restrain herself.

They lit citronella candles when the bugs came out, set up a boom box on the deck, and listened to Steely Dan as they ate.

Midway through the meal, Scott tipped his chin in Ryan's direction and said, "Alright, kid, so what's this I hear about a fake moon?"

"What about it?"

Scott buttered his bread slowly, perfect as a painter, catching every corner. "Your mom was saying you're big into conspiracies and junk." He took a bite of his bread, washed it down with yet another generous swallow of whiskey. He now had an empty wine glass, empty beer bottle, and half-empty tumbler of whiskey sitting on the table before him.

"Not junk," Lisa interjected. "Personally I find it fascinating." She smiled broadly at Ryan.

Scott snorted. "Fake moon, schmake schmoon."

Ryan was unaffected. "I like reading about that stuff," he said pleasantly.

Kimmy piped up, "Fake moon?"

Scott gestured toward Ryan with his thumb and spoke with a full mouth. "Einstein here"—he coughed into his fist —"thinks the moon is a hologram." A large bread crumb had attached itself to his goatee.

"I think it's *possible,*" Ryan said. "True or not, I like thinking about possibilities."

Lisa said, "I do too."

"Well, isn't that nice," Scott said. The crumb was still in the goatee. It trembled when he spoke but did not fall.

Poppy regretted that she'd brought up Ryan's conspiracy theories earlier—she certainly hadn't anticipated that Scott would use this as a source of mockery. It didn't help that Lisa was falling all over herself with interest. Poppy suspected

Lisa was just playing this up to maximize Scott's irritation, but who knew?

"Kids and conspiracies, man," Scott said. "I imagine you're a fan of that freaky Manson guy too."

Ryan said, "Huh?"

"That singer," Scott said, "who all the kids are into. The one with the white eyeball who takes his wiener out on-stage."

Kimmy said, "Gah-ross." She stuffed her index fingers into her ears.

The sound of Kimmy's voice seemed to have an immediate softening effect on Scott, even in his drunken agitation. He reached across the table to rumple her hair fondly. "You're right," he said. "Gah-ross."

"Oh." Ryan laughed. "Marilyn Manson. I don't care for his music. Guy's got some interesting politics, though."

"Figures."

Kimmy said, "Who would've made the moon, if it's fake? Why?"

Poppy tried to save Ryan. "We don't have to go down this path," she said, sending around the large bowl of sliced watermelon for the third time. "Let's talk about the weather instead."

But Alex was ready to jump in, having heard her brother's spiel at home before. "The government," she explained to Kimmy.

"The government! How come?"

Scott leered toward Ryan. "*Yeah.* How come?"

Ryan accepted a slice of watermelon. "Some people think

that the moon has been eroded in some way, or inhabited, or severely altered in appearance by extraterrestrials, and the government put a hologram in place to avoid mass panic on earth."

Kimmy said, "So there are aliens and the government knows, but they don't want us to know."

Ryan said, "It's just somebody's idea." He spat a watermelon seed onto his plate.

"It's a bunch of bull is what it is," Scott said, leaning back in his chair, gripping the tumbler with both hands as though using it to warm himself. "Kimmers, you keep listening to what they teach you in your classes at school. You can leave all the crazy ideas to all the crazy people."

John had been watching all of this quietly, and he exchanged a look with Poppy indicating that it would be best if someone else shut Scott up before he had to.

Poppy got the gist, but Lisa beat her to it. Lisa rose from her chair, went to Scott's, dug her thumbs into his shoulders, and said, "Let's go dish up ice cream."

He leaned forward. "Ow," he said. "That's no massage."

Lisa leaned in to pluck the crumb from his goatee, and Scott looked deeply offended, as though he'd put it there deliberately and she'd messed up the plan.

"Scott . . . now," Lisa said.

He followed when she gave him a severe look.

Lisa pulled the glass door shut behind them, but Poppy could still hear the crescendo of a fight in the kitchen.

Rae rolled her eyes like this was nothing new.

Kimmy turned back to Ryan. "Do you think the government is brainwashing us?"

Ryan cleaned the remaining melon from the rind, all the way down to white. "Could be," he said. He swatted a mosquito on his knee.

Kimmy said, "Like they're sending messages into our brains right now, like, *beep-boop-beep,* and we don't even know it? Like . . ." Kimmy's face radiated with possibility. "The government just made me say that, and they're making me say this . . . and this . . . and this . . ."

Alex said, "And they're making me say . . . this."

Kimmy was enthralled. "And me, say this!"

Poppy was relieved that this topic had already trumped any potential interest in the conflict indoors.

"We wouldn't even *know* if they were brainwashing us," Kimmy said, "so we definitely wouldn't know how to stop them."

Ryan said, "Some people think there's a way."

"To stop yourself from being brainwashed?" Kimmy said.

Ryan nodded.

"Well, what the heck is it?"

"If the government is sending things to our brainwaves electromagnetically, some people think you can stop them by putting tinfoil over your head."

Kimmy's nose wrinkled. "Really? Like make a little hat out of it?"

Ryan nodded. "Haven't you ever seen that in the movies?"

Kimmy looked at Alex. "We should do that, so the government stops making us think stuff and say stuff."

Poppy rose from her seat. "Let me go check on the ice cream, and I'll look into some tinfoil while I'm in there."

Inside, Lisa was dishing up ice cream and Scott was nowhere in sight.

Poppy said, "Did you send him to bed without dessert?"

"He didn't put up much of a fight," Lisa said wearily. "Pop, I'm sorry about him going after Ryan like that. I don't know what crawled up his butt. He looks sunburned, I imagine he's dehydrated, the whiskey went straight to his head. He's annoying as hell when he's been drinking, but he's usually not a mean drunk."

Poppy waved her hand dismissively. "It's nothing. Ryan's fine, takes a lot to ruffle his feathers. They're already on to something new out there. Tinfoil hats, matter of fact. Do we have some?"

"There's a roll in the drawer next to the sink."

Back outside, Ryan helped Kimmy and Alex fashion tinfoil hats while they all ate ice cream.

The sun had set, and the sky was a deep but electric blue with stars winking through, appearing to pulse at different rhythms.

Rae asked her mother, "Did you make Dad go to bed because he was being obnoxious?"

Lisa started to meander through a diplomatic answer about how tired he was, but Rae interrupted her: "Oh, save it." She ate a bite of ice cream and left her spoon dangling from her lips.

Kimmy tightened the point on the tip of her hat. "Daddy is one rude dude," she said.

Lisa took some pictures of Alex and Kimmy in their foil hats. Kimmy took hers off and tried to force it onto Rae's head, but Rae batted it away and smoothed her hair.

Eventually, Kimmy and Alex tired of the hats and crumpled them into little foil balls, which they flicked across the table into L-shaped finger goalposts.

Lisa and Poppy cleaned up the dinner dishes together, and Ryan announced that he was going to go for a night swim in the pool. He went to change into his swim trunks, and Kimmy turned to Alex. "We should have him teach us how to snorkel in the pool, since we kept getting ocean water down the pipes this afternoon," she said. "It'll be easier to learn without waves."

Alex agreed. The girls went to Ryan's bedroom and were surprised to find his door locked, so they bonked on the door and hollered in their request for snorkel gear.

Rae changed into her string bikini, which was made of spandex but designed to look like acid-washed denim. She met the others down at the pool and settled herself at the corner of it, on the second step of the entry point with the balance bar, so that she was submerged in water up to her chest but her hair remained dry. She sat cross-legged on the narrow stair.

The warm pool water was brightly illuminated from below, and chlorine steam lifted off the surface into the sultry night. The gentle churning of the ocean was faint, and a breeze glided through dry reeds. The air felt like a dangerous magic.

Ryan had two snorkels, and he was giving Kimmy and Alex their second lesson of the day, since their earlier attempt to learn in the choppy ocean had been disastrous. The girls giggled at each other's appearance in the full gear, goggles oversized and steamed up, the mouthpieces stretching their small mouths into cartoonish rectangles.

Ryan taught them how to paddle about, adjusting the pipe to the level and current of the water, to keep from getting a mouthful of it.

In the corner of the pool, Rae tipped her chin up to observe the sky and gazed in various directions, as though identifying constellations, thinking that Ryan would probably find this pose impressive. She recalled their conversation at the dinner table — fake moon, brainwashing. What was it that Ryan said he liked thinking about? Mysteries? She could be a mystery.

Alex and Kimmy slithered around the pool like bottom feeders, their ragged nervous breathing audible and mildly disturbing through the pipes.

Ryan dunked, then rose from the water and slicked his black hair back from his face. The golden lighting that rose from beneath the surface was majestic across his wet chest and face. He looked at Rae. "Is your swimsuit made out of jeans?"

"No," Rae said, her voice coming out shrill with nerves.

"It's just made to look like that. It's normal swimsuit material, see?" She snapped one of the spaghetti straps to demonstrate.

"Nice," Ryan said. "You wanna give the snorkel a shot once one of them's had their fill?"

"Oh, well . . ." Rae paused. "No, I've used one before, I already know how."

"Gotcha." Ryan dove back into the water.

This was not true—Rae had never snorkeled before—but she didn't want to put that goofy mask on her face, and she didn't particularly want to get her hair wet.

Ryan stayed underwater for quite a while, and when he reappeared at the surface, he slapped his chest, took a few heaving breaths, and said to Rae, "Do you know how long it's possible to hold your breath for?"

"Hmm." Rae pictured the tunnel her family had driven through that morning, with Kimmy insisting that everyone try to hold their breath for the entire length of it. Rae hadn't participated at all, Lisa gave up about ten seconds in, and Kimmy and Scott both claimed to have made it the whole way, gasping for air when the car emerged at the mouth of the tunnel and sunlight flooded them. Of course, it was obvious to Rae they had both cheated and breathed through their noses.

"Maybe two minutes?" Rae guessed.

"Times ten," Ryan said.

Rae stared at him. "Someone held their breath twenty minutes?"

Ryan nodded. "Twenty-one is the world record. They say

you pretty much train yourself to go to sleep, like hypnosis, to get yourself relaxed and your heart rate low enough."

"Wow," Rae marveled, pleased that Ryan had chosen to share this fact and this conversation with her and her alone, as Kimmy and Alex were still both fully submerged and out of earshot.

Rae thought quickly, grappling for a way to continue the conversation. She said, "I wonder if the guy with the record has lungs that are normal-sized, or if they grow when you do something like that." She thought this was an intelligent thing to wonder.

But before Ryan could respond, Kimmy, who had been looming closer and closer to Rae like a shark assessing its prey, suddenly burst to the surface. She spat the mouthpiece from her lips and yanked the goggles off. A deep pink ring surrounded her eye sockets and her lips were swollen.

"You just peed!" Kimmy shrieked at her sister, incredulous and full of glee. "I saw it!"

Rae's heartbeat surged. She felt heat flood her whole face. "No I didn't," she snapped. "I would never."

"I saw it!" Kimmy said. Water dripped from her hair to her bare shoulders. All her muscles were tight with the excitement of her discovery. "It was yellow and swirling like oil," she said, "and it came out from you and it was coming in my direction, like right *at* me!"

Rae tried to stay cool even as humiliation beat against her ribs like an animal. It was true, she had released a small stream into the pool. Who hadn't? Who didn't?

Rae said again, "I would never."

Kimmy turned to Ryan for validation, as Alex was still under the water. "I *saw* it," Kimmy said to Ryan. "Didn't you?"

Ryan wore a half-grin. He diplomatically offered, "It might've been me. It's so easy in the pool, just slips out sometimes."

Kimmy cocked her head to the side, eyes narrow, unconvinced. "I *really* thought I saw it come out from between Rae's legs," she said. "I was staring at Rae's knee when the yellow came out."

Ryan said, "It was probably my pee and just floated over that way." He gave Rae a nice soft look.

Rae tried to smile. Her ears felt full of something.

Ryan offered Kimmy a dopey shrug. "So I peed in the pool. Sue me!"

Kimmy laughed a little. She finally seemed satisfied with this explanation, albeit disappointed that the drama of her observation had so quickly dissolved upon Ryan's confession.

When Alex popped up to the surface a minute later, Kimmy said halfheartedly, "I saw your brother's pee in the water, it was floating toward me," and Alex giggled, but really all the fun was gone.

The two of them deposited their snorkels on the side of the pool and headed toward the deep end for somersaults. Ryan didn't initiate any more conversation with Rae, but contentedly stayed at her end of the pool and made sprays of water with his cupped fist.

Rae didn't know what to think. Could a boy like a girl who peed in the pool? Her mom wouldn't even pee in the same bathroom while her dad was taking a shower. Would Ryan go back to Wheeling and laugh with his friends about the girl in the swimsuit made of jeans who peed in the pool, right at her little sister's face? Oh God, Oh God. She would have to believe that Ryan was telling the truth, that he too had peed. The alternative — that he lied because he pitied Rae or couldn't bear her secondhand humiliation — was simply too awful to consider. *I hate my life,* Rae thought. Again and again she thought this.

John, Lisa, and Poppy were playing Spades inside, and once the children had changed out of swimwear and into pajamas, they joined for a few hands until John became too tired to continue.

Before dispersing for bed, they discussed plans for the next day.

John suggested a fishing trip; Barry had recommended a strip between Fripp and Pritchards Islands where someone had pulled in a bunch of flounder the other day. There were places where they could rent crab pots too, John said. Alex said she wanted to join him for that.

Lisa was hoping to check out the art gallery and maybe rent some bikes later in the week. She guessed that Scott would probably want to get another round of golf in.

Kimmy said, "Can I go into your room and put a tinfoil hat on Daddy while he's sleeping?"

Lisa said, "Let's just let Daddy sleep."

• • •

Scott was shirtless in bed, mouth agape, snoring lightly. The room smelled bad, of gas.

As Lisa got ready for bed, her thoughts turned to her conversation with Scott back in January when they had decided to invite John and Poppy on this vacation. She couldn't believe Scott had had the gall to accuse John of having a drinking problem. Scott had never once breathed a word of concern for any of his heavy-drinking friends, who frequently behaved as Scott had tonight; men in their forties and fifties egging each other on and drinking until they puked, a bunch of washed-up and depressing overage frat brothers. And *John* was the one with the problem? The hypocrisy was astounding. Of course, people were less inclined to toss the word "alcoholic" around when your drink of choice was twenty-five-year-old Scotch or a nice Bordeaux rather than Evan Williams or a forty. As in every facet of life, wealth wasn't only money, it was also protection, the benefit of the doubt. Anyway, Lisa couldn't tell Poppy what Scott had said about John back in January — Poppy would flip her shit. Better to save that anecdote for after the divorce.

Lisa brushed her teeth and leaned close to the mirror to examine a flaky bit of skin under her eye. Salt water always caused this. She spat into the sink and then applied cream to the dry spot.

She crawled into bed and squeezed foam plugs into her ears. She was a light sleeper, couldn't tolerate any noise from Scott. She faced away from him, toward the wall, which displayed a pastel watercolor painting of a gull standing at the water's edge, gazing stoically out at whitecaps and a pink sunrise or sunset. She closed her eyes.

Typically, Lisa loved this time of the day, when it was *over,* when there was officially no more that could possibly be accomplished or discussed. But tonight she found herself downright miserable in the silence of the room, with her own thoughts suddenly magnified. She realized she was feeling something she hadn't expected to feel on this trip: deeply, deeply sad. So sad, she was finding it difficult to breathe right. Her throat seemed too long or too narrow. She hadn't felt this sad and this far away from everything and everyone since the days following her mom's diagnosis. How could this be? She had thought that spending time with Poppy would be pure joy, that these days together would be a blissful reprieve from daily drudgery at home. But instead she was finding Poppy's radiant energy cruel in the way that it illuminated her own misery. Poppy was living a good life —that was undeniable. It wasn't a life that Lisa desired, at least not on its surface, not that husband or that home or that tax bracket. It was Poppy herself who had something that Lisa desperately wanted. Earlier, when she had asked Poppy if she ever imagined herself in another life, Poppy had said no without hesitation, almost incredulous at the question, as though it were rhetorical. This was what Lisa wanted most. She wanted to be so sure she was living the right life that that question seemed absurd. She wanted to stop feeling that somehow she'd gotten confused, fallen off course, and the right path forward had vanished altogether. She wanted to stop feeling like she was doomed, like all that lay before her were different wrong lives, and she was on the brink of committing herself to one of these *seriously* wrong lives for the rest of her days, leaving no possibility for escape or a redo. Lisa didn't want to feel that she was on the brink. She wanted to know that her life could be her home.

In their bedroom, Poppy changed into the old extra-large Mobil gas T-shirt of John's that she always slept in, and John lay in bed bare-chested, wearing only a pair of briefs with elastic that was frayed around the thighs. He had turned the TV on and was clicking absently through the channels. Eventually, he settled on *The X-Files*.

Poppy turned off the light and crawled into bed. The air conditioning was cranking, the room was cold. She watched Mulder poke at a skull with the tip of a pen. She said, "We've seen this one."

"Have we?" John handed her the remote.

Poppy said, "I wish I had more white clothing."

"Why?" John said, although he too had observed throughout the day that *everyone* on the island wore white. "You drop one pepperoni and the thing's ruined."

"Is that why we don't wear white?" Poppy said. "Because we drop pepperonis and they don't?"

John laughed. "No," he said. "It's because they can afford to replace everything they own, times ten, without a thought. Don't make any sense for us to buy things that can be ruined so easy."

"You're right," Poppy said. "Did you have a fun time golfing with Scott?"

"Guy's a self-centered loser," John said.

Poppy snickered. She propped up some pillows behind her so that she was elevated enough to comfortably watch TV.

John said, "I hope fishing's gonna get me out of golf for at least a day or two."

Poppy said, "Maybe his new friends from the north end of the course will invite him to go with them tomorrow."

"Wouldn't that be nice." John turned onto his side, facing Poppy, threw a heavy arm across her waist, and closed his eyes.

Poppy studied her husband's profile. His five-o'clock shadow, practically a full beard by this hour, was speckled with gray. He had a few curled dark hairs sprouting off the backs of his ears. One coming out of a small mole on his neck. Hair everywhere—he couldn't keep up with it, like trick candles on a birthday cake.

"Did you take your pills?" Poppy said.

"Mm."

Soon John's breathing became heavy. His fingertips fluttered.

Poppy watched TV for another hour and a half. When she started to doze off, she was awakened by footsteps in the hallway. Every room in the house had its own adjoining bathroom, so why would anyone have to be out wandering through the house? Maybe someone was up for a midnight snack. She was too sleepy to investigate. She turned off the TV, discarded the extra pillow from behind her, and snuggled into John. In his sleep, he made minor adjustments to his posture to accommodate her. Her bottom was tucked warm and tight against his crotch, his arm crossed up over her waist and chest, a comforting weight, a seat belt, and his nose pressed into the back of her neck. In the darkness, the cream-colored walls were gray, the blue curtains were gray, the green carpet was gray. Poppy formed herself into the curve of her husband's body and prayed the only thing she ever prayed, which was not so much a prayer as it was a threat.

When John went in for his back surgery a year earlier, he'd had an adverse reaction to the anesthesia. The doctors had quickly gotten it under control and he came out fine, but the scare was enough to rattle Poppy. Ever since and despite her best efforts, she was consumed by thoughts of her husband's death. It didn't help that he'd had such a tough go of it since the surgery, his continued pain a constant reminder of his mortality. If John had a bug bite on his neck, Poppy feared it was a tumor. If he scraped himself up at work, Poppy smeared the affected area with enough alcohol to sanitize a bullet wound. And now with the painkillers she had a whole new set of obsessions and concerns. John didn't fit the profile of high risk for addiction, but not all of them did. Poppy had been surprised by plenty of the people they knew at home who'd gone down that road. People with all the things you thought would insulate them, or at the very least help them rein it in: kids, church, newly renovated kitchens, committees, etc. You never knew. Well, anyway.

She trusted John with her life, but could you blame a wife for counting the pills in her husband's bottle each night, just to make sure?

The only thing that brought Poppy any measure of comfort when she was up in the night was addressing Death himself. *Don't you take him from me,* she admonished as she curled even tighter into her husband's big, warm, sleeping shape in that gray, artificially chilled bedroom. *Don't you dare take him from me.* See, Poppy didn't care when or how she went, so long as she was the first to go. This was her only demand. *Take me first.*

The basement bedroom was charming, with a white wicker chair that held several American dolls and some vintage copies of children's classics: *Peter Rabbit, The Rainbow Fish, Goodnight Moon.* There were two sets of sturdy bunk beds, the frames a striking dark-stained maple. Blue comforters. A box of Kleenex and two candles on the bed stand, one that smelled like cake, the other like fresh laundry.

Kimmy and Alex both opted for the bottom bunk. After this had been established, Alex had come up with the idea to remove the sheet from the top bunk and tuck one edge of it under the top mattress so that her bottom bunk was like the interior of a tent.

Kimmy immediately copied this idea. "I've always wanted a canopy bed," she exclaimed. "You are so smart."

Once the girls had been tucked in and were convinced the grown-ups were far from earshot, they got out of their beds, all toothpaste whispers and giggles, crept outside their bedroom and into the rec room, then up the stairs, slowly and quietly in case somebody was still awake in the main room, but no one was. The blue flashing light of a TV was on in John and Poppy's room, but that was the only sign of life.

The girls hadn't developed any sort of plan beyond "Let's sneak upstairs!" "Yes, let's!" "But we have to be careful in case anyone is still awake." "We can't get caught!"

But now that they were here, this space and everything in it held infinitely more intrigue than it had in the daytime. They snuck around the main room exploring, a need to touch everything, nighttime adrenaline surging. They wordlessly picked up coasters, set them across the coffee table in a nice pattern, collected and stacked them as they had been before. They drew fingers across all of the shelving, examined the dust they recovered. Lifted the cushions of the couch, sniffed beneath them, stifled giggles.

Eventually, the appeal of this activity was depleted and they returned to their bedroom. On the way, the girls were distracted by the fact that the TV was still on in Poppy and John's room, and so they failed to notice that, curiously, the light was now on in Ryan's bedroom, where it had been dark just a few minutes earlier.

Back downstairs, they crawled into their beds, tucked their canopy curtain flaps back so that they could see each other, and chattered happily in the dark. Kimmy said, "That was really fun."

Alex said, "I can't believe we didn't get caught, especially since my mom and dad are still awake watching TV."

"Would they have been mad if they caught us?" Kimmy said.

Alex thought. "Maybe a little."

Kimmy said, "I don't think my mom and dad would be too mad either. But it's still better that we didn't get caught."

It was quiet for a bit, then Alex said, "Maybe we should sneak outside tomorrow night. Not just out of our room, but like *outside* outside."

"Whoa . . . We would have to be really quiet and careful then," Kimmy said. "Because I think my parents would be really mad if they caught us sneaking *out*side."

"We could go out the rec room door down here," Alex said. "They wouldn't probably hear us then."

"You are so brave," Kimmy said. She lay on her stomach, facing Alex, the canopy sheet pulled back just enough for her to see across the room. Her eyes had adjusted to the darkness, and she could make out Alex's round head, wet teeth that gleamed.

"I think we should," Kimmy said. "Let's do it tomorrow night."

Alex said, "My dad keeps a flashlight in his tackle box. I'll try and steal it tomorrow morning when we go fishing, so you and me can have it for tomorrow night."

Kimmy said, "And my sister has that pair of really nice binoculars. I'll try to sneak into her room tomorrow sometime and get those for us too." Kimmy paused. "I'm not sure what we'd use them for, but it would be cool to have them with us when we sneak out."

"Good idea."

"It's a plan," Kimmy said, shifting her face to the very edge of her pillow, which was overly fluffed and practically suffocating her.

"It's a plan," Alex agreed, turning onto her left side, pulling her canopy flap down for the night, readying for sleep. Kimmy did the same.

After a bit, Kimmy said, "My dad's usually not so rude as he was tonight. He's actually a really nice dad. Even when my mom's pretty nasty to him, he's never mean back to her."

Alex said, "OK."

It was as quiet as a tomb for several minutes.

Eventually, Kimmy said, "I would shave my head like yours if my face was prettier," but there was no response.

7

KEATS WAS LATE getting in that night, and Roxie had fallen asleep on the couch, next to Leo. She wore a large Cleveland Browns T-shirt and nothing else. The TV was on but very quiet, one of those local channels that played around-the-clock community theater and talent show productions out of Beaufort. All the windows in their small apartment were open—they were trying to save on utilities—so the air was hot, heavy, strangely harder to breathe now than during the day, when the sun seemed to cut through it and open up the lungs. Roxie was perspiring in sleep and dreaming of thirst.

Keats entered the home quietly, expecting that Roxie would be asleep and hoping not to disturb her, but Leo startled to attention at Roxie's feet, the collar tinkled, the jaw muscles went tight. Leo emitted a cautionary rumble until he recognized that it was Keats.

Roxie yawned, sat up, and rubbed her eyes. Keats untied his work boots at the door, went to the kitchen sink, and washed his hands with dish soap.

Roxie kneaded Leo's haunches absently. "Time is it?" she rasped.

"Eleven thirty," Keats said. He opened the refrigerator and withdrew a Tupperware container of leftover lasagna. He brought this and a fork to the couch, where he took a seat next to Roxie.

She peered into the container. "That still good?"

"Smells fine."

"What kept you so late?"

Keats took a big bite and chewed slowly. "House on Greenmont I was telling you about?" he said. "Sewage backed up, shit all over the lawn. Had to drive into Beaufort to get the right part, then back a second time when the first one had the wrong attachment. Old pipes. Gotta have just the right connecting tube or it'll be backed up again in a week." Keats ate another large bite of cold lasagna, then licked ricotta from the fork. "How was your evening?"

In the far corner of the room the cricket started up. It had been in their apartment for weeks, although neither of them had set eyes on it. Its chirp was distinctive, uncharacteristically low-pitched, a loose whirring pattern that wheezed and swelled at the rate of human breathing.

"That darn thing," Roxie said. She combed through her glossy blond hair with her fingers, wincing when her wedding ring caught a tangle. "My evening was good. Took Leo out the pier before sundown, and I pulled in a good-sized mackerel, three or four pounds, using that new bar spinner."

"Nice. I haven't had any luck with that lure yet."

"He's out in the cooler whenever you wanna fillet him. It'll be fine for the night if you'd rather wait till tomorrow."

"I'll wait. So hot out, the guts'll stink to high heaven by dawn if I do it now. I'll do it in the morning, let the gulls carry off the scraps."

Roxie was quiet for a bit. "You OK?"

"Sure," Keats said.

"Lady from earlier isn't bothering you, is it?"

"Nah," Keats said. "Just tired."

It was hard to say which of them was more affected by interactions like he'd had with the red-haired woman that afternoon. It humiliated Keats and brought on some version of shame, but mercifully it evoked no sense of guilt whatsoever; he could still hold his head high because his conscience was clear. Roxie, on the other hand, shouldered a tremendous amount of unnecessary guilt. Even all these years later. Keats knew she put on a strong face for his sake, but the whole situation turned her heart to ash if she thought on it too long.

Keats reached over to squeeze her knee. "I'm just tired."

"That job tonight *did* take you awful long. I mean, you got the call, what, around three?"

Keats exhaled a long, whistling plume. "Yeah, round about then. Sometimes it drags out, you know how these people are, can't stand to have me out there hosing shit off their lawn while they sit down to dinner. Force a burger and a beer on me."

Roxie yawned again. "And yet you still come home hungry." She nodded at the Tupperware in his lap.

Keats grunted. "Bottomless pit."

"Anyway," Roxie said, her head lolling sleepily, "I need to get to bed. I'm trying to get a long run in early tomorrow."

After Roxie had left the room, Keats took his lasagna to the back window of their apartment, overlooking the ocean, and he stood there by himself, noticing the quiet corrugations of low tide and the wide beach stippled with large and small footprints. The brush decorating the landscape was still an awful mess since the storm that afternoon—big patches of it tangled in the fencing, brambles bundled together like tumbleweed, tough vines angled weirdly upright like broken black skeletons.

The cricket had gone silent for a minute or two, but now it started up again, purring and carrying on like a lovesick little buzz saw.

Roxie was fifteen years old when she first set foot on Fripp Island.

Vacationing with her parents on an exclusive and exotic island was no more or less miserable than living under the same roof with them in Boston for the rest of the year. Her mother was a drunk, and her father was a violent rageaholic. Both of her parents came from money, met at prep school, married at twenty-one. Roxie's father became a successful hedge-funder, and her mother worked several volunteer shifts a week in the accounting office of the Archdiocese of Boston. Roxie's parents despised each other and were dangerously addicted to their own dramas. Fights culminating in murderous threats and broken glassware were a regular occurrence. Roxie envied her classmates whose parents had gotten divorced and lived separately almost as much as she envied her classmates whose parents were happily married.

Keats's mother died of cancer when Keats was very young —he had no memory of her. His father, Joe Firestone, was the go-to handyman on Fripp Island, where he did jobs for half the homeowners. He worked hard and eventually saved enough money to afford a small, ramshackle cottage on the island, which smelled powerfully of cat piss and only had an outdoor shower. But after commuting to and from Beaufort for many years, actually living on the island was a dream come true.

Keats had been going to the public school in Beaufort, which was in walking distance from their home prior to the move, and he was working with his father only on the weekends. But once Joe bought the place on the island, it was wildly inconvenient for him to drive his fourteen-year-old son to school every morning, as no buses came to Fripp Island for pickups. For his whole life, Keats's only ambition was to work for his father; he had no desire to pursue anything outside of the family business. So one week into his eighth-grade year, he begged his father to allow him to drop out of school and work full time as Joe's right-hand guy. Joe agreed to this, on the condition that Keats would study from home to pass the GED, so that he would have the diploma should he need it down the line.

Once Keats was no longer in school, the two of them had time to renovate the cottage together, on top of the handyman work elsewhere on the island. They worked long, happy days together, sometimes on the same project if it required two sets of hands, and sometimes Joe would send his son out on house calls that he knew Keats would be able to manage on his own. Keats was capable, and a handsome and affable young man. He was quickly accepted by the homeowners' community. He and his father were known all across the island for their professionalism, friendly service, and reasonable rates.

Several years after Joe and Keats moved to Fripp Island, Keats met Roxie at a golf tournament. She was competing in the under-thirty women's division, and Keats was caddying for a woman whose toilet he had unclogged the day before. (Caddying was a great way to make a hundred bucks for a few hours of easy work, if his father didn't have other projects lined up for him.)

Wearing a T-shirt advertising an angry band, frayed denim cutoffs, and flip-flops displaying silver stacks of toe rings, Roxie looked like she hailed from a different planet than the other women on the course. She was also bored and playing terribly; she had by far the worst score of all the competing women. She struck up a conversation with Keats on the fifth hole, introducing herself and commenting on the humidity. He asked where she was from, and she said Boston. She asked if he'd been, and he said he'd never gone north of North Carolina or south of South Carolina. This stunned Roxie, who had been to Cancun and Hong Kong and the south of France and all over Europe three or four times, at least that many times to Hawaii, and she'd recently spent her birthday weekend in Key West, although she didn't mention any of this to him.

Keats said he liked how she had dyed the tips of her long blond hair blue. She said she used Kool-Aid to do it, and her mother kept threatening to cut it off in her sleep, like Samson and Delilah.

The two of them chatted in the sun and in the shade and then in the clubhouse when the tournament had ended.

Keats wasn't like the guys from Roxie's high school, who were all hair gel and dirty magazines and Lacoste polos. Keats had gentle eyes and a shy way of talking to her, head bowed and voice so soft, almost like he hoped she wouldn't catch every word.

He was eighteen years old at the time. He had never been on a date. Roxie was a sophomore in high school, and she'd had sex with two boyfriends, although neither of the relationships had lasted more than a month.

Roxie asked him which part of the beach he liked to hang out at, and at what time of day, and Keats described his favorite part of the island to her and said he was usually there around four o'clock in the afternoon, unless he was on a house call.

Roxie found him at his favorite spot at four o'clock the next day. He was throwing a tennis ball into the water for a little brown puppy to fetch. He waved when he spotted Roxie approaching, her rolled-up towel tucked under her arm. She wore a black bikini and round wire-rimmed sunglasses.

"Cute dog," she said.

Keats said, "His name's Leo."

They went for a swim together, then Roxie spread her towel out next to his. They chatted and laughed and tousled with Leo as the afternoon became evening.

Roxie was due back at her house for dinner with her parents at seven, but she said she'd try to come to the same beach at the same time tomorrow. She asked for Keats's phone number, and gave him hers.

The next day, they fished off Pritchards Island, scoped out some gators in the marsh near Gram's Diner, then got milk shakes.

The day after that, Keats was tied up with a house call until the evening, but he invited Roxie to join him for a fire on the beach around sunset.

On the final day of Roxie's vacation, her parents were registered to participate in a couples golf tournament, so she invited Keats to come to their house, where she wanted to make a few mixed drinks with her mom's gin while her parents were away.

Keats drank a beer or two with his dad now and then, but Joe drew the line at underage liquor, so Keats let Roxie mix up the drinks. Roxie said she had been doing this for years. They took their gin and tonics out to the pool and went for a swim. Keats told her he was pretty sure he'd replaced the pool filter at this house the previous summer. Roxie made him laugh with her impression of a dolphin, and they had a handstand competition.

She went to make a second round of drinks.

When she returned, Roxie said she was sad she had to leave the island the next day. She slipped into the water and blew bubbles to the surface. When she came back up, Keats said, "Me too."

After they had finished their cocktails, Roxie took his hand and led him out of the pool and inside, to her bedroom.

She hesitated for a moment, looking incredulous when he told her he'd never even kissed a girl. They couldn't go all the way, she said, because she didn't have condoms, but they could do other things.

Roxie's parents had gotten into it on the ninth hole at the tournament. Her mother went to the clubhouse and ordered a triple vodka soda, and her father stormed straight back to the house by himself.

He found Roxie and the maintenance boy in bed together, and Keats wasn't even one foot out the door before Roxie's father was on the phone with his attorney up in Boston, then with the local police department.

Despite Roxie's tears and rage and threats and protestations, her father moved forward with the statutory rape charge.

Joe Firestone put up his house as collateral in order to afford a decent attorney for his son's trial.

Keats was arrested and pled no contest, of course; Roxie was fifteen years old at the time of the incident, and he was eighteen.

He was given a light sentence on account of Roxie's refusal to participate in the trial, and after multiple appeals she made directly to the judge, attempts to intervene on Keats's behalf. Keats was able to avoid prison by agreeing to a stint on probation, and his name would be placed on the sex offender registry for eight years.

Joe Firestone was relieved that his son could avoid jail time, but he ended up losing the cottage as a result of the financial burden caused by the whole ordeal. Once the house was gone, the only affordable rental he could find on the island was a tiny loft apartment above the garage of a homeowner for whom they had worked for many years. It was too small for two grown men, but they made it work.

Business suffered. People looked at them differently.

A year or so later, before Keats had turned twenty, Joe was diagnosed with pancreatic cancer, and he was gone within months.

Roxie battled her father every step of the way. She wasn't able to prevent him from bringing charges against Keats, but she swiftly began the process of legally emancipating herself from her parents. She remained in touch with Keats in the time following the incident, despite a court order that they have no contact until she turned eighteen.

She begged Keats for his forgiveness long after he'd assured her that it wasn't necessary.

She loved him. Somehow, and she didn't know if she would ever be able to understand this fully or accept that she was deserving, but somehow, amid all of this, Keats had started to love her, and he kept on loving her too.

Roxie returned to Fripp Island midway through her senior year of high school, as soon as the legal emancipation process was complete. She didn't have her diploma or a penny to her name.

She moved into the loft with Keats and got a job at Gram's Diner.

They kept to themselves, knowing how people talked.

Keats didn't get nearly as many calls as he and his father had prior to the incident, but he still found a fair amount of work through a few loyal homeowners who gave him the benefit of the doubt, despite having heard the rumors. Between his handyman jobs and Roxie's tips from Gram's, they made enough to keep up with the rent on the loft, the utilities, groceries and food for Leo, and the occasional night out in Beaufort, and whatever was left they put into savings. Their goal was to have two thousand dollars saved by the time they left Fripp Island for good.

Roxie learned what sort of meals she could make for under five bucks for the two of them: spaghetti, bologna on Wonder Bread, casseroles of hamburger and potato. Fish and crab they caught themselves and ate with melted margarine, a slab off the brick-sized block of the cheap stuff, which was slick and yellow as an egg yolk. They ate ice cream that came in a bucket.

On days off together, they took Leo to the beach and went for swims and walks and napped in the sun. They crabbed and fished and retrieved recycling from all the condos, sorted through the glass bottles and aluminum cans and took them to the collection site at the Piggly Wiggly in Ashby, where they would get fifteen cents for every recyclable. In the evenings, they played Cribbage and Spider Solitaire; they watched sitcoms on a tiny rabbit-eared television set and sunsets from the deck.

Keats eventually proposed marriage with the engagement ring his mother had worn—his father had kept it for all the years since her death—and they were married one October afternoon at a courthouse in Beaufort.

They intended to leave Fripp Island as soon as Keats's time on the registry had expired. They were eager to go, but if they were to move while he was still listed, they would be required to alert all their new neighbors to his status, which would of course contaminate relationships in any new community. So the plan was to head south with as many of their possessions as they could pack into Keats's truck as soon as his time on the registry was up. They had a few small fishing towns picked out on the coast of Georgia, where they thought they could happily start a new life.

Five months. Assuming the paperwork went through, they would be in Georgia by Christmas.

8

POPPY WOKE AT five o'clock the next morning, when the air was still blackish blue and certainly not cool, but not yet hot. She shuffled to the closet for her running shoes and sports bra, dressed quietly so as not to disturb John, and went down to the kitchen. She boiled water on the stove and stirred in a spoonful of instant coffee, just like she did every morning at home. She had noted yesterday that the house contained a French press and an espresso maker, but she preferred her instant. Better flavor. She didn't care what anybody said.

When she stepped out onto the back patio to do her stretches, she noticed a set of footprints in the sand leading from the house to the beach. She did not see a return set of prints. It entered her mind that Scott, in midlife-crisis mode, might have gone skinny-dipping, and she decided not to follow the footprints to investigate.

She drank her coffee, walked around to the front of the house, and out to the street, where she took a left. She planned to go to the tip of the island and back, a two-mile circuit.

Cicadas buzzed and air-conditioning units roared. The air smelled of fish and gasoline and sweet blossoms. *Poom-poom-poom-poom-poom,* her tennis shoes padded softly along the footpath. She passed gorgeous modern condominiums with entire walls of glass. Sprawling plantation-style homes with white-pillared porches and immaculate lawns that looked too good to be real, surrounded by sand and scraggly brush. Every tenth house, it seemed, was not a mansion but a small shanty with a beat-to-hell roof and pastel wooden signs stuck crookedly into the ground near the entrance, messages like *Seas the Day* and *Peace, Love, and Sandy Feet.*

Poppy stopped to cough into a fist. The humidity down here, even at this early hour, felt like it was about a thousand percent. She glanced at her watch; somehow she was keeping a good ten-minute-per-mile pace. She carried on down the path, enjoying glimpses of ocean between the houses. The sunrise was still at least half an hour away, but the world was slowly awakening to its presence, the sky going navy overhead, rosy at the horizon, stars retreating. She admired the palmetto trees, hardwood live oaks, magnolias, some barkless species that she didn't recognize.

A huge gray teardrop of a wasp nest was attached to a nearby telephone pole. Poppy would have liked to suit up and take an industrial-sized can of Raid and a baseball bat to it, like a piñata. She loved an excuse to be merciless.

Soon she had to stop again. She coughed and wiped a thick film of sweat from her face with the hem of her shirt. She stretched her muscles. *Damn,* this humidity was really doing a number. Her lungs tickled like the dickens and she couldn't seem to get a good breath in or a good one out. She guessed she had about a half-mile to go to her intended destination, so she decided to power through until she had gotten at least that far. She'd walk some of the way back if she had to.

Poppy jogged a quarter of a mile and noticed a parking lot up ahead next to a small, ramshackle blue building with a sign out front that she couldn't yet read from this distance. When she sniffed the air, the wonderful aroma of breakfast reached her. Bacon and coffee and maple syrup. She drew closer and saw that the sign read *Gram's Diner* in pale green cursive. Several cars and golf carts were parked in the lot. Poppy sniffed the air greedily; sugar, coffee, and fat.

She had to slow to a walk again by the time she actually reached Gram's. The humidity was too much. She was drenched with sweat, her breath was shallow. A terrible throbbing cramp was spreading through her belly.

She paused in front of the restaurant and peered absently into the windows at the sweet and cozy-looking scene within. Most of the patrons at this early hour were locals, Poppy gathered; tanned to jerky, with mounds of bleached yellowy hair bundled into unruly ponytails or contained beneath faded pastel caps. Most of them were elderly, although there was also a table of young surfers who were eating eggs in their wetsuits.

A voice to Poppy's left, from the side of the restaurant, startled her.

"You worked up quite a sweat," a woman's voice said. "Need a glass of water?"

Poppy turned. The woman was leaning against the building, smoking a cigarette, and wearing a teal skirted apron over denim shorts and a T-shirt. She was thin, young, early to mid-twenties, very pretty. Large, pale blue eyes. Glossy blond hair pulled into a long, loose braid. She waved her cigarette in the general direction of the entrance. "Just go in and ask. They don't bite." She smiled. Her teeth were too straight and too white, like too much money had been spent on them.

Poppy coughed and wiped sweat from her face with the collar of her T-shirt. "No water necessary," she said. "I just wasn't prepared for the humidity. Hell, it's *nasty* out here."

"Takes some getting used to. I grew up in Massachusetts, so I know how it is when you're not accustomed. You from up north?"

"West Virginia," Poppy said. "So . . . sort of."

The young woman took a long drag from the cigarette.

"Massachusetts, you said? You're a long way from home, then," Poppy said.

"This is home now," the woman said. She tap-tap-tapped a bit of ash from her cigarette, then stared silently at the beach for a long moment.

Gathering that the girl didn't wish to offer more on the topic of home, Poppy gestured toward the inside of the restaurant and said, "You work in there?"

The girl nodded. "Roxie, by the way." She put the cigarette back in her mouth, wiped her hand on the apron, and extended it to Poppy.

"Poppy." As she shook the girl's hand, a great, ticklish outburst rose from her lungs and she had to step back and cough harshly.

"You sure I can't get you anything?" Roxie said, her young face creased with concern. She patted Poppy's sweating shoulder. "You're welcome to come on in and sit in front of a fan for a minute. I'm a runner too. Same exact thing happened to me first time I tried to go for a run down here. I gave up a mile in."

Poppy coughed again. "So'd you give it up for good, then?"

"No," Roxie said. "I still go couple mornings a week, when I'm not working. You just need to stick with it, the body adjusts to the humidity. But you look like you should at least sit down for a minute, take a rest."

"Actually," Poppy said, taking a breath in through her nose to settle her lungs, then lowering her voice, "if you can keep a secret . . ."

Roxie's eyebrows arched.

Poppy nodded down toward Roxie's hand. "I quit cold turkey when I got pregnant with my first, eighteen years ago, but I still sneak one now and then when I know I can get away with it. My husband would kill me. But I swear, nothing sets me straight like a cigarette."

Roxie laughed and passed the cigarette Poppy's way.

Poppy raised it to her lips. She pulled long and hard on

the Camel. Her eyes rolled back and she moaned deep and low with pleasure. Then she released a slow stream of white smoke through her nostrils, savoring the tidy thrum of the nicotine, the way it set her whole body right. Hell, the whole world.

Poppy made a move to return the cigarette to Roxie, who said, "Nope, that's all for you. You earned it. You enjoy that."

Poppy took another drag and gazed out into the gray-blue morning. "Sorry to interrupt your break *and* hijack your cigarette."

Roxie said, "I'd take your company any day over the creeps who interrupt my break to talk my ear off about how far under par they were yesterday." She paused to stick her tongue out the side of her mouth. "Sleazy rich losers. They're *relentless*."

"Gross," Poppy said. "I used to work at a restaurant. I know the type."

Roxie tossed her golden braid over her shoulder and glanced at her watch. "Time for me to head back in," she said. "Take it easy out there, OK? Don't overdo it."

Poppy said, "Reckon I'll be walking most of the rest of it. Thanks again for the cigarette."

"Anytime."

Poppy looked back into the diner, a charming scene with checkered tablecloths, framed photographs of fish and sailboats and beaches and sunsets, and old-fashioned stainless-steel napkin dispensers and sugar jars on every table. She thought perhaps she'd bring John for breakfast tomorrow morning, request Roxie for their server so they could leave her a generous tip. She and Roxie might share a fun moment or a wink as they told John how they had met this morning while Poppy was out for a run, but they would deliberately leave out the part about the cigarette.

Poppy always got a warm, happy, and hopeful feeling when she was around young women who worked in restaurants. It made her feel like the world really didn't change all that much, that life was still good, people were still alright. There was still a lot to recognize and like in one another. She left the diner and made her way up the street to her intended destination, where she paused to stretch against the coin-operated binoculars that faced the beach.

Seagulls dove and stabbed at things in the water. There was a decent swell, and she imagined the surfers would be out there riding it at any moment. She listened to grunts and the ping of rackets from nearby tennis courts. The sun was beginning to rise over the water, the tiniest sliver of gold appearing at the horizon, the brightness of it violent against the dark and distant ocean. She enjoyed this view for a bit, the gold swelling and appearing to pulse against the sea as the sun worked its way up and out, gradually setting the horizon on fire.

Then she headed back toward the house, jogging for short intervals, the stomach cramp finally shaking loose, her body finally feeling strong.

With Roxie's indictment of "sleazy rich losers" on her mind, Poppy's thoughts turned to what Lisa had said yesterday about the likelihood that Scott was having an affair. Just when they were coming up on their twentieth anniversary and everything. It made Poppy hot and queasy with spite.

When they were teenagers, Poppy had been the one the boys flocked to, with boobs already in the eighth grade, the big hair and big personality, the naughty jokes. Lisa was her awkward sidekick, gangly and pale, taller than all the boys in the class, which was such a humiliation that she experimented with a hundred different postures to conceal her height, until she pinched a nerve in her neck. But within months of graduating from high school, Lisa began to appreciate her long legs and show them off with short shorts and miniskirts. She developed curves and learned how to apply makeup that suited her green eyes and pale complexion.

Poppy and Lisa started dating John and Scott around the same time.

John was part of the small crew hired to renovate the patio of Luigi's, where Poppy and Lisa waited tables. The project only took a month, but in that time John became friendly with the restaurant staff, who would bring him lemonade and garlic bread when they could sneak it without the manager noticing.

John had dropped out of high school several years earlier, when his father died and his mother spiraled into depression. John was already working construction in the summertime, and his grades were not good enough to propel him into any other field, so he left school in order to support his mother until she was able to get back on her feet. That never really happened, so John never returned to school and never left construction.

Poppy asked him out on a date as the renovation project at Luigi's was wrapping up. She liked his crooked, pinched-off smile and gentle eyes. She said, "So are you going to take me out to dinner or what?" He stared at her like she'd just asked if he wanted to go to Mars. She said, "Good God, that's a look! You're about to offend me. So sleep on it, then. I get off around eight tomorrow."

John was waiting in the parking lot the next night at 7:45. He wore khaki pants and an ill-fitting jacket over a flannel shirt. They went to dinner at the Half Moon Diner, spent four hours there, and then kissed outside her house.

Soon things got hot and heavy, but John didn't want to go all the way and sleep together until they were married, because his parents had raised him that way. When Poppy learned this, a few more dates in, she proposed on the spot. They got married at the courthouse two weeks later. Everyone said they were acting like total maniacs except for Lisa, who knew Poppy better than anyone.

For their honeymoon, they spent one night at a cottage on Middle Creek Lake. They picked up groceries on their way to the cottage, and John stunned Poppy that evening by roasting a chicken. He explained that he had been doing the cooking at home since his mom had lost the will to look after herself.

Poppy was John's first. John was Poppy's . . . well, who was counting? John didn't seem to give a shit. Poppy was prepared to tell, but she was relieved when it was apparent that John wasn't going to press her for a number.

She got up early the next morning to make him breakfast, eager to impress her new husband, especially after his masterpiece the night before. She had never cooked an actual meal in her life, outside of cereal and toast and powdered macaroni and cheese from a box.

Thirty minutes later, she delivered John a rubbery, grayish omelet the size of a pizza, on a serving platter meant for hors d'oeuvres.

"Good Lord!" he exclaimed, sitting upright in bed. "What'd you do, use all dozen eggs?"

Poppy nodded. All she wore were knee-high blue socks and a greasy dish towel slung over her shoulder. The omelet teetered precariously toward John and he recoiled.

"Is that . . ." John stared at the thing. "Why does it smell like . . . did you put cinnamon in it?"

"Like a special pancake."

John laughed uncontrollably while Poppy sputtered angrily like a steaming teapot. Her nipples were bright and erect, pubic hair matted sideways like a crooked toupee, goosebumps covering her bare arms. "Well, if you're just going to sit there laughing at me while this beautiful breakfast gets *cold* . . ."

John took the omelet from her and set it on the bed stand, then he pulled her back into bed.

Scott had become a regular customer at Luigi's during his years in law school at Wheeling University. He usually went to the restaurant with two or three of his buddies, and they would sit at the bar drinking Peronis and watching sports on the TV. He started chatting up Lisa one day, dazzled by her beauty and small-town naïveté. Scott was in his final year of law school and almost thirty at the time; he had worked in sales for several years before deciding to pursue law. For their first date, he took her to his campus, where they walked around and he showed her the buildings where he went to class and the small cathedral where he attended mass, then they went to dinner at the only French restaurant in Wheeling. As soon as Scott passed the bar and received an offer from Raslowe & Associates, he and Lisa became engaged and moved up to Warrenton, just outside of D.C., where they had lived ever since.

Their relationship made perfect sense. Despite her humble upbringing, Lisa had always had a taste for the finer things. She lusted after the clothes she saw on soap operas and the handbags that the wealthy college students carried around. She tried to eliminate the distinctly West Virginia aspects of her Southern accent. Lisa always knew she was going to end up with money. It was never a question of *if,* just a question of *when* and *who.*

In the months leading up to their wedding, Lisa converted to Catholicism in order to appease Scott and his parents and so that the priest at Scott's home church could officiate. Baptism, first communion, confirmation, the whole she-bang. Lisa privately found the whole process ridiculous and humiliating—taking classes alongside eight-year-olds, pretending she cared to know the difference between schisms and the sacraments — but for Scott's sake she fulfilled these requirements without complaint.

Their reception was a lavish affair at the country club Scott's parents belonged to. Poppy got rip-roaring drunk, picked a fight with the DJ, and wore Lisa's garter around her own head for a while. Lisa thought it was all a gas, but Scott's mother was appalled and insisted on calling a cab for John and Poppy, back to the Super 8 where they were spending the night. Scott's mother said to John, "The Super 8? You didn't get a room at the Plaza? We got the special rate and everything, specifically —" She cut herself off, but the meaning was clear: *We got the special rate specifically for people like you.*

John said, "We're just fine, thanks, ma'am," and he refused the twenty that she tried to stuff in his palm for the cab when it approached. Poppy was loudly whisper-slurring, "What are you doing? John, take that money! John —" as he ushered her into the car.

Scott and Lisa honeymooned in Cancun.

Lisa called Poppy on the second day and complained of the affected accent that Scott put on when speaking to the hotel staff and the sycophantic way he asked for a blow job. Poppy was snorting with laughter until she heard tears in Lisa's voice.

"Oh, no," Poppy said. "I thought you were joking. But it can't be *that* bad, right? You're jet-lagged."

Lisa sniffed. "You're right, I'm just in a funk."

Poppy said, "Have a margarita and take a nap." She paused, then lowered her voice. "And if it *is* that bad, well, listen, I'm sure it's not too late to get it annulled. You've got options."

It was a shaky start, but things settled down after the honeymoon.

Things were quite good for a while, actually. Scott and Lisa did a lot of traveling over the next few years. Lisa got into yoga and organic cooking and expensive skin-care lines from the Home Shopping Network. Then she got pregnant.

And now, somehow, both couples were approaching their twentieth anniversaries. *Twenty years?* Amazing how time could slither away from you, that sly bastard. Blink and a year is gone. Get a good night's sleep and when you wake your kids are half grown.

Back at the house, Poppy was surprised to find Rae awake —it wasn't yet six thirty. Rae was seated on a barstool at the kitchen island. She was still wearing her yellow pajamas, but her hair looked neat and combed-through, her face bright, possibly a little makeup, features wide awake as though she had been up for hours. She was drinking coffee and reading from the same novel she'd had on the beach the day before.

Poppy said, *"Hola."*

Rae said, "Hi."

Poppy knelt. She removed one shoe. It stank, so she put it back on, loosened all the laces, and shuffled around with untied shoes. She poured herself a glass of water.

"You're an early bird for a teenager," Poppy observed.

"My kid would sleep till noon if I'd allow it. You drink black coffee?"

Rae nodded. "But my mom makes me do half-decaf."

"I see," Poppy said. She caught a glimpse of her own reflection in the toaster. Hair huge, a clown's wig, sprung free from the rubber band and bobby pins. Face still red with exertion and slick with sweat, she observed, "I look like I escaped from a mental institution." She hoped this would elicit a giggle from Rae, but it did not. She fluffed her hair up even bigger. "Cavewoman?"

Rae tented her book on the counter before her, tucked her hair behind her ear, and said, "You smell like smoke."

An ice cube slid into Poppy's mouth and she crunched it. "You don't miss much, do ya?"

"Do you smoke cigs?"

Poppy gazed at Rae. "On rare occasions. I bummed one from a nice young lady up the road. My lungs were giving me hell."

Rae said, "Do Ryan and Alex know you smoke?"

"No," Poppy said. "And neither does John. So let's keep this between you and me, missy."

Rae smiled, sly like a cat.

"I'm serious," Poppy said. "John finds out I'm still smoking cigarettes, it'll be . . ." Poppy stretched her lips wide over her teeth and drew her thumb across her neck.

Rae was still smiling. "Do you guys fight?"

"Me and John?"

Rae nodded.

"Everybody fights with the people they live with. They're the ones whose shits you gotta smell."

Rae laughed, finally, and Poppy felt she deserved a prize. But a moment later Rae's face darkened and slipped into something far away.

Poppy said, "Your mom says you're big into horses."

Rae nodded.

"Now tell me the truth," Poppy said. "Are you more into the horses, or the cute guy who wears the tight pants and gives riding lessons?"

Rae stared at her. "My mom told you about Lucas? Oh my *God*. That figures."

"Hah, I gotcha," Poppy said. "No, she didn't tell me anything about anybody."

"Oh." It took Rae a moment to decide how to respond to this. Lucas was sort of cute, nothing like Ryan, though. Lucas was pale and skinny as spaghetti. And for that matter, Rae was pretty sure Lucas was into the Korean girl who rode the Appaloosa named Strudel. Rae didn't really give two hoots about who Lucas was into, but it *was* annoying when someone whose league you were out of didn't pay you any attention at all, like you were totally useless, a lost cause. Well, anyhow, she didn't figure Poppy needed to know any of this, so she said, "Lucas is gay."

Poppy clucked her tongue.

Rae slid off the stool to refill her coffee. Her toenails were painted fire-engine red, so neatly done that Poppy wondered if it was a professional pedicure.

Poppy dampened a dishcloth with cold water and held it

to her forehead. "Humidity'll kill ya out there," she said. She decided she would have something to eat, wash her hands, and brush her teeth a second time, before John woke, so that he wouldn't smell cigarette on her. She took a banana from the large wicker bowl that Lisa had filled with fruit, and peeled it. Rae took her coffee back to the island counter and returned to her book.

Poppy sniffed her fingers to make sure the banana overpowered the cigarette.

Rae sipped her black half-decaf coffee and curled her red toenails around the legs of the barstool.

In Ryan's bedroom, his heart was still slamming against his chest as he set his backpack at the foot of the bed, brushed sand from his legs and feet, and removed his T-shirt. *Christ Almighty!* This was way too much adrenaline for six o'clock in the morning. His mom had nearly scared him shitless when ten minutes earlier he'd caught a glimpse of Poppy finishing up her run and approaching the house. Ryan was coming in from the beach, so was on the opposite side of the house from Poppy, but he happened to see her out on the sidewalk. He stopped dead in his tracks in the side parking area, completely still so as not to attract her peripheral attention, until she was out of view. Once he was confident that Poppy was inside, Ryan swiftly entered the house using the lower-level entrance in the rec room down by the pool, which he had left unlocked. Inside, he crossed through the rec room, used the back stairway to make his way up to the bedroom level, and waited out of sight until he heard voices in the kitchen—his mother and Rae—before making a fast break for his bedroom.

In the safety of his bedroom, Ryan sat on the end of his bed and panted. He knew his mother went for early-morning runs at home, but hadn't imagined she would keep up the routine here. It hadn't even occurred to him.

The sweat at Ryan's underarms became cold and crispy in the overly air-conditioned room. He shivered.

Of course, if Poppy *had* seen him, he probably could have talked his way out of the situation by claiming he was down at the beach enjoying the sunrise by himself. But it was so unlike him to be up early in the morning that Poppy might have demanded more information. She might have searched his backpack. She might have asked Rae if she had seen Ryan coming or going or knew what he was up to.

Lisa scrambled eggs and fried sausage links and toasted white bread for breakfast. Everyone filled their plates and ate on their own time. The *Today* show was on in the main room that connected to the kitchen. Katie Couric marveled about a pig that saved its owner by running up the street for help when the man collapsed in his yard, and Al Roker went on about the heat wave in the Southwest. A newspaper had appeared on the front porch during Poppy's run and was now fully dismembered. Lisa brewed more coffee and prepared a second package of sausage links.

Poppy went to Ryan's bedroom to wake him—at eight-thirty, when he was the only one yet to make an appearance.

He was still sleeping, shirtless, arm flung over his face to block the sunlight.

Poppy pinched his earlobe and said, "You need to put sunscreen on the top of your ears today."

Ryan opened one sleepy, small eye at her.

"Rise and shine," Poppy said. "Everybody else is up and hanging out." She ruffled his hair. Ryan had Poppy's hair. Black and coarse, the texture of steel wool, and it seemed to radiate heat. It wasn't worth trying to comb or keep up with hair like this after one day on the beach; just cram it under a hat or pull it into a ponytail and leave it until the end of the week, then expect to use a bottle of conditioner and rip out knots the size of mice.

Ryan swatted his mother away gently.

"What'd you do," Poppy said, "stay up watching the sci-fi channel till two o'clock in the morning?" She looked over at his dresser, where the dead crab from yesterday was floating in bright blue liquid, in a juice glass from the kitchen. "Speaking of which, what'd you find out about your crab fungus?" she said. "Cure for cancer?"

Ryan chuckled and sat up in bed. He rubbed a hand over his bare chest, which was already deeply tanned from one day in the sun. He had more hair than Poppy remembered.

She nodded toward the crab and said, "*Please* throw that thing away before it starts to stink, ya weirdo."

Ryan made a move for his towel and toothbrush.

Poppy said, "You want eggs and sausage and toast?"

"Please and thank you," Ryan said over his shoulder.

Back in the kitchen, Poppy and John loaded the dishwasher. John commented to Lisa how much he had enjoyed the coffee, and Poppy, who only ever made instant at home, acted offended. Lisa said she had been getting her coffee from the same organic beanery in their area for years—she was hooked on the stuff, convinced it was the best around. The guy who ran the beanery had lived in Maui and worked on a coffee plantation for ten years.

From across the room, Scott piped up, "Guy's a con artist. I saw him at Walmart once with a whole cartful of Folgers."

Poppy said, "Really?"

Lisa giggled. "Scott likes to give me grief about my organic this-or-that." She seemed genuinely amused by Scott's accusation, and it pleased Poppy to see the two of them bantering good-naturedly this morning.

Together they talked over their plans for the day.

John and Alex would leave soon for the bait shop, then head directly to the pier out by Pritchards Island, where Barry, from the golf course, had talked up the fishing. Lisa and her girls planned to check out an art gallery when the place opened at ten, then make their way down to the beach. Poppy and Ryan would go to the beach first thing—both were eager for a swim.

Scott was just announcing that he might come to the beach for a few hours, then go to the driving range after lunch, when the house phone rang.

Poppy startled and leapt to answer it, but Scott was closer and got there first.

Scott was cheery and familiar with the caller, offering an

occasional "Sure thing!" and "You bet!" He glanced at others in the room as he carried on the conversation.

When the call ended, Lisa said, "Who was that?"

Scott explained that yesterday he had exchanged phone numbers with the guys he met on the golf course, and one of them was calling to invite him to join their round of golf.

Lisa said, "Fine by me."

Poppy said, "Fine by me."

Scott looked around the room. "No one's gonna beg me not to go? Really? Well, then I guess I'll go."

Rae said irritably, "Why don't you quit talking about it and just go, then."

Kimmy sang, "Go away, Daddy! Shoo-shoo, fly away!"

Scott said, "You girls are harsh." He threw a balled-up napkin across the room at his daughters. Rae ignored it completely. Kimmy picked up the napkin, tightened it between her palms, and hurled it back.

Scott put it in the garbage, then went to his room to gather his things.

9

ALEX'S WILLINGNESS TO bait her own hook and the technique she employed had always impressed John. He recalled his own squeamishness when he was a kid, didn't reckon he'd done it himself until he was in his early teens. That was around the time he had started hunting with his own father, too. John had cried when he made his first kill, a squirrel with a .22, and his father told him it was OK, that if you *didn't* feel something the first time, there was probably something wrong with your head.

Even after John had killed a few turkeys, a rabbit, and a buck, there was still something about baiting a hook that could make his stomach go a little undone. Actually *feeling* something writhing for its life — not seeing it twenty yards out from your shotgun, but feeling it right there in your fingertips — that was the part that could make the heart weak.

But not Alex. She'd twist up a thick old night crawler five different ways, knot it into itself, pull the ends to tighten it, even as the thing struggled mightily to muscle its way free. Then she'd stick the hook through, catching as many surfaces as possible, purple guts oozing, the worm's flesh working in and out like an accordion—she'd do all of this like it was straight-up nothing. She'd ball up the worm so tightly on the end of the hook it looked like a tiny Christmas ornament; no way a fish could steal a nibble without getting the hook. She didn't even flinch.

The two of them positioned themselves two-thirds of the way out the pier, right where Barry had said the current was likely to attract the big ones, and they sat next to each other. The cement of the pier was steaming after the rain in the night and the early heat of the day.

John had spent a few bucks on a bag of ice and filled his cooler on wheels in hopes that they would have at least a few fillets to take back to the house. He put the heavy cooler behind him to serve as a backrest. Alex hummed contentedly as she lightly bounced her pole to try and drum up some interest underwater.

An old fisherman was making his way in from the far end of the pier. He had a big red lump of a nose that was mushy and creased as a piece of chewed gum, and he wore a khaki bucket hat, flip-flops, and a lightweight shirt riddled with dark red and brown stains. He carried a pole and a tangled swath of netting.

As he drew near, John said, "Any bites?"

"Not a one," the man said. "Reckon that rain yesterday stirred up some stuff, brought some big schools of sardines through. Nobody's hungry today. But maybe you'll have better luck than me." He nodded down at Alex. "You too, son. Hope you snag the big 'un."

Alex said, "Me too."

John put a finger to his brow and murmured, "Alright now."

As the fisherman continued on his way, John glanced sideways at Alex to see if she had been fazed by the "son" comment, but if she had noticed it at all, she certainly didn't seem to care.

They sat for a long while without a bite, the sun broiling their heads.

Occasional whitecaps broke against the pier to offer the small relief of a misty spray.

Eventually, Alex pulled her worm in and rearranged it on the hook. She added a weight to her line, recast, bounced it. After a few more casts, she got up and switched to the other side of the pier.

After a bit, John called over to her, "Awful hot out here. We oughta try and make it out earlier tomorrow. Six or seven o'clock. Beat the heat."

Alex said, "Sure." She was quiet for a moment, then she said, "Daddy, do you like them?"

John glanced over his shoulder at her. She was still facing away, out across the water.

"Who?"

"That other family," Alex said. "Mr. and Mrs. Daly. Rae. Kimmy."

"Oh." John reeled his line in, pulled at a string of brown seaweed that had attached itself to the bait, and recast. "Mm-hm," he said. "Do you?"

He watched over his shoulder again as Alex's round buzz

cut tipped back and forth, left to right. "I like Kimmy a lot," she said, "though she annoys me a little bit sometimes."

"How so?"

"I don't know, she's just . . . *silly* sometimes."

John laughed. "What's wrong with silly?"

"There's a difference between funny and silly. Don't you think so? I like funny people. But sometimes Kimmy's not funny. Sometimes she's just silly."

John knew exactly what she meant. He didn't want to encourage a judgmental streak in Alex, but he also couldn't help the swell of pride he felt at the idea that his daughter was not and would never be a *silly* girl. He could imagine Alex saying things like, "Oh, get a life," to girls who were late to class because they were too caught up doing makeup in the bathroom, or when they cried because the boy they had a crush on didn't return a call.

"I *do* like Kimmy," Alex said decisively. "I'm not sure about the rest of them, though."

They fell quiet. Several minutes later, Alex reeled in her line and examined the worm. "It's dead now," she said. "And most of the blood's drained out." She dangled it over in John's direction. "See?"

"Yup."

"No wonder I'm not getting any bites with this floppy old thing." She removed the flimsy worm remains from her hook and reached into the Styrofoam cup for a fresh one.

John said, "You can do another one or two, but let's not waste all the good bait today if we're not gettin' a single bite. Like that guy said, today just might not be the day."

Alex rejoined John on his side of the pier. She swiftly and methodically attached a fresh worm to her hook. Mashing, knotting, stabbing. Slime. Guts. She wiped her dirty fingers on her thigh. Her skinny legs dangled over the concrete. She cast her line.

After a bit, Alex said, "A predator is like a bear, right? Or a shark?"

"Yup."

"Somethin' that hunts somethin'."

John nodded.

"So, humans are predators?"

John considered this. "I'd say so."

Alex gazed out over the water and bounced her line.

The art gallery was a bust; it featured the work of only one artist, who had a special talent for producing watercolor sunsets that were indistinguishable from one another except for the placement of a few faraway and poorly rendered seagulls.

Lisa, Rae, and Kimmy returned to the house and went to their rooms to change into their swimsuits. As Lisa tied the straps of her halter-top bikini, her eyes fell on Scott's white leather golf glove. It was on the floor, on the far side of the dresser, half hidden by a bath towel that had been carelessly tossed in the same vicinity.

In all the years Lisa had known him, Scott had never once forgotten a single element of his golf getup. He took an inordinate amount of pride in his gear—more so than in his actual play. *Must've been in a rush,* she thought, and as she recalled now, it did seem that Scott had been itching to get out the door this morning after he took that phone call. The others must have scheduled an early tee time.

Lisa carefully situated her white wraparound cover-up at her shoulders, and arranged it to display one classy inch of cleavage. She tightened the tie at the waist. She pulled her hair into a low ponytail and put on her wide-brimmed straw hat, then went to the kitchen to pack a small cooler and wait for the girls.

Down at the beach, Ryan appeared to be sleeping flat on his back, a T-shirt shielding his face from the sun, and Poppy was paging through an old *Good Housekeeping* magazine that she had found in the rec room. Poppy waved as Lisa and her girls approached. Poppy's skin was deep red-brown and gleaming with sunscreen and sweat. Lisa set up her umbrella next to Poppy and silently applied sunscreen to her arms and legs.

Kimmy immediately went for a swim.

Rae dragged her beach chair and book to the edge of the water, where she sat with her bottom half-submerged. She wore a swimsuit that Lisa would have forbidden if Rae had had even an ounce more in the way of womanly curves to fill it out. It was a tiny string bikini, bright green, with gold glitter and stripes that matched her gold hoop earrings. As it was, on Rae's late-blooming, scrawny fourteen-year-old frame, the strings that tied over her hip bones and hung across her rib cage were about as suggestive as ribbon around plywood.

Lisa finally settled in next to Poppy.

"How was the art gallery?" Poppy said brightly. She was sipping from a Bud Light in a Texaco koozie.

"It sucked," Lisa said distractedly. She fiddled with the tie on her cover-up for a moment, then said in a low voice, "Pop, I swear to God, I'm about to blow my lid. I'm trying to keep it together for the kids, but . . ."

Poppy took off her sunglasses and stared at Lisa. "What's up?" she said.

Lisa swallowed. "These new *golfing* buddies of Scott's?" she said. "The phone call? He said he was going to go play a *round* with them this morning?"

"Yeah?"

"Just now when I was up at the house I found his golf glove in our room."

"He forgot it?"

"You don't know how he is with this stuff. The fancy gear, that glove, it's like his *thing*. Hear me out—I was willing to accept that. The glove. But then . . ." Lisa paused, took a deep breath, and placed her palms out, facing the ground, as though it was moving beneath her and she needed to steady herself. "But *then* I went to the kitchen to fill up a cooler, and on the kitchen table, near all the brochures and takeout menus and stuff that came with the house, I saw both club passes sitting there."

"What are those?"

"He got them when we crossed the bridge onto the island yesterday, when we got the parking pass and the golf cart voucher and the fishing voucher. If you plan to golf, they give you the club pass, which you need for admission to the course. Scott got two, one for him and one for John. They would have used them when they played yesterday."

"OK . . . And?"

"So both passes are still at the house," Lisa said. "Scott didn't take either of them."

"Oh," Poppy said, understanding now. "Ohhhhh." She winced. "Yes . . . ," she said, choosing her words carefully. "If it had been the glove *or* the pass, it wouldn't seem like anything at all, but—"

"And the whole thing smelled fishy to me already yesterday," Lisa said. "When he disappeared with strangers during that storm for well over an hour, left John to sort out the stuff with the cart, I thought that was awfully strange. But I wasn't going to make a fuss about it. But now this? With all this . . . it's pretty obvious what's going on, wouldn't you say?" Lisa's white chest was speckled with angry red at the sternum. "He's cheating on me *here*, on our *family vacation*," she hissed. "Pop, that bastard is with another woman on this very island, right at this very moment."

Poppy winced again. She reached over to lay her hand on Lisa's wrist.

Words tumbled from Lisa. "I know I talked a big game yesterday, fine with Scott having an affair, blah-blah-blah. I really thought I was, and I really think I would be, if it wasn't on this island. I mean, what the *hell?* Did he make arrangements for his mistress to stay here all week, somewhere across the island? Or is he just, what, picking up local escorts? Hookers, I mean. Prostitutes. How does that work?"

Lisa was trembling, and her voice had risen to a volume where Poppy was concerned that it might wake Ryan.

Lisa had tears on both cheeks, dripping to her collarbone.

Poppy swallowed. She held her friend's hand tightly in her own, then pulled it to her lips and kissed Lisa's fingers. She whispered, "I'm sorry."

Before Poppy could say more, her eyes were drawn to the beach, where Kimmy was on her way toward them, shivering and clutching her elbows.

Lisa sighed mightily. "OK," she whispered. "I need to keep it together for the girls. I'll have to find a time to confront him when it's not going to blow up in front of everybody." Lisa sniffed in long and hard and wiped the tears from her face. "I'll have to find a way to control myself until the time is right."

Poppy massaged Lisa's shoulder. All the words of comfort or consolation that rose to her tongue seemed small and insincere. Lisa shuddered from the base of her spine as though an ice cube had been pressed to her neck. She pinched her nostrils and straightened up as Kimmy drew near.

Kimmy wrapped a Tweety Bird towel around her shoulders and shook her hair out wildly. Then she looked to her mother and Poppy for affirmation.

Poppy said, "Nice moves."

Kimmy did the whole routine again.

Lisa said, "You should re-up on sunscreen, your nose looks pink."

Looking a bit dazed from her head-banging, Kimmy gazed behind them, toward the house.

"Goodie, Alex is back," she announced.

Poppy turned to look over her shoulder. John and Alex were making their way to the beach. He was hopping and swiveling awkwardly to avoid prolonged contact with the scorching sand. Alex wore flip-flops and knee-length board shorts over a red one-piece swimsuit.

When they had made it down to the others, Poppy teased her husband, "Hey there, first-timer."

John set his towel next to hers. He yanked his white T-shirt off over his head. His chest was strong and brown. His belly was big but tight as a drum, abdominals toned from years of physical labor, beneath the years of fast food and Budweisers.

"Huh?" John said, rubbing sunscreen on his face.

"You ever been to the beach before?" Poppy said. "Doncha know to put something on your feet? Sand's about a thousand degrees on a day like this." She reached over to rub a smear of sunscreen on the backs of his knees.

Alex stood with her thumbs hooked into the belt loops of her board shorts and said, "We didn't get a single bite."

Kimmy said, "Not one single bite? How boring. Were you so bored? We were bored too. The gallery was such a drag." Poppy could tell from the way Kimmy said this, and from the accompanying gesture—chin in the air, a graceful flop of the hand—that she was repeating her mother's words verbatim and feeling quite pleased with herself for delivering this sophisticated observation as though it was her own.

Alex picked at a callus on her palm. "I'm hot," she said.

Kimmy said, "Do you want to go for a swim?"

The two of them bounded toward the water. They passed Rae, who was motionless at the water's edge, nose in her book, and splashed with high knees, hands in the air, losing their balance and tumbling full force into the waves. They bounced and dunked and kicked, their laughter and high-pitched squeals reaching far up the beach.

Poppy glanced at Lisa, whose eyes were hidden behind large sunglasses. Poppy wished she could warn John that serious trouble was brewing between Lisa and Scott, so that John wouldn't stumble innocently into some question or topic of conversation that would send them all down a dark path. Poppy could still feel anger radiating off Lisa—the air between them crowded and noisy with conflicting and dangerous frequencies. Fortunately, it seemed John would not be sitting near them right at this moment. Still standing, he stretched his back and rubbed his eye sockets with his knuckles and puckered his face in the bright sun. Poppy said, "Did you forget your sunglasses too?"

John nodded. "'Fraid so. These pills . . . my friggin' short-term memory . . . Anyway, I'm gonna go for a swim."

Poppy was tempted to join him, preferring the thought of John and his easy company to further conversation with Lisa, but she felt it would be better for her to stay and offer Lisa the opportunity to say more, if there was more to say.

Once John was out of earshot, Lisa said, "Should I follow him?"

Poppy was confused. "John? Into the water?"

"No, *Scott*," Lisa said impatiently. "Tomorrow, when he goes to 'golf.'" She air-quoted. "Catch him red-handed. I don't want him to think he can weasel out of this — plausible deniability."

"True," Poppy said.

"Or the other option, if I knew I could hold my tongue, I'd just wait until we're home," Lisa said. "That would probably be the best way to handle it, because I don't know how he's going to react when I bring it up. Depending how the conversation goes, what if he . . . I don't know, Pop, what if I confront him here, and he drives off and disappears for the rest of vacation? The girls would be . . . For it to happen like that, on vacation . . ."

"You really think he'd fly the coop?"

Lisa mashed her lips together in thought. "Not really," she said. "But if he did, or if anything happened to upset the girls . . ."

"If he's cheating, and if the two of you split up, the girls will be upset whether it happens now or ten years down the road. That's inevitable and it's not your fault, it's just life," Poppy said. She scratched at her itchy scalp through black hair that had become a sun sponge, as hot and greasy as tar.

"I might murder him," Lisa said, humorless. She ran a finger along her brow, catching delicate tiny bulbs of sweat. In the sunlight, her red hair looked like it had been spun with gold. Poppy marveled at her best friend's beauty, despite the grim, sickly expression that Lisa now wore.

Lisa turned to face Poppy. "What should I do?" she said in a voice that was suddenly as small and defenseless as the first murmurings of a child.

Poppy was so hot she was finding it difficult to concentrate on Lisa, even in her moment of great need. Her mind had melted to slush. Words swirled. She rubbed her eyes and screwed her face around, trying to force some blood to her brain.

She took Lisa's hand. "I think you should take some deep breaths, maybe go for a swim, maybe go inside and have a glass of wine and a lie-down . . . Things will shake out how they're gonna shake out." Poppy stopped speaking when she saw that Ryan, who had been napping on his towel several yards away, shifted his position, appearing to wake. "None of this is your fault," Poppy continued in a lower voice.

Ryan slowly worked his way up to a seated position and looked casually their way. The T-shirt that had covered his face was now draped around his neck like a shawl. "Hey, Ma," he said. "I'm gonna go in for a snack. You want me to bring you anything?"

"No, I'm fine, hon," Poppy said.

She watched Ryan for a bit as he loped sleepily toward the house. It was curious, she thought, how lackluster Ryan seemed today, given his high energy yesterday — thrashing in the waves with Kimmy and Alex, collecting crabs and shells and scampering around like a little kid all day, no need for a nap. Maybe he slept poorly last night, she thought. She'd ask him before bed tonight if he wanted the air conditioning adjusted lower or higher in his room, or if he wanted a different pillow.

Beside her, Lisa suddenly inhaled so forcefully her throat rattled, and she scrambled to her feet, sand kicking out to both sides. "*No,*" Lisa whispered under her breath. Then she said "NO!" again, and this time it was a cry, loud and anguished. Then she was running toward the water, her cover-up wrap dress undone and flapping out at her sides like huge, lopsided white wings.

Poppy's startled gaze reached the shore, Lisa's destination.

Next to Rae's beach chair was a chocolate Lab, nuzzling up to Rae's neck as she draped an arm over its back. The dog's tongue was long and pink against Rae's face. Keats Firestone stood there, lean and muscular in swim trunks and a backwards hat, smiling down at Rae, the dog's leash wrapped loosely around his wrist.

"*Oh, shit,*" Poppy breathed.

She rose from her chair, not particularly wanting to be at Lisa's side when the confrontation took place, but wanting to be close enough that she could get a good read on the situation and intervene if necessary.

Poppy began to jog slowly in the direction of the water just as Lisa was reaching Rae's beach chair. Poppy couldn't hear the language Lisa used, but she could make out some very emphatic words spoken, accompanied by a shooing motion. Then Keats turned abruptly, pulled the dog by its leash, and started speed-walking back from where he had come. Poppy watched as he speed-walked, then he jogged, then he ran.

When Poppy reached her, Lisa was holding her sunglasses in one hand, wiping her face with the back of her wrist. Her face was splotchy red on white, like peppermint, and she was shuddering with uneven breaths.

Rae sprang up from her beach chair, outraged and incredulous. She stared at her mother like Lisa had just shot the Labrador in the head.

Lisa gasped for breath and waved her hands around her face as though deflecting insects. *"I'm sorry,"* she wheezed.

"What the *hell?*" Rae hollered. "That was *so embarrassing!*"

Hoping that Lisa would collect herself and avoid revealing more to Rae, Poppy stepped between mother and daughter to address Rae directly. "What happened?"

Rae spoke quickly, bewildered and irate. "That guy was walking by, and his dog was really cute so I sort of whistled at it, and the dog came over real friendly, and I was just petting it, and my mom" — she pointed violently toward Lisa, as though she were on the stand and had been asked to identify the perpetrator in the courtroom — "Mom came running up, totally crazy, and said to that man, 'Stay away! You stay away from her!' Waving her arms like, like the guy's trying to murder me with an ax. And then" — Rae sputtered, still in disbelief — "he took his dog and left. Well, *you* saw," she appealed to Poppy. "You saw. They just left after my mom scared them off. What the *hell?*"

Rae's hands were angry little white balls.

Poppy stole a quick glance over her shoulder at Lisa, who looked shell-shocked. Shoulders low, hands cradling her own elbows. Face long and open. Poppy felt a surge of pity for her friend, who had been through the ringer in the past hour.

Poppy turned back to Rae. Her mind worked fast. "Chocolate Labs are notoriously aggressive," she said.

Rae crumpled her brow, looking skeptical.

"It's true," Poppy ventured, eyebrows high and persuasive. "Especially toward kids. They can get aggressive really fast. *Violent.*"

Delivering this quick lie with such conviction, Poppy half wondered if it was true.

Rae's expression was still dubious.

Poppy lowered her voice to a softer pitch. "Your mom has had a really hard morning," she said, looking Rae directly in the eye.

Rae snorted. "Oh, *really?* A hard morning? Because the art gallery sucked? I didn't know that was enough to make a person lose their freaking mind and scream at a stranger, chase him off the beach."

"I yell at strangers every day," Poppy offered. She reached out a gentle hand to Rae's shoulder. "Let's just let it go. It won't happen again. Right?"

Poppy turned around to confirm this with Lisa.

Lisa was bent and fanning her face, gazing at the horizon. "Of course not."

Out in the water, John, Alex, and Kimmy were swimming happily in a gentle surf that broke over the sandbar, oblivious to what had taken place at the shore.

Kimmy danced and spun in circles and slapped at the water's surface. John was floating on his back, only his face and belly visible except when a swell rose beneath him and he paddled mildly with windmill strokes to ride it. Alex was at his side, dog-paddling haplessly. It occurred to Poppy that they should probably put Alex in swimming lessons. They rarely vacationed at the beach; too far away, too expensive, but it would be good if she at least knew some basics.

Lisa said, "I think I'll get into the water for a bit."

"Good," Rae scoffed. "You could definitely stand to cool off."

Poppy said, "Let's all go in the water. It's sweltering out here." She realized she hadn't yet seen Rae swim at all.

Rae said, "I don't want to get my hair wet."

Poppy groaned and made a playful move like she was going to splash a bunch of water on Rae's head. "We'll just wade, then," she said to Rae. "Come on, skinny-mini."

Lisa removed her cover-up and draped it over Rae's beach chair, then entered the water.

Behind her, Poppy and Rae slowly walked into the water side by side, Rae wincing dramatically at every small wave that reached new heights on her goose-bumped body.

Poppy said, "It's not that cold, you weenie."

Rae laughed.

Poppy said, "Have you and Kimmy had swimming lessons?"

Rae nodded. "But only for a short time and when I was really little, like four or five years old. I don't remember anything I learned."

"Kimmy looks pretty comfortable out there."

"She's not," Rae said. "Well," she amended, "she may be comfortable, but she's *not* a good swimmer."

"No?"

Rae shook her head. "She practically drowned last summer when we were in Florida. All of a sudden she got su-per-scared and frantic. The water wasn't that deep and the waves weren't that big, she just panicked."

"Goodness," Poppy said.

"Did Alex and Ryan have swimming lessons when they were little?" Rae asked.

Poppy shook her head. "I was just feeling bad for never putting them in lessons, but it sounds like maybe lessons don't do a whole lot of good anyway."

Rae watched her mother dip herself up to her neck in the water, then she said, "What's going on with my mom?" It seemed her irritation with her mother was finally giving way to concern.

Poppy said, "She's got a lot on her mind."

"Like what?" Rae adjusted the clasp on one of her hoop earrings.

"Well . . . She just wants this to be the perfect vacation for everyone."

"It probably *would* be if she wasn't so stressed."

Poppy said, "Well."

Shivering, Rae turned back to face the beach, the water now at her waist. She saw Ryan, who was returning from the house with a bag of chips and a Gatorade. Rae's eyes narrowed to focus on him intently for a few seconds with a severe sort of expression on her face. *Ohhhh*, Poppy thought, turning away to conceal her own grin. This was a new thing, but it made perfect sense. A crush on Ryan would explain why Rae was wearing this ridiculous bikini and hoop earrings, why she didn't want to mess up her hair, associate with the "little" girls, or engage in their play. *Poor thing,* Poppy thought. Ryan was far more interested in a dead crab in a glass than in some fawning fourteen-year-old.

Poppy recalled asking Lisa yesterday if Rae was into boys yet, and Lisa's confident, dismissive "Nah." *Sheezus,* Poppy thought. How out of touch must Lisa be? Her poor daughter was practically foaming at the mouth.

Rae interrupted Poppy's thoughts. "It's too cold," she said. "I'm not going in any further." Eyes still on Ryan, Rae struck a runway-model pose, arms behind her head, arched back. It looked like she aimed to keep it up for a while.

"Suit yourself," Poppy said, diving in to dunk her head, then paddling out to the sandbar.

Lisa made her way over to Poppy. "Thanks for stepping in, with Rae. Sorry. I really just *lost* it for a minute—"

Poppy waved a hand in the air to end the apology. "It's nothing."

Lisa was still wearing her hat, but she removed it now, handing it to Poppy to hold while she dunked. Her long hair stretched and corrugated like seaweed in the current. She emerged from the water like a goddess, face soft and mild, red hair sleek, neck long and graceful, breasts full and textured with goosebumps. She looped her hair into a rope and squeezed water from it.

Poppy handed back her hat.

Lisa was quiet for a bit, then said, "You still don't think we should tell anyone? About Keats?"

"You think we *should*? You don't think chasing him and his dog off the beach will keep him away for the next few days?"

Lisa squeaked air in through one corner of her mouth. "I guess you're right. When he looked at me there," she said, "he definitely recognized me from yesterday at the house."

"So then he knows that *you* know about the registry," Poppy said. "At least I'd think that's what he would assume every time a person gives him looks or, you know, chases him down the beach."

"You're probably right," said Lisa. "That should be enough to keep him away."

Poppy thought for a moment, then said, "And anyway, the way Rae told it, she whistled the dog over. It sounds like she approached him rather than the other way around."

Lisa scooped water in her palms, a faraway look in her eyes.

Poppy said, "Lisa . . . Lisa?" She felt like she was calling to her friend through a tunnel. "Are you gonna make it?"

Lisa turned to her and said coolly, "I don't really have a choice, do I?"

10

POPPY HAD THE idea to make sandwiches for everyone and bring them down to the beach around one o'clock that afternoon, along with chips and beers and cookies and Capri Suns, sunscreen, ChapStick, magazines, Frisbees, dry towels . . . Everything imaginable, thereby eliminating the need for anyone else to go in the kitchen, so that Scott and Lisa would have privacy to hash things out when he returned. Lisa helped Poppy make the sandwiches and fill a cooler and a basket with all of these supplies, then Poppy returned to the beach and Lisa stayed in the house to await Scott's return.

An hour passed with no sign of Scott. Restless, Lisa retrieved a cluster of green grapes from the refrigerator, ate a few, then picked up the phone and dialed her mother's number. Might as well get this out of the way before she had to deal with Scott. As the phone rang, she danced her toe across the hardwood floor and picked at a shred of grape flesh stuck between her teeth, fighting the onset of nerves that always accompanied these calls.

Lisa loved the feeling of *after* a phone call with her mother

—of being done. Having it accomplished. The *before* made her skittery with dread. It was worse now that Carol was sick, because there was the added fear of bad news from the doctor, but Lisa had felt this way about calling her mother ever since leaving home over twenty years ago. Every time she dialed that same home number, unchanged since before she was born, Lisa felt she was on the edge of something bad, something that would hurt. Carol had never once spoken words of judgment against Lisa for her life choices, but some dark and cold space persisted between them and they couldn't quite seem to bridge it, no matter the frequency of their phone calls nor the warmth of the sentiments expressed.

Lisa was petrified that her mother would someday say a thing that would gut her, like, "Do you miss me?" But she knew her mother would never say this.

Carol sounded winded when she answered. She'd had to move too far and too fast to get to the phone.

Lisa said, "Hi, Mom."

Carol heaved, a small grunt. "Let me just . . ."

Lisa pictured her mother easing herself back into the blue recliner where she spent her days, gingerly accommodating all the aches as she sank into the chair.

"Take your time," Lisa said. "You should really keep the phone next to your chair."

"I do." Carol sighed. "But I forget. How's the beach?"

"It's nice," Lisa said. "Sunny. The house is great. The girls are loving it."

"And how's Poppy?" Carol asked this with such fondness

and familiarity that Lisa felt a jolt of painful longing. Her mother always spoke of Poppy with affection and gratitude when describing the appointment Poppy had taken her to or the meal Poppy had delivered, and this had never bothered Lisa. But somehow it felt different today, since she and Poppy were here vacationing together; they were on equal ground. It seemed unfair that Carol should ask about Poppy this way, with this lift to her voice, like thoughts of Poppy were a greater pleasure than a phone call from her own daughter.

"We're having a ball," Lisa said. "How are you feeling?"

"I wish they'd fix my TV. They keep saying they'll send a guy."

"Are you sleeping alright?"

"Mm-hm."

"Taking your pills?"

"Sure."

Lisa was out of questions. She wanted to ask her mother, *Do you miss me?* and *Where did we go off track?* and *Will we be able to fix this before you're gone?* But all of these questions died long before they reached her throat; they were knotted somewhere low inside her. She wanted to ask, *Do you wish I was a different person?* Instead, she said, "OK, then, I guess. Love you."

Carol said, "Love you."

Lisa hung up the phone and ate another grape. She gazed out the window and down to the beach, where everyone was in the water except for Rae, who was lying in the shade of an umbrella, small and curled like a snake. Lisa thought of herself at age fourteen and the little life she had shared with her mother. The wallpaper in the kitchen featuring rows of cherries that had faded to pink. Carol bent over the bathtub doing laundry by hand after the machine broke and they didn't have the money to replace it. The smell of Wonder Bread toasted for ten seconds too long. Tears warmed Lisa's eyes and the world became bright and blurred. Nostalgia, she'd once been told, was one of the most powerful and least useful sensations. God, did it hurt.

She winced as she recalled how stubborn and cold and cruel she had been to her mother when she was Rae's age. Nothing was right, nothing was enough, and she was so consumed by the injustice of this that she was brimming with spite and disgust. Lisa tried to remember if Poppy had been this way as a teenager, and thought not. Poppy had always been ferocious yet sure-footed. Lisa wondered what a mother can do to give her daughter a sure footing when the daughter is so convinced that the world, the very ground she walks on, is ill suited to her existence and conspiring against her every step.

Down at the beach, Ryan had decided to go for a walk after overhearing several other beachgoers who were seated nearby discussing a swarm of jellyfish that had washed up on the shore the night before. The sand, they said, was littered with the small, transparent, circular bodies. Ryan approached the group and asked how far away the jellyfish were.

A man in a wetsuit said, "About fifteen minutes thataway," thumbing north. "Whole beach covered with 'em. Happens every July." He held up a fist to indicate the size. "Moon jellies. Ten thousand of 'em."

The woman next to him sported two brick-red French braids that reached all the way to her hips, and she was so thickly freckled that her skin had an odd grayish hue. She said, "They're worth seeing, if you've never seen 'em."

Ryan announced to the others in his group that he was going to check out the jellyfish. John and Alex both appeared to be sleeping, with shirts over their heads.

Kimmy leapt to her feet. "That sounds cool. I'll come with you."

Rae, who was fanning her face with her book, was horrified by her sister's audacity—Kimmy's unbridled enthusiasm at the opportunity to spend one-on-one time with Ryan was downright mortifying.

Rae set her book at her side and removed her sunglasses to glare harshly at Kimmy. She hissed, "You can't just invite yourself along on his walk, you nitwit. Obviously he wants to go by himself."

Rae's eyes darted toward Ryan, expecting a private look of appreciation. To Rae's dismay, Ryan didn't even glance in her direction. His eyes were on Kimmy, who had visibly shrunk at her sister's reprimand. Kimmy twisted her arms uncomfortably around each other. She said, "I guess that's true," and made a move to sit back down on her towel.

Instead, Ryan said, "It's fine, I don't mind the company."

Kimmy looked to Rae for approval, or permission, or maybe to punctuate this small victory.

Rae said softly, "I just thought . . ." Then she shoved her

sunglasses back onto her face and stared hard at the water. She felt like a balloon that had just been popped, wormy and shapeless now, trash.

Ryan said, "You should come too, Rae, I think it's gonna be cool." He cracked his knuckles and the muscles of his brown forearms shifted and bulged.

Instantly, Rae was full and soaring. *Of course!* Now she understood—this was what Ryan wanted all along; he was just too shy to ask Rae, and only Rae, to accompany him.

She feigned a few seconds of indecision before agreeing, then she stood and brushed sand from her elbows. Her binoculars were strung over the back of her chair, and she picked them up and put them around her neck. She was hopeful that Ryan might ask to borrow the binoculars when they got close to their destination, that he would lift them to his face and his warm, tanned eye sockets would press against the black eyepieces. It would be something she could offer him, something they could share.

"Let's go," Ryan said.

"Which way?" Kimmy asked, and once Ryan had pointed, she darted down the beach to pop into the water for a cool-down before the walk.

This left Ryan and Rae to walk side by side at a leisurely pace. Their hands were so close that with the slightest extension of the fingertips or shift of a wrist, they could have been touching. Watching Kimmy peripherally and smiling knowingly to each other, they seemed like a couple and Kimmy a sidekick, the third wheel, their annoying but necessary companion.

Rae's heart belted out a symphony as they walked together this way, dizzy with lust and possibility. A little engine of desire inside her revved and screamed, *Yes!* She imagined that a little engine inside of Ryan was feeling and screaming the same thing.

Kimmy was the first to spot the glut of beached moon jellyfish, since she was in front of Ryan and Rae.

She waved her hands over her head and called, "They're like see-through donuts! Can I touch them?"

Ryan did not ask to borrow the binoculars, but broke pace with Rae to jog out ahead and reach the enormous expanse of jellyfish, which were suddenly everywhere, such thick coverage in places that they overlapped one another. The sight was impressive and also mildly unsettling—a reminder that the world was actually quite strange if you bothered to notice, like glancing up to see a full moon in broad daylight.

"Yeah, you can touch them," Ryan called to Kimmy. "These ones don't sting."

Rae jogged the short distance to catch up to Ryan and Kimmy, though she was disgusted by the sudden carpet of jellyfish at her feet, a massive, squishy slew of them.

Kimmy held a jellyfish near her face, sniffing it.

Ryan observed that a couple dozen yards up the beach, the abundance of jellyfish ended as abruptly as it had appeared. Must have been a huge bloom of them traveling together, he thought.

Rae poked at one with a toe, hoping she did not appear uninterested in Ryan's great passion. She could learn to tolerate this stuff, she supposed.

Ryan said, "There are thirteen different species of moon jellies. Some scientists say they're the oldest multiorgan species on the entire earth. Meaning, like, seven hundred million years."

Rae was so fixated on Ryan as he spoke—not the information he was spouting off but the shape of his lips around each word, the glistening of sweat on his brow, and the brilliance of his black curls under the sun—that she wasn't watching Kimmy, even from the corner of an eye. So Rae was horrified when she finally looked Kimmy's way after Ryan had finished his spiel, and discovered that Kimmy was stuffing two jellyfish down the front of her swimsuit, placing them right over her nonexistent breasts.

Kimmy massaged them theatrically through her swimsuit and did a little dance.

"They're like those things you put on in front of the mirror the other day," Kimmy gleefully pointed out to Rae.

Rae was stunned into silence.

Kimmy continued, "You know, those chicken cutlet things Mom keeps in her underwear drawer. You put them in your bra the other day. I saw you."

Kimmy was clearly so delighted at having made the association between the size and shape of the jellyfish and that of Lisa's silicone bra inserts that she was completely oblivious to Rae's reaction and to Ryan's discomfort at bearing witness to this. He was staring intently at the ground before him, shuffling some jellyfish around with his toes. Kimmy wouldn't stop. She would never stop. Now she struck a pop-star pose: chest out, booty out, lips out, and she said to Rae through her shoved-out lips, "I saw you put those things in your trainer bra and you stood like this in front of the mirror."

Kimmy exaggerated the pose even further and then broke it, collapsing into giggles.

Rae's face was so full of angry blood she thought her whole brain might shoot out through her nostrils.

It was true, of course.

The girls had first discovered the cutlets years ago while putting away folded laundry, and Kimmy had carried one down to the kitchen, where Lisa stood over a steaming pot. Kimmy held the cutlet up like a dirty Kleenex and demanded, "What the heck is this? It was in your drawer with your undies."

Rae had followed closely behind her sister, sharing Kimmy's curiosity about the cool, fleshy blob, but, as usual, lacking Kimmy's will for confrontation.

Lisa was stirring something in the pot with a wooden spoon. She looked over her shoulder and laughed when she saw what Kimmy was holding. She balanced the spoon across the top of the pot so she could face her daughters while she explained. "Sometimes ladies buy dresses or shirts that don't fit right around the chest. Around their *breasts*," she clarified. "So then sometimes ladies use these things to make a garment lay better over their breasts."

Lisa took the cutlet from Kimmy so she could demonstrate. She lifted her shirt and tucked it beneath her bra.

Kimmy said, "But you don't need that, Mommy, your
breasts are pretty big already."

For some reason, this made Lisa laugh really hard. "I'm
glad you think so," she said. "But they were even bigger,
quite a *lot* bigger, actually, when you were a baby and breast-
feeding."

Kimmy said, "So, after me and Rae sucked all the milk
out of them, they shrank."

"Exactly," Lisa said. She patted the cutlet beneath her
shirt.

Rae had forgotten about this exchange and the existence
of the cutlets entirely until a few weeks before this vacation,
when Lisa finally agreed to purchase a few training bras for
Rae, who was a late bloomer. Rae was dying to know what it
would look like when she grew breasts of her own, and fold-
ed-up socks didn't quite lie right under the training bra, so
she decided to give the cutlets a try. She retrieved them from
her mother's drawer and went to the full-length mirror. She
tested out a few different poses, not realizing, of course, that
Kimmy had been watching all this. *God,* that little *weasel,*
that sneaky little spying *snake.* Rae should have known that
without locking her bedroom door, she ought to assume
that everything she did was under Kimmy's sneaky spying
eyes.

Even so, Rae thought now, still staring at her sister in
outraged disbelief, the sun white and terrible in her eyes,

Kimmy should have the good and decent sense not to bring this up in front of Ryan. First the thing with the pee in the pool, and now this?

"Kimmy, you're a liar and an idiot," Rae said in a tone laced with venom.

Kimmy's happy laughter ceased immediately, and she looked like she had been slapped.

Ryan started to hum and he walked slowly toward the water, clearly wishing to avoid any further involvement with this conflict.

Kimmy withdrew the jellyfish from her swimsuit and placed them at her feet. There were tears in her eyes when she straightened back up.

"Rae?" she said.

"I can't even look at you."

"What did I do?" Kimmy murmured.

Rae said, "You are such an embarrassment." But even as she said this, she was losing steam. Witnessing Kimmy's genuine confusion softened her. Kimmy wasn't a bad girl or a bad sister, she was just a dumb one.

Rae sighed, looking out at the water, then at Ryan, then at her little sister. She said, "You just don't talk about things like that."

"Why? I didn't know."

"Now you know," Rae said. "You just don't." She forced herself to extend a hand to gently pat Kimmy's wet head.

On their way back, Kimmy ran ahead once again, darting in and out of the shallows and bending for shells.

Rae was quiet for a long while, mired in indecision over whether or not she should acknowledge the cutlet conversation with Ryan.

Her thoughts were interrupted when her eyes fell on a girl who was walking toward them from the opposite direction. The girl looked about Ryan's age, maybe a few years older, but regardless, she was fully developed where it mattered. She was very pretty, with a tanned, athletic body and long black curls that tangled around the strings of her white bikini. Rae instantly despised the girl. The confidence with which Rae had walked with Ryan on the way to see the moon jellyfish twenty minutes earlier, the certainty with which she regarded their mutual attraction, had all but faded since the cutlet conversation. And Rae could only imagine what was going through Ryan's head as this perfect-looking girl approached, this person who definitely did *not* require cutlets to fill out the cups of her bikini. Rae felt deeply ashamed of her own existence.

Because she was so attuned to the girl's body and Ryan's body language, Rae picked up on a subtle but distinct exchange between the two of them. As the girl drew close, she straightened up as her eyes fell on Ryan with something like recognition. Ryan straightened up too. And then Rae detected the smallest cautionary shake of Ryan's head, as in, *Not now,* or *Not here.* The girl tipped her chin up at Ryan to indicate some understanding.

When the girl had passed, Rae was left to grasp at an explanation. *Did Ryan know her?* Rae wondered. How *could* he know her? They were so far from his home in Wheeling and had been on the island for only one day and one night. And if for some reason he did know her, why hadn't the two of them exchanged words? Rae puzzled over this for a few minutes. Failing to come up with a good working theory, and failing to summon the courage to ask Ryan directly if he knew the girl, Rae cycled toward different possibilities. She began to second-guess her perception of the interaction. Maybe she had been wrong about the recognition between them; maybe that was just how hot people regarded one another.

Beside her, Ryan knelt to pick up a small shell. He examined it and then passed it to Rae. "Pretty, huh?" he said.

The instant he spoke to Rae, everything was right again. They were together, not apart, and she could agree that the shell was pretty. She held it in her hand as they continued up the beach.

Perhaps, Rae considered, this new idea causing her to brighten and open upward, perhaps it was not caution that Ryan had conveyed to the girl with that small shake of his head, but disinterest. Perhaps the girl's look had been suggestive, a proposition, a *hail fellow hot person* look, and Ryan's had meant *not interested, don't bother,* or even *can't you see I'm walking with my girlfriend?*

To Rae, that last scenario seemed totally possible. It seemed like a miracle that was actually totally possible.

Back at the family beach setup, John and Alex had woken from their naps and gone into the water to join Kimmy and Ryan.

Poppy was back, freshly sunscreened, with a new maga-zine from the stack in the recreation room. She was on her third Bud Light since leaving Lisa in the house to intercept Scott on his return. She was guzzling beers because she was a nervous wreck. She was way too keyed-up for a nap, although she probably could have used one. Worst of all, she couldn't unload this burden on anyone, at least not yet. Nothing agitated Poppy more than having to keep a secret, but John was a wretched liar. There was no way John's entire demeanor wouldn't change if she clued him in on what was going on, and how Scott had really spent those lost hours during and after yesterday's storm.

Poppy startled when she heard someone behind her, and she looked over her shoulder to see Scott approaching in swim trunks and a white shirt, sunglasses concealing his eyes. The sun was bright white across the sand behind him, and he was like a mirage. His posture was low, sagging like wet laundry. He carried a rolled-up towel and a small cooler, as though he intended to stay. Her heart started zooming with adrenaline, and she quickly turned back toward the beach so that she wouldn't stare.

Was he crying behind those sunglasses? Was he pissed off? Was he wearing his wedding ring?

Scott unfurled his towel on the sand next to Poppy and took a seat there.

She cleared her throat, aiming for a cheery and casual greeting. "Hey," she said. "How's it goin'?"

Scott didn't look at her, nor did he respond right away. He stared out at the ocean, then lowered himself and sat cross-legged on the towel as though about to embark on meditation. His hands were in his lap.

Finally, he murmured, "Fine." He sounded like he had just fought a war.

Oh God. Poppy felt a jolt of sympathy spike through her. Was it over? Had Lisa announced that she was leaving him? If so, there was no reason to pity Scott, of course; after all, he had spent the past three hours in some other woman's bed. But, *oh God,* was it really happening this way, this soon? Poppy rapid-fire swallowed several times to will her voice calm. She noted that he was wearing his wedding ring, but that meant nothing. They were probably going to put on their best face, wedding rings and niceties, at least for the rest of the vacation, for the girls' sake.

She thought of Lisa, up at the house. She must be an absolute *wreck,* Poppy thought; she must be completely crushed and inconsolable. She must have sent Scott down here as the ambassador so as not to raise suspicions between Rae and Kimmy if both of their parents were absent for too long. Poor Lisa must really be in a state. Poppy wanted to check on her. She also wanted to tell Scott that he wasn't doing a very good job of pretending things were normal, that if he didn't buck up, Kimmy would take one look at him and immediately demand to know what was wrong. But she knew it wasn't her place, and that it would be better if Scott didn't know what she knew. She suspected that the entire charade could easily fall to pieces and all would be revealed if anything caused Scott's emotional state to teeter and tip.

Beside her, Scott was removing his shirt. His skin sagged

more than Poppy remembered. His nipples looked sunburned. His crucifix bounced against a tangle of black and gray chest hair.

Then he rose without a word, scooping himself up off the sand, and looked around for a moment before locating the largest shovel the kids had brought, its red plastic blade the size of a dinner plate. Scott took the shovel a few yards out, midway between Poppy and the water, and started to dig.

He dug like a professional, both arms, a good anchor at his core, pitching sand over his shoulder. As he dug deeper, the sand became darker. Soon his whole body was slick with sweat, his face deep red; he was baking out there in the direct sun. He paused from his digging only once, to stand back and assess his progress, then he used his shovel to scrape a perimeter into the surface, marking off the intended size and shape of the hole. Poppy was transfixed. Scott dug and dug, stepping into the now three-foot-deep hole to work it from a different angle, then stepping back out, up onto the beach, to expand it.

Poppy couldn't look away. Scott's red face had become purple. Sweat now poured from him.

On and on he went. Surely he must be exhausted, she thought, but his movements were still tight and practiced. Digging and digging, like he had been born for this and this alone.

Suddenly concerned that he was driving himself toward cardiac arrest, Poppy got up to intervene.

"Hey, dude," she called as she approached. Part of her

was afraid that if she startled him, he'd let out a primal scream, bludgeon her on the head with the plastic shovel, and drag her out to sea.

Scott did not directly acknowledge her, but he stepped back from his hole and stared into it as she joined him at his side. He was panting, his skin was deep red-brown and crinkled like beef jerky, and he smelled sharply of raw onion and booze.

"Jesus," said Poppy, disturbed by the hole now that she was looking at it full-on. "Nice grave you've got yourself there." It was the perfect size and shape to hold a coffin.

"Guess so," Scott said, humorless.

"You know," Poppy said, "just last week a lady at some beach in Florida died in a big hole some nincompoop had dug for shits and giggles."

"Huh," Scott grunted.

"Heard about it on the news," Poppy said. "She was out for a walk at nighttime, the tide was on its way in, she slipped into some big hole right along the beach, just like this, water came up and over her, hole caved in, and she was swallowed up by sand."

Scott said, "She had to've been drunk."

"Maybe," Poppy said. "What compels you to dig something like this, anyhow?"

Now that he had paused from his mission, the heat and fatigue seemed to be setting in, and Scott looked drawn and unwell, unsteady on his legs.

He tossed the shovel to the ground next to the hole.

Poppy said, "Why don't you go for a swim, cool off a bit?"

Scott spun like a robot following commands. Poppy watched just long enough to make sure he didn't die of heat stroke before reaching the ocean.

As soon as he had entered the water, Poppy hightailed it to the house.

She found Lisa seated on a barstool in the kitchen, sipping a glass of white wine and paging through an old copy of *Redbook*.

Poppy said, "Hey," in a gentle voice, went to Lisa, and wrapped her arms around her.

Lisa patted Poppy's forearm but did not exactly reciprocate the hug. Her eyes were dry, her expression cold.

Poppy said, "How'd it go?"

Lisa sipped her wine and turned the page of the magazine. "Did you talk to him just now?"

"Yeah. Very weird. He spent the last who-knows-how-long digging a hole on the beach. Grave-sized, perfect to bury a person."

Lisa chuckled through her nose.

"He seemed wrecked," Poppy said. "Like he just got his gut punched. I figured that the two of you had it out"— Poppy blew air out the side of her mouth—"and that it did not go so well. He was looking *rough*."

Lisa closed the magazine before her and looked at Poppy. "I know," she said. "That's how he was acting from the moment he stepped in the door."

Poppy gazed at her. "What do you mean?"

"I was all charged up to confront him," Lisa said, "but then he walked in like *that,* all mopey-dopey, like some mean kid stole his lunch money. I was so taken aback. I didn't know what to make of it."

Poppy said, "What could . . ."

"That's what I keep trying to figure out. I'm like . . . Did things go south with the other woman? Did she leave him? Did he find out that *she's* cheating on *him?* Did he find out that I knew? Was he suddenly struck with some crisis of conscience?"

Poppy chewed her bottom lip.

Lisa scooted the bottle of white wine across the counter and retrieved a clean glass from the dishwasher. She poured Poppy two inches of wine and sat back down on her barstool.

Poppy said, "You're right, that's definitely not the way you'd expect a guy to be acting if he was running around with some other woman, everything hunky-dory."

"Exactly."

Poppy sipped her wine. "So you didn't confront him?"

Lisa shook her head. "I just asked him how golf was. He said, 'Fine.' I had already picked up on the mood, and I was like, 'Doesn't sound like it was fine,' and he started undressing and mumbled something like he hadn't played a very good game."

"He undressed in front of you?" Poppy said.

Lisa nodded. "I thought that was funny too. Like, if he had spent the past four hours in bed with another woman, he might be nervous about stripping down in front of me, worried what I might see or smell, but he didn't seem to have a second thought about it."

Poppy frowned. "That *is* odd. He was either *totally* sure that he had covered all his tracks, or he wasn't actually . . ."

Lisa was nodding. "I followed him around the bedroom while he was undressing, and I pointed to his glove in the corner of the room. I was still fired up and hoping to catch him in a lie. I was like, 'You forget something?'"

"Yeah, and?"

"And he was like, 'Forgot my damn glove, got a blister,' and he held out his thumb to show me." Lisa demonstrated. "I didn't examine it up close, but it looked legit, and he was so casual about the whole thing, not a moment's hesitation or nerves. I got no sense whatsoever that I was catching him in a lie."

"Strange."

"After he went down to the beach just now," Lisa said, "I stuck around and did a little snooping. Pockets of his golf shorts. Wallet."

"What'd you find?"

"Nothing."

Poppy drank more wine. "Are you thinking . . ." She hesitated. "What are you thinking?"

Lisa sighed. "His behavior was so . . . so *dark*, right? I'm thinking maybe I was wrong about another woman. Is that crazy? Maybe he really *did* just forget the glove, and the pass. Maybe one of the other guys lent him their pass."

"Why the mood, though?"

"He said he played a bad game," Lisa said again, with a shrug.

Poppy said, "I don't think my eleven-year-old kid would get that bent out of shape about a bad game."

"Mine either," Lisa conceded. "But Scott *really* hates to lose, he's always been that way. Well, and anyway, he can be sensitive."

"Sensitive?"

"I've told you before, I think he might be going through some midlife thing. Do men go through menopause? He's been sort of in and out of a funk the past few years. *So* moody. On cloud nine one minute, then totally morose, like you just saw, the next. It's weird. Since we stopped having sex, I've been assuming it was another woman that has him so manic, but maybe I've been wrong." Lisa grew quiet. She said, "I don't think I know him at all anymore." A deep exhale came out jerkily and she rubbed her eyes. "I called my mom," she said, in a surprising shift.

"How's she doing?"

"She misses you." Lisa chuckled, then her face darkened. "Pop, do you think she's going to make it?"

Poppy nodded assuredly.

"What if she doesn't?" Lisa posed this so innocently that for a moment Poppy saw her face as it was when they were children.

What would happen if Carol didn't make it? *Well,* Poppy thought, *the things that always happen.* A funeral. A burial. Casseroles. The emptying of a house and sorting of the things within it. That's what would *happen.* What didn't seem clear was what sort of unspoken wounds Lisa might sustain. There was love between Lisa and Carol, of course, but there was something else too, which Poppy had sensed long before Carol's diagnosis. It was in the way they talked about each other, always loving in their words, never, ever a harsh word, and yet . . . There was a stiffness there, a formality one might use when describing a stranger. This wasn't *not love,* but it wasn't a kind that announced itself readily.

Lisa wiped her eyes. "Well. Jeez." She laughed softly. "I thought this was going to be a relaxing vacation. I swear I didn't bring you along to be my therapist. But let me tell you something. You are my favorite person in the world, and that's including the person I married and the people I gave birth to."

Poppy laughed. She kissed Lisa's forehead and felt a pang of discomfort, realizing she couldn't honestly say the same of Lisa. Lisa was a very distant fourth in Poppy's life. Maybe not even. *Yikes.* Better not to discuss rankings ever, with anyone.

Lisa seemed unbothered by the silence. Eventually, she straightened up and refilled her wine. "I'm just gonna try and keep things cool between Scott and me for the rest of vacation. I want Scott to get as much quality time in with the girls as he can, so hopefully we can all have some good memories of this week regardless of what happens down the line."

"I concur," Poppy said. She rinsed her wine glass. "Do you want to come back to the beach?"

"Not just yet," Lisa said. "I'm going to have another glass

of wine, maybe lie in bed for a few minutes. You go on ahead."

Everyone had reconvened at the beach umbrella by the time Poppy returned, except for Scott, who was out in the water. It appeared that he, or someone, had filled in the grave he'd dug while she was gone. Rae had returned from her long walk. John, Ryan, Alex, Rae, and Kimmy were playing a rousing game of Twenty Questions.

Poppy fanned her greasy face with both hands. The shade of the umbrella was wonderful after the sweltering walk from the house.

She was relieved to observe that Kimmy seemed entirely unaffected by her father's mood. As usual, Rae wore a slightly sour and indecipherable expression, and Poppy expected that she too was oblivious to her parents' troubles.

Poppy said, "I'm gonna go for a quick dip."

Rae said, "Where's my mom at?"

"She's having a quick rest at the house," Poppy explained. "She wanted to get out of the sun for a few minutes."

Rae said, "I'm gonna go in for a little bit too."

Poppy didn't see much use in trying to talk Rae out of this; it would only draw attention to the situation if she objected to Rae going in. "OK, hon, but I think your mom might be taking a nap in her room. I'd let her sleep if you can, she seemed really tuckered out."

Rae looked mildly insulted by the suggestion that she was going inside in order to spend time with her mother. "I just want to get out of the sun," Rae said. "I don't care if she's sleeping."

As Poppy approached the water, Scott was facing away, staring at the horizon, bobbing with the gentle rolling waves. She dunked and paddled out his way, and when she reached him, she said, "Glad to see you're still with us."

Scott turned. "Huh?"

Poppy nodded toward the shore. "When I saw the grave was all filled in I got worried."

Scott pinched his nostrils.

"I'm joking," Poppy said. "But . . . is everything alright?"

"What's that?"

"It seemed like you were in such a mood when you got back from golfing. Then digging that hole and all."

Scott reached up a hand to slick back his hair in a glamorous sort of gesture. Poppy's eyes fell on a bubble of bright red the size of a pencil eraser at the base of his thumb. The blister.

"Just played a bad game," Scott said. "That's it. I hate to lose. I'm over it, though. There's always tomorrow. Or the next day."

"Tomorrow or the next day?"

"Sure," Scott said, adjusting his sunglasses. "I'll definitely want to play another round with those guys before we head home. Gotta redeem myself."

Poppy reared back. "Oh, come *on*, you really think that's a good idea?" she said. "Disappear for four hours and come back in such a funk you have to go for an hour-long swim before you can spend time with your family? And you're gonna do it all again *tomorrow or the next day?*"

"Jesus, lady," Scott said, taken aback by her tone. He scowled at her.

"Isn't that why you *go* on vacation? Isn't that the point? To spend time with your family? You're here to make memories with your girls, aren't you? It's like you're trying to come up with ways to piss off your wife. What're ya thinkin', man?"

Poppy didn't give a shit what happened between Scott and Lisa once the vacation was over, but she'd had about enough drama for the rest of the week. The two of them were treading on thin ice, thinking they could get through vacation with their daughters none the wiser if they kept this up.

Scott said, "You really think Lisa even cares what I do? Pop, you know we've got our problems. I know Lisa confides in you, and I'm fine with that. She talks to you more than she talks to me. My wife can't stand me!" He seemed half amused by this, but there was also an edge to his voice, there was a wound. "Anyway, I figure I'm doing Lisa a favor spending half the day on the golf course. Otherwise we're gonna be at each other's throats all day."

Poppy considered this. "You might be right, actually," she said.

"Of course I'm right," Scott said. "My wife really and truly hates me. Serious. She doesn't want to touch me with a ten-foot pole."

"Are you saying . . ." Poppy paused. She didn't want to reveal too much. Even if he wasn't lying about playing golf,

an affair still seemed the best explanation for their troubles
—the erratic sex life, the emotional gulf between them, the
callous resentment. "Are you saying you don't think you've
given her any reason?"

Scott grew quiet. He stared far out over the charcoal
ocean. "I don't know," he eventually said. "I often wonder."

Poppy felt a sudden pang of consternation. Unsure of
herself. She pictured Scott (if he really was innocent in all of
this) seeing his wife day after day and wondering in earnest,
What have I done to deflate her yet again? This made Poppy
seriously sad.

"Sorry I snapped at you," she said. "I take it back. What
do I know?" She blew her wet nose into her wet fingers and
rinsed them in the ocean. "I don't know nothin'."

Scott laughed. "You're OK," he said. He took off his sunglasses, dunked, surfaced again.

He looked old and tired, eyes as red-rimmed as a hound's.

The possibility that she might have misjudged the situation with Scott and Lisa depressed Poppy in curious ways.
Was it possible for two people to fall this badly out of sync
with each other without either of them being to blame?
No discernible letdown or betrayal, just . . . the love ended?
God, could that happen? No, no, that didn't just happen to
people. It couldn't. There had to be more, had to be something Poppy didn't know.

11

THE FAMILIES DINED outside that evening: corn on the cob, grilled pork chops, salad with walnuts and peaches, store-bought key lime pie and Cool Whip. The air was very warm but silky and light, less humid than the previous evening. Sunburns were turning to suntans, eyes bright against browned faces, toes cracked from hot sand and salt. It surprised Poppy how pleasant the company felt around the table, considering the drama from earlier in the day. Lisa and Scott seemed relaxed in one another's presence. Kimmy and Alex made daggers out of their corn cobs and prodded each other. Ryan wore a sleepy, affable smile. Even Rae seemed to be in good spirits.

Everyone helped clean up the meal when they had finished, loading the dishwasher, corn cobs and fatty edges of pork to the garbage, a quick Windex wipe-down of the table.

The entire group played a few hands of Crazy Eights, then Poppy went to get some fresh air on the patio.

The sky was hazy, a gorgeous, dreamy shade of pink.

Poppy poked her head back inside. "Anyone wanna walk up the path toward the golf course through that jungly part before it gets dark? Might see some wildlife, dusk's the best time."

Ryan said, "I'm in."

All the others quickly agreed to join as well.

Poppy led the way, using a little map from the pamphlet provided at the house. "We'll cross the road up there," she pointed, "then take the footpath, and when the trail forks we're gonna go left into the woods instead of right to the golf course. Our path will lead through some marshy bits. There should be a wooden bridge for us to cross. Supposed to be a pretty lagoon up the way."

"What sort of animals?" Kimmy said. She tossed a small shell up and down in her hand, and when she dropped it on the ground, she gave it a kick.

Poppy read from the pamphlet. "Says here we're likely to see herons, loons, pelicans, turtles, deer, raccoons, and . . ." She paused dramatically and swooped her face down, near to Kimmy's. "*Gators,*" she snarled.

Kimmy said, "I'm not even that scared. I've already seen some gators here, they just lay around and don't do anything. Right? They wouldn't eat a person. Well, maybe like a baby if you dropped it right on top of them, but it wouldn't just up and eat a *person* person. Right?"

Alex turned to her brother. "What *do* gators eat?"

Ryan said, "Worms when they're little, move on to bigger stuff as they grow. Fish and turtles and birds. Squirrels. Whatever they can catch."

Lisa said, "Nobody on Fripp Island has ever been killed by a gator. I looked it up before we came."

Poppy said. "Seriously?"

Lisa nodded.

Of course she did, Poppy thought. Lisa studied the local sex offender registry in the weeks leading up to the vacation, for Christ's sake, so why *wouldn't* she look up deaths-by-gator?

Poppy stuffed the map into the back pocket of her denim shorts.

Kimmy and Alex ran ahead of the adults with a burst of spastic energy. Poppy and John were next, followed by Scott, who walked with his hands looped behind him, like a maître d' sent to check on everyone's meal. Lisa had engaged Ryan in further conversation about wildlife on the island; she claimed a particular interest in birds of prey.

Rae brought up the rear of the group, and she observed all the others before her. Poppy and John were holding hands. Poppy was half the size of her husband. Maybe a third of him. Rae wondered how sex worked for a couple like that. Poppy on his lap and bouncing like a Pomeranian was the only way Rae could picture it.

Rae couldn't remember the last time she'd seen her own parents holding hands. Had they ever? Yes, she recalled the two of them holding hands while walking to mass on Sunday mornings and on walks around the neighborhood and during Friday-night movies at home, draped all over each other like teenagers. These memories awoke a painfully sweet nostalgia in Rae, as though her whole body had been bathed in gentle light. She knew her parents still loved each other, surely they must, but they never touched anymore, and it hurt her to recall a time when they did. Not that she had ever liked that—in fact, back when they used to kiss on the lips, Rae would cover her eyes and beg them to stop. But the distant memory of those times, the knowledge that that warmth was once present between them and now was not, sent a powerful rush of sadness through Rae. It was surprising to feel something so intensely that for once did not directly involve her. It *did* involve her, though, she thought with sudden indignation. It wasn't fair for something to be ripped away before you had the chance to decide if you should cherish it. It wasn't fair for the people you lived with every day to change.

"...Now, *herons* are typically monogamous for one breeding season," Rae overheard Ryan saying to her mother.

"And how long is that?" Lisa chirped, like a total moron. "Their breeding season, I mean."

"A year."

Even I know that, Rae thought, her sadness turning to disgust. Why was her mom being so idiotic, and why was Ryan politely accepting it, patiently explaining things to Lisa as though she was fresh off a rocket ship from Mars?

Eventually, they reached the secluded lagoon, with a narrow wooden bridge overlooking it. They lined up shoulder to shoulder along the bridge to admire the scene. In the deep shade and dusky light, the water looked as black as ink. Lily pads decorated its surface, and bright orange flowers lined its perimeter.

Ryan was the first to spot the fawn. He inhaled sharply and whispered, "Nobody move . . . Look across the way."

Everyone froze in place and looked to the far side of the
lagoon, where a startlingly small and beautiful fawn was approaching the water's edge. Its body was no bigger than a
two-liter bottle, its arched back thickly spotted with bright
white thumbprints. Its little face was so sweet it took your
breath away, eyes black and large, white spots on the bridge
of its nose and lining its upturned ears.

The fawn stepped cautiously toward the water's edge on
matchstick legs that seemed to bend wrong, ill suited to support even this tiny thing. The fawn nosed down to a pink
bloom that rested on a lily pad. Would it eat the flower or
simply smell it in appreciation? It was such an impossibly
gorgeous moment, it seemed the world might end right
there, in a dreamy poof of smoke.

Kimmy's breath came out in sharp and desperate bursts
—it was just too beautiful and too exciting to bear. Even
Scott was touched and transported by the scene, a quiver
rising within and awakening a nameless desire so intense he
almost could have mistaken it for sexual arousal.

Poppy had a disposable camera in her pocket, and she
made a move for it, slow and steady, willing the fawn not to
scamper off. Just as her fingers closed around the camera in
her pocket, the fawn made a sudden move, and for one split
second Poppy regretted her greed for a picture, certain that
her movement, careful as it was, had caused the creature to
panic.

But in the next moment it was clear what had startled the
fawn, when the head and upper torso of an alligator surged

out from the black water, as thick and strong and ugly as a demon. Lily pads spread in both directions, except for one that was attached to the gator's thickly textured back as it gripped the fawn by its front leg and pulled it into the water, whipping its powerful head back and forth to stun the fawn.

The gator was fat and warty — a horror, a monster — and once it had the fawn in its grasp, its jaws opened only once, in a swift and measured move to grip higher on the fawn's leg. The poor animal screamed, high-pitched and pure as glass, as the gator dragged it fully into the water.

The small lagoon was not deep, and even after it had been dragged several feet from the edge, the fawn could clearly be seen thrashing, releasing tortured shrieks. Blooms of bright red blood reached the surface of the water. The fawn continued to kick, and when a breath shot out from its wild nostrils, so did a spray of blood.

Everyone stood in silent, stunned horror except for Kimmy, who let out a blood-curdling cry directed at no one in particular: *"Do something!"*

Before anyone could stop him, before he rightly knew himself what he was going to do, Scott was running down the wooden bridge to the far side of the lagoon where the fawn was still fighting, three or four feet from the water's edge. Scott wrestled a thick dead root from the ground near his feet, jumped on the thing to break it into a manageable, baseball-bat-sized weapon. He took a step into the water, soaking his sandaled feet, and Lisa screamed, "Scott, *no!* Stay *back!"* But her voice did not reach him — at least not the part of him that wished to acknowledge or obey her—and he waited only a few seconds before he got a clear view of the gator's head, then he went for it with a two-armed, over-the-head, ax-to-chopping-block swing. The stick met the reptile's thick skull with a satisfying thud, like he had just struck a bed of clay.

The gator reared back in stunned surprise, unclamped its jaws, and moaned deeply. The fawn, released from the gator's grip but too weak to stand or flee, remained where it was.

The gator's head emerged from the water, and without hesitation Scott struck it a second time, with the same accuracy and success he'd shown on the first swing. This time, the gator appeared to lose consciousness for a few seconds. Its huge head bounced, then lolled lopsidedly. Shortly, the gator came to, grunted, and slunk back into the lagoon and out of view.

The fawn panted at the water's surface and Scott let out a desperate sound. He dropped his weapon, stepped farther into the water, and leaned down to grip the animal around its torso. He pulled it from the water, cradling it with both arms over his chest, like a baby. His wrists were covered in black slime from the lagoon. Blood poured from the fawn's neck. Its legs were splayed, tiny and limp as ribbons, down over Scott's belly. It wheezed. Its black eyes were glossy with pain. Blood and more blood, a steady torrent from its neck.

Scott looked down at the animal, his face stricken, and he didn't make a move to bring it any closer to the others nor lay it to rest elsewhere. The fawn's blood quickly soaked

Scott's shirt. Its mouth was open, pink tongue visible and erect, no bigger than a coin. Scott didn't move.

Next to Poppy, John whispered, "For fuck's sake," which would have registered surprise in her—John never cursed—had it been under less shocking circumstances.

John said, "Pop . . . go now. And take them with you." John nodded in the direction of the others on the bridge.

Still too stunned to speak, but understanding John's intentions, Poppy made a move to corral everyone else back from the bridge, toward the path from which they had come. All of them left willingly except for Kimmy, who stood her ground until Lisa picked her up and wrapped her legs around her waist. She held Kimmy tightly, swaddled like a baby against her chest, and they all hustled away from the lagoon.

Tears streamed down Kimmy's cheeks as she stared back over her mother's shoulder, craning her neck to see. "What's going to happen?"

Poppy walked quickly, trying to encourage everyone to keep pace, and said, "You don't want to know. You don't want to be there for it."

Kimmy said, "Will they save it? Can they stop the bleeding? Can they bring it back and we'll feed it with a bottle?"

Lisa said, "I don't think so."

"Why? What's going to happen?"

Rae's face was pale and drawn. She said, "They're going to kill it, Kimmy. It wouldn't be able to live, so they're going to kill it."

Lisa said, "Rae, for heaven's sake."

Ryan looked at Alex, attempting to gauge her response to all of this. Alex had been hunting and fishing with her father enough times for Ryan to assume that her reaction to a natural death would be measured, and it was. Alex shed no tears, and she had left the scene willingly, accepting the inevitable outcome.

Poppy said, "That was a terrible thing to see."

Kimmy said, "Poor Daddy, having to hold that poor thing while it dies."

Rae snorted.

Kimmy stared at her sister. "You don't feel bad for Daddy?"

"He would have left it alone if he had half a brain," Rae said disdainfully. "It would be dead already, and it wouldn't have suffered as much if he'd just let it go."

"Rae!" Lisa said. "Jesus *Christ!*"

Poppy coughed. "OK, everybody. We saw something terrible. Let's not fight."

They walked in silence for a while, and eventually Alex murmured, "She's right."

Ryan was the only one who heard his sister speak, and he leaned down. "What'd you say?"

"Rae's right."

Ryan nodded and placed a finger over his lips, indicating that he agreed but it did not need to be restated.

At the lagoon, as soon as the others had disappeared down the path, John approached Scott, who was still cradling the fawn against his chest. Its breath was thin and uneven.

He said, "Why don't you set that poor thing down."

"I know she's lost a lot of blood, but I think we can save her. Here . . ." Scott made a move to hand the fawn off to John. "Here, you hold her a sec. If I take off my shirt, we can wrap it . . ."

John took a step back, refusing to handle the animal. He said again, "Set that poor thing down."

Scott sputtered, "Well, but we can't just leave her here to suffer."

"I don't intend to," John said, drawing his Swiss army knife from his pocket.

"Oh God," Scott moaned from deep in his belly. Saliva drooped from his bottom lip. The fawn squirmed against Scott, but he didn't seem to notice. "Oh God," Scott said again. He looked like he was seriously contemplating running off into the woods with the fawn, never to return.

"Get a grip," John said, and he examined the blade of his knife. He spat on it.

Scott said, "Please don't."

Disgusted, John said, "You don't have to watch, but you've drawn this out enough."

Scott blinked, suddenly aware that John's ire was directed at him. "I just wanted to save her," Scott said, talking loudly over the terrible sound of the fawn's labored breath. Its nostrils twitched, its eyes rolled in semiconsciousness.

John grunted, "For crying out loud, put that animal down."

Scott put the fawn down, turned his back, and hiccupped

as John drew a swift, deep cut through the animal's neck. It was dead in two seconds. John rinsed his bloody fingers and the blade in the water of the lagoon.

Without turning around, Scott said in a broken voice, "Should we bury her?"

John rose to stand, and his knees cracked. "Not sure why you're so convinced it's a *her*. Anyhow, I reckon we'll leave it right where it is so that gator can finish it off."

"You kidding me?" Scott hiccuped again. "After all this, you're just gonna let her body get ripped apart by that *bastard* in there?" He nodded toward the dark water. "You really want this precious little thing to go out in the most undignified manner —"

"Reckon you already accomplished that," John interrupted him, pitiless.

Scott was flabbergasted. He turned toward John, and his face was slimy with tears and mucus. "You're the one that *hunts*," Scott said venomously.

"Yeah, I do." John nodded. Proud. Not a speck of remorse or chagrin. "Maybe that's why I understand the importance of a fast kill. And the virtue of eating the meat, or letting some other hungry creature at it, putting it to good use one way or another. That's how the food chain works, you know." John was fuming now. He spat. Not at Scott or the dead fawn, but angrily into the water. "Maybe that's why I'd rather let nature run its course than prolong some poor creature's suffering just so you can cradle it in your arms and whisper sweet nothings."

Scott stared at him. "You are sick," he said. "You think I did that for *me*?"

"Well, you certainly didn't do *it* any favors, did you?" John nodded at the crumpled, bloody carcass at his feet.

Involuntarily, Scott glanced down at the fawn, then had to look away. "I'm about to puke," he muttered.

John rolled his eyes and snapped the blade of his Swiss army knife back into place. "Take all the time you need," he said over his shoulder, heading toward the path.

John walked briskly. He stretched his back, tight from the drama, and returned the knife to his pocket. He wondered what sort of scene might await back at the house—if Ryan and Alex would be trying to comfort Rae and Kimmy with explanations about the natural order of things.

Where the woods had gone eerily silent as they all stood in appreciation of the beauty of the lagoon, moments before the attack, it was now alive once again with tittering birds and hissing insects.

12

LATER THAT EVENING in her bedroom, Rae was fluttery and restless, her mind shuttling between Ryan and the man with the Labrador from the beach this afternoon. The man liked her, that much was clear. Although it hadn't been immediately apparent to Rae, as soon as Lisa intervened it was obvious. Lisa wouldn't have reacted the way she did if she hadn't thought the man was interested in Rae. Even so, the forcefulness of her mother's reaction perplexed Rae. Sure, the man was a little older. He was fully a *man,* not a boy, but probably no more than ten years older, Rae guessed, and ten years was the age difference between her parents. So if there was anyone who had zero business judging what sort of attraction there might have been between Rae and that man, it was Lisa.

In any case, even Lisa's tantrum on the beach hadn't been enough to defeat Rae. The more she thought about it, the more validated she felt by the attention from the man, because it stood to reason that if that man in his twenties didn't think Rae was too young for him, then seventeen-year-old Ryan *definitely* wouldn't think she was too young for *him.* Rae was now circling her room in her pajamas, the TV on but muted, so that she could fully focus on practicing her look.

This look was one that Rae had been working on for a while, eager to perfect it so it would be available when the time came to put it to use. Unlike most of Rae's other looks, she had not learned this one from her mother but from girls in movies and on soaps and sitcoms. It was the look a girl gave in response to something wonderful that a boy had said moments before he kissed her. He would say, "You're beautiful," or "You're amazing," or "I think I love you." And the girl would look soft and big-eyed and a little mysterious, like she had a secret, as she whispered, "Thank you," and tipped her chin up in preparation to be kissed. Of all the looks Rae needed to learn, this was the one that mattered most.

Rae said "Thank you" to the armoire, looking deeply into the knobs at eye level. "Thank you," she whispered and dipped to the lampshade. Then to herself, in the mirror. "Thank you," she breathed to the blinds, then to the TV. "Thank you." Rae circled around and around the room, practicing that whisper, practicing that mysterious smile, practicing how to receive love.

All of Alex and Kimmy's sneaking-out plans were in place. Alex had snagged the flashlight from John's tackle box this morning, and Kimmy had snuck into Rae's room earlier this evening, before the walk, to take the binoculars.

After their parents had tucked them in and gone to their own bedrooms for the night, Kimmy bolted upright, pulled the binoculars from beneath her pillow, and put them around her neck. "Are you ready?" she said. "I still feel like doing it, even after the deer and stuff. Do you? Are you ready?"

Unfortunately, though, Alex's stomach cramp had returned moments earlier. It was worse than it had been before, and she moved from her bed to the floor, where she could writhe more freely. She moaned softly.

Kimmy sat next to Alex on the floor in the dark room. "Do you want me to get your mom?" she said.

Alex shook her head. "It was almost this bad this afternoon, but then it got better. I think if I just wait a minute it'll go away."

Kimmy said, "We don't have to sneak out tonight, not when you're feeling so bad."

Alex said, "We'll see. Just . . ." She turned onto her side and curled her knees to her chest like a pill bug and groaned.

Kimmy was distressed. She touched Alex's forehead with the back of her hand, as she had seen her own mother do when she and Rae were ill. She brushed her fingers across Alex's arm in an attempt to soothe her. Alex moaned louder.

Kimmy said, "What should I do?"

Alex bolted upright and said, "Oh, *crap.*"

"What?" Kimmy said, lurching upward herself, involuntarily mimicking Alex's every move.

Alex said, "Kimmy, close your eyes for a minute."

"What?"

"Just close your eyes. I'll tell you when you can open."

Kimmy blinked. "Are you playing a trick on me?"

"No," Alex insisted. "I promise. Please, just close your eyes."

Kimmy obeyed.

Alex undid the tie on her pajama bottoms, which were a lightweight blue cotton, and she reached all the way in beneath her underwear, dipped her index finger in, then pulled it out. Even in the dark room she could see the blood.

A strange and desperate noise slipped out of Alex, and Kimmy's eyes snapped open.

"What?" Kimmy said.

Alex held up her black-red syrupy fingertip.

Kimmy said in an awestruck voice, "Oh my gosh, did you start your period?"

Alex nodded. And for some reason, tears oozed to her eyelids, even though she wasn't particularly upset by the presence of blood nor the idea of menstruating.

Kimmy noticed the tears, and she swiftly retrieved the box of Kleenex from the bed stand and handed Alex two tissues — one for her finger and one for her tears.

Kimmy placed her hand on Alex's forearm and said, in the most grown-up and comforting voice she could muster, "You're a woman now, Alex, it's nothing to be sad about." She stroked Alex's bald head fondly. "You're just growing up. I wish I would start my period too, I can't wait until I do. Really, I wish it was happening to me too, right now. Lucky you, becoming a woman."

Alex listened to these words of reassurance and hazily nodded her head in a show of appreciation to Kimmy.

Kimmy was so encouraged by the gesture that she went on, "I really shouldn't say this because I know she's not happy about it, but" — Kimmy leaned forward to whisper this highly confidential piece of information—"not even Rae has got her period. She's waiting and waiting, she's got maxi pads ready in her bathroom at home and everything. She wrote in her diary about how bad she wants it, so she can be a woman. She hasn't gotten hers yet and she's *fourteen*, Alex, so you are so lucky that this is happening to you now."

Alex did not respond to this but stared at the blood on her finger, twisting her wrist to see it in different light.

Kimmy said, "Should I go upstairs and get a maxi pad from your mom or my mom?"

Alex nodded. "My mom," she said. "I'll stay right here so I don't get it on anything."

Kimmy left the room and went up the stairs to the main floor. She was prepared to knock on Poppy and John's door, but before she had reached it, her eyes were drawn to movement in the kitchen.

She walked along the hallway toward the kitchen to investigate.

Rae was at the refrigerator, returning a magnum of screw-cap white wine to the shelf. The refrigerator door suctioned shut with its gentle *foomph*, and Rae turned toward the hall. She held a mug in her left hand. She still hadn't noticed her sister, although Kimmy was now in plain sight.

Rae was wearing her pink pajamas from Victoria's Secret, size triple-extra-small, and still the waistband hung loose over her bony hips and the shoulder seams were nearly at her elbows. Rae had begged Lisa to take her to Victoria's Secret for bras and panties last month, and Lisa had eventually acquiesced. Once they got there, though, all of the lingerie was way too big, so they had settled on this set of pajamas and a few training bras.

Halfway back through the main room, Rae saw Kimmy. Rae startled, her eyes flashed, the mug teetered, a few drops spattered on her bare foot.

Kimmy took a few steps toward her sister and Rae backed away.

Kimmy whispered, "What are you doing?"

"Nothing," Rae hissed. "I just got up for a cup of juice. What are *you* doing?"

Kimmy wanted to tell, but a loyal instinct stopped her — she wouldn't tell anybody about Alex's period except Alex's mom. Not even Rae. It wasn't anybody else's business.

Kimmy said, "I came up for juice too." She took another step forward and looked down into Rae's mug. The contents were not orange or purple — the colors of the juices in the house — but a pale yellow, like pee. Kimmy leaned toward the mug to sniff it, and Rae moved farther back.

"That doesn't look like juice," Kimmy said, her nose close to the mug.

Rae rolled her eyes so far they were all white. When her irises returned, they fixed sharply on her sister. "Get out of my way, Kimmy," she said, moving to pass her.

Kimmy moved directly into Rae's path, looked down into the mug once again, and whispered, "Is that *wine*?"

Rae's pretty, angular jaw went tight and square as she ground her back molars together. Her nostrils flared. "What are you doing with my binoculars?"

Kimmy had forgotten she was wearing them. "Me and Alex were just going to play with them," she said dismissively. "Rae . . . is that wine in that cup?" Kimmy felt her heartbeat whirring faster and faster. Blood flooding her skull. "You have to tell me if that's wine," Kimmy said, "or I'm going to tell Mom on you."

Rae exhaled a damp, sour cloud. "You should really learn to mind your own business, you little . . ." Rae hesitated, crafting the perfect insult. "You sneaky little snake," she said, curling a finger around the strap of the binoculars, then letting go so they bounced back hard against Kimmy's belly.

Kimmy recoiled.

A mean snarl crossed Rae's lips. She could see that this was the only course of action. Insulting her little sister's integrity would be the only way to make her submit, the only way to guarantee that Kimmy wouldn't tattle.

"I was going to forgive you for making up that thing with me peeing in the pool. And this afternoon, when you did that thing with the jellyfish down your swimsuit and told Ryan the story about me trying on Mom's breast thingies," Rae said. "I was going to forgive you for those, and I was even going to forgive you for spying on me when I tried them on at home in the first place. For snooping on me." She paused to put a contemplative finger to her lips. "But *this*?" she hissed. "Now you're stealing my binoculars and sneaking around the house following me, waiting for something new, something you can tattle on or something you can use against me in front of somebody else?" Rae's lips pressed together so tight they went colorless, and she shook her head slowly once again, as though she were both sad-dened and impressed by her own resolve. "I can't forgive you for the way you are," she said matter-of-factly. "I can't forgive you for being a snake."

Kimmy's eyes grew large and watery. She started to bab-ble and weep. "Wait, Rae, that's not even why I'm — I came up because — I'm not a snake, see, the binoculars —" But Rae had already waltzed past her and down the hall toward her bedroom.

Kimmy followed after her sister, launching quiet but des-perate protests.

Before entering her room, Rae leaned close, roughly snatched the binoculars off over Kimmy's head, and whis-pered, "Don't you dare follow me into my bedroom. Don't you dare follow me *anywhere* ever again." Then Rae disap-peared into her room and the lock clicked.

Kimmy ground her tears into her eye sockets with the heels of her hands. She felt wrecked, empty, indignant, and hopeless. Shortly, though, she realized that she couldn't wal-low in self-pity. She remembered why she had come up in the first place, and she knew that she must retrieve Poppy for Alex during this important time. She must somehow move past the terrible and unfair thing that had just hap-pened with Rae, for Alex's sake.

Kimmy knocked quietly on Poppy and John's door, and when Poppy answered, hair in a crazy ball atop her head, face scrunched up, Kimmy whispered, "Alex started her pe-riod and she needs a maxi pad."

"Oh, *really?*" Poppy's sleepy face leapt to life, and she said,

"I'll be right down. I'm just gonna pop into the bathroom to grab a few things."

Kimmy tried to contain her tears as she made her way back downstairs.

Fortunately, Alex appeared not to have moved, and the light was still off in their bedroom, so Kimmy could blow her nose and compose herself in darkness. It seemed like Alex was still crying too — several newly crumpled tissues had appeared at her side. Kimmy took Alex's clean hand and gave it a comforting squeeze, and they held hands until Poppy arrived in their bedroom a minute later.

Poppy kissed Alex's forehead and offered her a Motrin. She explained that she didn't keep maxi pads around, but the liners she had would probably suffice, and she also had tampons, if Alex wanted to learn to use those, so that she could swim tomorrow.

Poppy kissed Alex again, examined her daughter's face, and said, "You doing OK? How do you feel, starting your period?"

Alex shrugged. "I'm OK. I don't really care, so I don't know why I can't stop crying." She giggled, which quickly brought more tears.

This opened the floodgates in Kimmy — she began to cry too. She cried because she was hurt by Rae's accusations and names, she cried because Rae was drinking wine, and this seemed a cause for major concern, yet already Kimmy knew that she couldn't — she wouldn't — rat out her sister and so would have to keep a big, terrible secret. She cried because she hadn't taken the binoculars to spy, she hadn't been spying at all, it was an accident that she'd seen what she'd seen, but Rae would never believe it. She cried because she missed her stuffed animals at home, and because Alex had started her period and she didn't even seem glad about it, whereas Kimmy couldn't *wait* to start her period, there were so many girls who couldn't wait, and here Alex had hers and she didn't even care. She cried for the dead fawn. She cried because of course the moon was not fake. Of course this dumb old world was exactly the way it seemed.

Poppy stared at Kimmy and said, "What's gotten into you?"

Kimmy shrugged helplessly, took a Kleenex, continued to cry.

Poppy said, "It's OK, it's been quite a day. It's gonna be A-OK, girls," and she offered comforting hugs to both of them.

The girls continued to cry for a bit longer, until the tears turned to laughter, and Kimmy reached for Alex's hand again and they began to laugh really, really hard all of a sudden, and everything felt better, and OK.

Eventually, Poppy and Alex went to the bathroom to clean up. Alex was appalled at the blood and the mess, but Poppy said it was nothing—she'd bled more from a paper cut. Alex had had the presence of mind to grab fresh undies in her bedroom, so she got changed and freshened. Poppy showed her how to use a tampon. As Poppy walked Alex back to the bedroom, she leaned down and whispered, "I know *you're* going to be just fine, but your roomie in there ... Whaddaya reckon's got her so wound up? Do you think it's the deer?"

"Beats me," Alex said. "Maybe she just really hates the sight of blood."

13

POPPY WOKE AT five o'clock in the morning, instantly as bright and alert as if someone had crashed a cymbal at her face. She had slept soundly after the incident with Alex and Kimmy, and now felt strong and energetic as she moved from the bed to the other side of her room, where she plucked her running clothes from a pile of dirty laundry. She hadn't wanted to commit herself to any more runs on the island after the humidity had given her such a hard time yesterday, but today she woke feeling so intensely good, she could hardly wait to get out there and work her muscles until she hurt. In the bathroom, she dumped John's pills into her palm and counted them. Satisfied with the result, she returned them to the bottle. Even though it had been months at the same dose and not a single slip-up, every time she counted she feared the worst. She didn't know why she was so convinced the world was out to get John.

In the kitchen, she boiled water and poured it into a mug with instant coffee. She stretched as she waited for the coffee to cool enough for her to guzzle it.

She double-knotted her shoes.

Outside, caffeine and early-morning adrenaline zoomed

through Poppy. She took a left out of the driveway, planning to run the same route as yesterday, except today she wouldn't stop at Gram's Diner for a cigarette.

The air smelled wondrous. Sand crunched beneath her feet on the concrete sidewalk. The moon was still bright above her, white as cream against the navy sky. She started to sing Madonna's "Thief of Hearts" quietly to herself. She felt zippy and strong. Today she might even do a few push-ups and crunches when she got back. Today she would make that pitcher of frozen margaritas she'd been talking about. Today would be a wonderful day.

Five minutes into the run and still feeling like a million bucks, Poppy spotted another runner approaching on the opposite side of the road. A thin young woman, long tanned legs, long blond braid that swung back and forth like thick rope, white T-shirt, and blue mesh shorts. When she got closer, Poppy called out, "Oh, hi! Good morning!" as she recognized her acquaintance from the day before.

The young woman paused in her stride, and her face brightened with recognition.

"Morning!" the young woman called. "I'm impressed you decided to give it another go after yesterday." It looked like she wouldn't mind pausing to chat, so Poppy jogged over to join her on the other side of the road.

"How funny, running into you again," Poppy said. "You got the morning off work?"

Roxie nodded. "Lunch shift today, don't have to be in till eleven." She wiped sweat from her chin into the collar of her white T-shirt.

"How long of a run you doing?" Poppy said.

"If I tell you, you're gonna think I'm insane," Roxie said.

"Then you must."

"Two laps around the island."

"The entire thing, twice? What's that, twelve miles?"

Roxie nodded. "Thirteen."

"Good God! So what mile are you on now?"

Roxie looked down at her watch. "Somewhere between eight and nine. I live just up that way"—she thumbed behind her—"but I drive across the island to start my run at that end, so I finish on a two-mile downhill."

"You're gonna run an entire half-marathon before the sun's even up," Poppy said.

Roxie nodded. "Being out like this in the quiet of the early morning . . . it sets me straight." She bent back her left leg, gripped her foot, and pulled it up to her buttocks, stretching out her quadriceps, releasing a sigh as the stretch warmed up through her body. "Why do you go this direction?" Roxie asked.

"Huh? Oh." Poppy gazed at the street ahead. "I saw on the map that the whole way to the tip and back would be two miles from our house. Just figured that was a good destination. You know, little overlook at the beach access up beyond Gram's."

"I guess," Roxie said. She brushed her lips absently with the tip of her braid. She nodded in the direction she was headed. "If you go *that* way, though," she said, "you get to run through the magnolia grove."

"What's that?"

Roxie repeated the quadriceps stretch on her right side. "The road narrows and you're suddenly surrounded by magnolia trees. They reach across over your head, like a canopy." She made a rainbow in the air with her hand. "The smell is magnificent."

"That does sound nice," Poppy said. "You said it's that-away?" She nodded back in the direction from which she had come.

"Yeah," Roxie said brightly. "Why don't you join me? From here it'll be about a mile to the grove, about the same distance you wanted to do anyway, and it really is worth seeing."

Poppy fanned her fingers in the air. "I'll slow you up."

"I'm a tortoise, not a hare," Roxie said. "What are you, about a ten-minute mile?"

"Sure."

"Come on," Roxie urged her. "Running goes so much faster when you've got company, doesn't it?"

"I guess you're right."

"Come on, then," Roxie said, *come on*, gently taking Poppy's elbow and guiding it so they were both facing south.

"OK, OK," Poppy said. "But you set the pace. I do *not* want to slow you down."

They started off together. Roxie smelled of apples and laundry detergent. Not a trace of body odor, even after eight miles—Poppy was amazed.

A seagull flapped onto the street near them and poked at a french fry flattened into the concrete. Poppy kicked at the bird when they got close — the gull didn't give a shit. It stared at her like it wanted to fight.

Poppy said, "You're never gonna guess what we saw last night."

"Here on the island?"

Poppy nodded. "I'm not going to make you guess. We saw a gator maul a baby fawn at a lagoon just up the way."

Roxie drew all her breath in. "Yikes."

"We were all there," Poppy said. "Kids too. All eight of us. Staring at this little fawn, I made a move to snag a picture, and then a gator flies up out of the water, gets the thing by its neck, and drags it into the water."

"That must have been awful," Roxie said. "I've seen them go after birds and squirrels, but never a deer. And just a baby . . . Fawns are so sweet. That sounds terrible. Blood everywhere? What happened?"

"My friend's husband tried to save it," Poppy snorted. "Went after the gator with a big old stick."

"Did it work?"

"He scared off the gator," Poppy said, "but not in time to save the deer. The rest of us left, and my husband stayed behind to help with the mercy kill."

"Poor thing."

"My husband hunts, so he's used to the blood. Not used to seeing it on a baby animal, not used to having to kill a thing with his Swiss army knife, but so it goes."

"And the kids?"

"They seemed fine," Poppy said. "My kids are tough

cookies. The other two . . . well, their older one's a piece of work. She was being a real shit, giving her little sister a terrible time, making it much worse than she'd've had to. And their little one, she was the most traumatized, had a good long cry about it. But she was fine soon after."

It was quiet for a bit, then Roxie said, "Where did you say you're from again?"

"West Virginia," said Poppy. "And lest it cause any confusion, my family's vacationing with my best friend from childhood—*they* are the rich ones. They got some all-inclusive package, we're just along for the ride. My family? We could never afford this. Vacation to us is All-You-Can-Eat Hotdog Day at the county fair." Poppy lowered her voice as though the two of them were joined in conspiracy against everyone else on the island. "Rich people, though, *yech!* Right? All of 'em except for my best friend, of course. Lisa's fine." She slapped at a mosquito on her shoulder. "Anyway, you're from up north, you said?"

Roxie nodded.

"How'd you end up on the island?" Poppy said, momentarily forgetting that Roxie hadn't seemed too keen on discussing the subject yesterday morning.

"My family vacationed here when I was a kid," Roxie said. "My parents, sorry to say . . ." She gestured toward the condominiums they passed. "*Yech,* like you said. We'd rent a gorgeous beachside place for a week, my mom would still find things to gripe about. Curtains didn't match the wallpaper. Sheets smelled mildewy. And if it wasn't something about the house, it was my dad—they'd be at each other's throats all week long. And I was an only child, so I didn't have anyone to run off and play with just to escape." Roxie shook her head at these memories. "Anyhow," she said, "how I actually ended up living here, that's a long story and it'd bore you to tears."

"Probably not," Poppy said.

Roxie shrugged mildly and didn't offer anything further on the matter.

Poppy pointed out their rental house as they passed it, on the far side of the street. "That's my home base for the week," she said. "Pretty nice digs. The green one with the white shutters."

"That one there?"

Poppy nodded. "I'm pretty sure it's haunted. I swear to you, the last two nights, I *swear* I heard footsteps a couple different times. And everybody's got their own bathroom attached to the room, so I don't know what causes . . . Well, anyway."

Roxie said, "Some people think this whole island's crawling with ghosts."

"Really?"

"Sure, there's tons of spooky folklore," Roxie said. "Pirate ship set fire to a boat full of orphans coming from England, just off the coast. All the orphans on the boat died in the water but now inhabit the island as ghosts. Some people say they can hear the children singing at night."

Poppy said, "I do not like that."

"The Gray Man is another one."

"Who's that?"

"Legend started up in Charleston. A guy set out to visit his fiancée, but he and his horse got trapped in quicksand in the marshes near Pawley Island. They say the ghost always wears gray and wanders up and down the coast when a storm is on the way, looking for ladies with broken hearts. See, he's still trying to find his fiancée. He wants to protect her from storms."

"I'd punch him in his gray ghost face," Poppy said, "if he tried to talk to me."

Roxie laughed. "Half the people who live on this island claim they've seen him. They've always got some new story. That's what happens when you wait tables—you see the same-old-same-olds every single morning, and they're forever coming up with new material."

"Sounds that way," Poppy said. She breathed in through her nose and out through her mouth to prevent a stomach cramp.

Roxie said, "You said you used to work at a restaurant too, right?"

"From junior high till I was almost thirty," Poppy said.

Roxie ran a palm along the back of her tanned, graceful neck and wiped the perspiration on her mesh shorts.

Poppy glanced at her watch. She felt like a million bucks. She felt she would be fine running twice as fast, twice as far. Roxie was right; a running partner made all the difference. Young people could really do wonders for the middle-aged, Poppy thought. All that vitality, that get-up-and-go.

Roxie said, "So what do you do for work now?"

"I'm in the bounce house biz."

"Come again?"

"For birthday parties and carnivals and stuff. I rent 'em out, blow 'em up, clean up the puke."

"Interesting," Roxie said. "Never occurred to me somebody would do that for a living."

"It's a drag," Poppy said. "Money's alright, though."

Roxie slowed her pace and sniffed the air. "Smell that?" She held her arms in the air and slowed to a complete stop, as if standing still would intensify the aroma. "We're close."

Poppy lifted her chin, nose to the air. "Yes," she said, the air suddenly sweet with blossoms. "Smells like honeysuckle."

"It's just up ahead."

They jogged another quarter-mile, around a gentle bend, and, "Wow!" Poppy said, inhaling the air, thick with the sweet aroma of the white blooms. The great branches of the trees, heavy with broad, dark, glossy leaves, reached across to meet overhead, some of them interlacing like fingers.

"Wow!" Poppy said again wondrously, standing still with her chin tilted up to the sky, the scent of the blooms dizzying. She filled her lungs with it.

They stood in a comfortable, lovely silence for a bit. Poppy felt like she was in the Garden of Eden. She jumped to grasp a bloom and pull it to her face, couldn't quite reach, and missed. Roxie hopped to retrieve it easily, and she pulled it down and handed it to her. Poppy buried her nose in the warmth of the white petals, then she let go, and the branch sprang back upward and bounced. A soft breeze skimmed over her face. A few sandpipers speed-walked across the sidewalk before her, looking aimless and distressed, like they were lost and running late for an important meeting.

Roxie cracked all her knuckles, then her neck.

"I reckon I should head back," Poppy said. "If I go any further, I'm setting myself up for a hell of a hike back. But thank you for letting me join you and bringing me to this place."

"My pleasure." Roxie knelt to tighten the knot on her shoe. "I'm off tomorrow and I'll be running the same route at the same time, if you care to join again."

"Tomorrow?" Poppy said. "Yes, that should work. Tomorrow will be our last full day on the island, boo-hoo. We need to be out by ten o'clock the following morning."

Roxie tucked a loose strand of hair into her braid. "You'll wanna make the most of your last full day then, right? Get an early start?"

"Good point," Poppy said. "Let's plan on it. I'll meet you right in front of our place, same time."

"Perfect." Roxie gave her a half-hug, hip to hip, then she trotted off.

Poppy watched Roxie as she ran, admiring her calf muscles shifting with each stride, that graceful frame, the silky braid, looking like it was straight off a Pantene commercial.

The run back to the house passed quickly, as Poppy was still filled with a bright and youthful energy, the distinct feeling of high hopes.

When she got to the house, she poured a glass of ice water and went out to the patio to watch the sun rise. She did some stretches and ran an ice cube over her forehead.

Then she tiptoed into her bedroom, where John appeared to be sleeping soundly on his side, holding Poppy's pillow to his chest, just the way he held her when she was next to him. She had noticed that John often shifted to this position when she left the bed for a midnight snack or an early-morning run; he'd pull at a pillow or place the comforter so that it was bunched before him, to make a Poppy-like form to hold in sleep.

She peeled off her running clothes, which smelled of an unpleasant synthetic type of sweat. She took off her bra and underwear too, everything damp with sweat. Completely naked, she crawled into bed, pulling the pillow from John's arms and nestling herself in its place, facing him. She threw an arm over his broad shoulder. She put her nose on his neck and felt him swallow. She kissed his Adam's apple, and it vibrated as he made a gentle *"Mmm,"* sound, waking to her touch. Half asleep, he ran his hand clumsily down her side, then between her breasts. She shivered. She whispered, "It's gonna be an hour before anyone else is up."

He smiled, his eyes still closed. He said, "Mm?"

Poppy nuzzled her face into his neck, which was rough with two days' worth of unshaven stubble. She exhaled through her nose right into his jaw, and he giggled, ticklish. He whispered, "Did you have a good run?" and turned to lie on his back.

Poppy moved up onto her knees, then up over his belly, straddling him. Since his surgery, sex was easiest with her on top. They had tried out other ways, but this worked best. Poppy liked being on top anyway. She liked to see his face and touch it and direct the pace of things, and she could fairly predictably climax at the same time he did, because she could tell when he was close: a sudden look in his eyes that was at once ferocious and completely defenseless.

She eased herself on top of him and leaned forward to kiss his hair. Many kisses, all over his forehead and into his hair and scalp. He put both hands on the back of Poppy's head, in her hair, and whispered, "Love you, Pops," and she said, "Yeah, yeah, yeah," feigning impatience, and he laughed softly as she pressed herself hard against him.

All the good old moves, the tried-and-true, as steadfast and predictable as clockwork. Sex had changed once kids entered into the mix, of course; it had to be quick, had to be quiet. Then a bad mattress, then a bad knee, then the bad back; various circumstances necessitated a certain kind of sex, and over time, that kind of sex had become the only kind. Well, and anyhow, they'd been together twenty years, for crying out loud. Poppy didn't have anything new to show John at this stage of the game anyway—no new dirty talk, no new tricks. Why bother? What did she have to prove? She melted onto him, astounded at how good it still felt, that same old, dear old dance. She wondered if they'd still be doing it twenty years from now, when the kids were long gone and she and John were old, wrinkled, and lazy. Then she wondered about twenty years after *that*. If they'd still be doing it when they could barely see, barely hear, barely move, when all that was really left of life was the feelings.

After Poppy and John showered, they got an early jump on breakfast before Lisa was up, so that Lisa could relax and enjoy a meal without assuming all the work of preparing it. Poppy mixed up a sausage, egg, and cheese casserole with ingredients they already had around the house, and John went out to pick up a dozen donuts from Sweetie-Pies, the famed bakery across the island.

Ryan was the first to wake. The casserole still had twenty minutes of baking time, and John had not yet returned with the donuts.

Poppy said, "You got a better night's sleep than our first night, I take it?"

Ryan nodded. "Like a log." He removed the rubber band from the newspaper that sat on the counter and started reading the front page. Poppy leaned over the counter to sniff him. "Are you wearing cologne?" she said.

Ryan wriggled away. "It's called *deodorant.*" He went to the refrigerator and poured himself a glass of orange juice. "I'm gonna be on the patio. Let me know when the casserole's ready?"

"Yeah, hon," Poppy said.

Several minutes later, Poppy was unloading the dishwasher when the phone rang behind her, and she was so startled that she dropped a steak knife on the floor.

She put the phone to her ear. "Hello?"

Silence. No voice, no dial tone.

Poppy held her palm over the mouthpiece and rammed the speaker end to her ear. *Who the . . .* Several more seconds passed. Was that breathing at the other end of the line? A man. Was it *heavy* breathing? Could be.

Poppy took her hand off the mouthpiece and said, "Hello?"

A man's voice, deep and soft, said, "Hello."

Poppy said briskly, "Are you calling for Scott? To play golf?"

A few seconds of silence, then the man said, "No."

She sputtered, "Well then, who *are* you? . . . Huh? . . . Well?"

The man didn't speak, but he didn't hang up either.

"*Nothin'?*" Poppy barked.

When the man didn't answer, Poppy hung up the phone so hard it jangled against the wall mount. "Hell with that guy," she muttered to herself. Some sicko getting his jollies calling random numbers on the island and breathing heavily into the phone if a woman answered.

As she returned to the dishwasher, the name Keats Firestone flashed through Poppy's head. She tried to ignore it. She put a few dishes away and fanned her face with a pamphlet on the counter. Well, shit on a stick. She wished she hadn't had that thought. *Keats Firestone.* Poppy didn't *really* believe the call had anything to do with Keats, but, well, she'd rather rule it out so she could forget about it altogether. If it weren't for the kids here, if they hadn't had that second encounter with the guy . . . It would be better for her just to trace the call so she could know and put it out of her mind.

Poppy grabbed a pen and a takeout menu from the counter and returned to the phone. *Alright, creep. Where ya calling from?* Poppy dialed *69, and a woman's automated voice came on and introduced the Caller ID service. When the woman recited the originating number of the call, Poppy was so surprised by the area code that she almost dropped the phone. The area code was not local, but belonged to Wheeling, West Virginia. The caller was somebody from home.

14

KEATS WATCHED THE morning news and ate a soft-boiled egg on a piece of toast while Roxie showered after her long run.

She came out of the bathroom in her blue terrycloth robe, a towel wrapped around her hair, turban-like, and she carried a large bottle of moisturizer. She took a seat next to Keats on the couch.

He said, "Need a rubdown?"

"Not today. My foot's the only part of me that's cramping up, and it isn't too bad." She squeezed a dollop of moisturizer into her palm and rubbed her hands together to warm it. "You know that lady I told you about yesterday who bummed a cigarette while she was out for a run?"

Keats nodded absently, eyes on a commercial for mortgage refinancing.

"We bumped into each other again this morning," she said. "Isn't that something? She's staying in one of those green houses up by Millard's Cove, and she'd just started out north when we ran into each other. I convinced her to turn back and go see the magnolias with me. We ran a few miles together."

"Imagine that helped the time go by."

Roxie nodded. She shook the towel around her head free, and wet hair fell to her shoulders. "We're probably going to meet up and run together again tomorrow morning." She cracked her big toe.

Keats patted Roxie's bare knee, which was peeping out from her robe.

"She and her family are from West Virginia," Roxie continued. "Sounds like they don't have much money. They're with another family who got an all-expenses-paid deal, so they're just along for the ride." Roxie propped her foot up and examined a callus. She rubbed the underside of her foot with both thumbs, working at a cramp. "It's nice to meet down-to-earth people on the island every now and then. You know? Easy to forget they exist."

Keats scraped the prongs of his fork over a bit of sticky golden yolk that remained on his plate, to create a striped design.

Roxie sniffed the air, then punched the couch cushion next to her, releasing a cloud of dust and dog hair that hung suspended and colorless in the morning sunlight. "Yuck," she said.

Keats said, "Talk to the dog, then. Tell him to quit sheddin'."

Roxie laughed. "When we leave the island," she said, picking at a loose thread on the couch and patting the cushion, "this old thing's staying behind."

"Fine by me," Keats said.

• • •

John entered the house whistling, a large, greasy white box full of donuts under his arm. Poppy took the donut box from him, set it on the kitchen counter, and held a finger at her lips.

In hushed tones, Poppy told John about the phone call, the heavy breather. She showed him the number of the originating call, which she had called back and gotten no answer after twenty-some rings. Then Poppy explained that she had called the directory service to find out where in Wheeling the call came from, gotten the address, and discovered it was a pay phone on Mercer Avenue. She had ruled out anything concerning her parents. She had ruled out anything concerning Carol, or anyone who might have been calling on Carol's behalf. There was no reason such a person would have called from a pay phone, she thought, and no reason they would have declined to speak when given the chance.

The two of them tried to picture the exact location of the address in Wheeling. As far as they could remember, Mercer ran for a few blocks downtown, near the university parking garage. Nothing of particular note in the area.

John seemed more intrigued than concerned.

Nothing scared John, a quality that Poppy found both re-assuring and incredibly annoying. Years earlier, a serial killer had escaped from a maximum-security prison in Paden City, under an hour away from their home, and John didn't even think to deadbolt the front door the night the news broke. Poppy stared at him flabbergasted the next morning. She pointed at their door. "John," she said, "a granny could kick that thing in. You're practically begging that serial killer to waltz in and slit our throats!" John found this terribly funny, but he also promised to deadbolt their front door until they received word that the killer had been apprehended.

Poppy studied his face. "You're not worried."

John shook his head. "I'm sure there's a good explanation. Not worth making a fuss about."

"Do you think we should ask the kids?"

John considered this. "I guess we could, long as it's low-key and doesn't get them wound up. I'll ask Alex about it while we're out fishing. See if she knows anybody who ever makes calls from a pay phone, or if she can think of anyone who'd be trying to get in touch with her."

"OK," Poppy said. "I'll run it by Ryan sometime this morning too."

She gazed outside. Ryan had finished his orange juice. His legs were crossed and propped up and the newspaper was spread over his thighs, but he didn't appear to be reading.

John and Alex ate their breakfast and left for fishing before any of the Dalys had woken. Poppy served donuts and her sausage and egg casserole to everyone as they showed up. She had tried her best with Lisa's special coffee and the French press, but it somehow came out both too thin and too gritty, so Lisa started a fresh pot.

Kimmy was the last member of the household to surface. Rae was at the coffee table, still in her Victoria's Secret pajamas and working on a jigsaw puzzle when Kimmy entered the room. Rae offered a bright and energetic "Morning, Kimmers!"

When Kimmy didn't acknowledge her sister, Rae threw a pen cap at her head. Kimmy swatted it away. She was not in a mood to be joked with. She hadn't slept well, stewing all night about the fight with Rae and listening to Alex's intermittent moaning and thrashing about with cramps, despite the Motrin that Poppy had given her.

In the light of a fresh day, the world felt significantly less grim to Kimmy, but the fight with Rae still smarted, and she was determined not to accept any niceties.

But Rae wasn't giving up easily. "Kimmy," she cooed from the sofa, "come sit next to me. I need your help with the puzzle."

Kimmy didn't look in her sister's direction.

Rae patted the cushion next to her. "You look so pretty. Are you wearing one of your new Lip Smackers?" Rae had given Kimmy a set of Lip Smacker glosses in various flavors for her birthday several months ago—it was a special present, Kimmy treasured it very much, and Rae knew this.

Kimmy glanced sideways at her sister, but offered nothing.

"Are you?" Rae pressed forward. "Which one are you wearing?"

Kimmy sighed through her nose.

"What's that?" Rae encouraged her gently.

"Root beer," Kimmy muttered, already feeling far too susceptible to Rae's attempts at reconciliation.

"It looks really cute." Rae scooched down the couch so she was closer to Kimmy, and she sidled up to her. She took

Kimmy's hand and pulled it downward so that Kimmy's face was near hers.

Rae whispered, "I didn't really mean what I said last night." Her breath smelled like the maple donut she had just eaten. "Forgive me?"

When Kimmy didn't respond immediately, Rae tugged needily on her hand, then kissed Kimmy's fingers like an overzealous admirer.

"Forgive me?" Rae said again.

Kimmy hated herself for so easily succumbing to this obvious manipulation, but attention from her older sister was so rare and felt so impossibly good that she couldn't help herself. Rae had even called her pretty, and that meant so much coming from Rae.

"Forgive me?" Rae asked a third time, and Kimmy nodded.

"Cool," Rae said, dropping Kimmy's hand and returning to the puzzle.

Kimmy said, "I'll help you with the puzzle in a minute." She went to the kitchen to select a donut.

Kimmy felt so instantly restored by the interaction that it didn't occur to her that Rae had somehow secured her forgiveness without saying "I'm sorry." It didn't occur to Kimmy that Rae had never once in their entire life together said "I'm sorry."

Ryan was still outside on the patio, finishing his second donut, shirt off now, soaking up the early-morning sun. He was bent over the newspaper with a pencil, tackling the crossword.

Scott announced that he was going to drive off the island to the nearby town of Beaufort for an hour or two, to check out a classic car show featuring Mustangs from the 1960s. Lisa showed no sign of surprise or objection to this, so Poppy figured they had already discussed it. Scott must have been right with what he'd said yesterday, Poppy thought, about giving Lisa space even if it was at the expense of family time together.

"Bye, girls," Scott called to Rae and Kimmy, who were working, heads down, on the jigsaw puzzle. He came over to do a special choreographed high five with Kimmy. She made him stop and start over several times until they got it just right.

Then she sang, "Daddy, if you're leaving us, you have to come back with presents for us."

Scott laughed. "If you say so."

Kimmy saluted and said, "Later, alligator."

Rae didn't say anything, but looked up briefly once her father was halfway to the door, as though to confirm that he was actually leaving.

Once he had gone, Lisa drew close to Poppy and spoke softly enough that the girls wouldn't overhear. "We figured it's better if we steer clear of each other as much as we can without being obvious," she said.

"Did you talk anything through last night? Resolve anything?"

"No, except for a pact to keep it civil for the girls. I told him we need to talk when we get back home. *Really* talk. Get serious about making some decisions."

"How'd he respond?"

"He agreed," Lisa said.

"At least you can agree on that."

Lisa reached behind her neck to tighten the knot on her bikini, a red one today. It seemed Lisa had a new bikini for every six hours. This one was particularly sexy, with a gold hoop at her sternum that connected the bra cups. She was beach-ready, sunglasses holding her hair out of her face, cheeks already gleaming with sunscreen, a white see-through cover-up skirt high on her waist. Bright red lipstick to match the bikini. Poppy felt like a schlub in the same navy one-piece they had all seen before, the only swimsuit she owned, her hair still wet from the shower but rapidly expanding with frizz as it dried.

Lisa moved across the room to wipe down the kitchen table with Windex. "Can you believe tomorrow is our last full day?"

From the living room, Kimmy wailed, "I *never* want to leave!" She turned to Rae. "This is the best place we've ever been. Don't you think so?"

Rae shrugged. "Every place I've ever been is pretty much the same." What she meant by this was, *I feel pretty much the same way every place I go.* No matter where she was, the world always refused to give Rae what she felt she was owed.

Poppy said, "Are you guys done with your breakfast? Let's get our butts down to the beach."

Kimmy leapt to her feet, puzzle pieces scattering to the floor.

Poppy finished loading the dishwasher while Lisa massaged sunscreen into Kimmy's back. Then she stepped onto the patio, where Ryan was still hard at work on the crossword. "You ready to hit the surf?"

"Let's do it." Ryan folded up the newspaper and squinted into the sky behind Poppy, his pupils instantly shrinking to specks, his dark brown irises red and green and gold in the direct sun.

John and Alex were having much better luck today. After only an hour casting off the pier, they had gotten dozens of bites, and John had already pulled in two midsized speckled trout and a flounder, while Alex snagged a pinfish. John had come optimistically prepared once again with a cooler full of ice. He was pleased that he'd have a few fillets to take back for Poppy to fry up. The pinfish would be measly, but the trout would probably provide six ounces apiece. Enough for everyone in the house to have at least a little.

As was John's practice, once he had removed the hook from the ensnared fish, he bopped the fish on the head with a mallet, hard enough to kill it instantly, before throwing it on ice. Alex, as always, watched this process unflinchingly, but she did not ask to participate.

A year or so earlier, while fishing out of John's motorboat on Baker Lake, Alex had asked to kill the first bluegill they caught. She'd seen her father do it a hundred times before. And while it was trickier in a motorboat than on a cement pier, you simply held the thing on the floor of the boat with a foot and your left hand and bopped it with the mallet in your right, and John had no qualms about letting Alex do it. He had seen her hammer nails with great precision and whack baseballs into center field; he didn't think she'd have any trouble offing a six-inch bluegill with a single swing.

But she did. She let up with her foot a split second before the mallet struck, and the fish flipped in that moment, moving enough that Alex made only partial contact with the head, not nearly enough to effectively stun it. Blood poured from the fish's gills and it thrashed hard against the bottom of the boat, continuing to impressively catch a few inches of air. Alex gasped and squeaked as the fish thrashed and bounced, and instinctively she slapped at the thing with her hand while it was in the air. She ended up batting the fish clean over the side and into the water. She held the mallet in her right hand and stared up at John with surprise, and then shame.

"It's OK, hon," he said gently. "You almost had him."

Alex peered over the side of the boat.

John said, "Can you see him down there?"

Alex nodded. "He's bleeding really bad." She sniffed and added softly, "He's swimming really slow in a little circle." She looked up at her father with tears in her eyes. "He's going to die."

John said, "Well, he was gonna die either way."

"But . . ." Alex peered back over the side, looking like she might try to reach in with her hand and scoop the fish out but realizing she wouldn't be able to reach it. "But since I messed up, he's suffering," she said. She looked up at the sky and then wiped her eyes on her forearm. "I'm sad," she said.

"It's good to feel sad sometimes," John said. "You did just fine, though, you did your best. I bet you'll get the next one, and every single one after that."

It was a good lesson, John thought. It was good to feel how bad it was for something to suffer unnecessarily.

Their fishing success today had been so quick and so surprising that John had almost forgotten his promise to try to find out if Alex knew anything about the Wheeling phone booth caller. He turned around to adjust the ice in the cooler behind him to make sure all their fish were covered, then he cast his line and remarked, as casually as he could manage, "Hey, by the way, you happen to know anyone from home who uses a pay phone?"

"Like in a booth?" Alex said.

"Yeah."

"Not really. I mean, if somebody's mom's late picking them up from school, sometimes somebody'll use the one in the lobby to call home or something."

"Right," John said. "But nobody that you know of uses one, like, often, right? Or, nobody has maybe a dad or older brother you know of that uses one?"

Alex shook her head disinterestedly.

It was quiet for a while.

Alex acted as though she might be getting a nibble and bounced her line, but nothing came of it.

John decided to take the conversation further. Though he

didn't suspect the caller from home was anything to worry about, it couldn't hurt to have a little bit of a chat ... He couldn't remember the last time he and Poppy had the Good Touch, Bad Touch talk with Alex. They had made a point to do that with both kids, he was sure of that, but he couldn't remember how long it'd been, which probably meant it had been too long.

John cleared his throat, adjusted his posture, and said, "There's no one from home you can think of, other than your friends from school, who ever tries to get in touch with you on the phone. Right?"

"Like who?"

"I don't know," John said. "Like a teacher, or one of our neighbors, or one of your friends' dads ... I just mean, nobody like that ... You've never had any sort of private relationship with somebody like that, right?"

"What the heck do you mean, Daddy?"

John cleared his throat and said, "We've talked about good touches and bad touches—"

"Oh my gosh, Daddy." Alex's cheeks flushed and brightened fully to bubble-gum pink. "Yes, we've talked about that, and they also talk to us about that at school. I know what all that stuff is, like molesters and stuff. Oh my gosh, why do you want to talk about such gross stuff?"

John instantly felt so reassured by this response that he laughed. Then he stopped abruptly, not wanting Alex to think it was a laughing matter.

"I just wanted to make sure," he said. "It's been a while since we've had that talk, and I want to remind you, don't ever be scared to say something to your mom or me. About that kind of thing, or any kind of thing."

"I know, duh," Alex said. She paused. "Did you bring this up because I started my period last night?"

"No," John glanced at her stiffly. "Nothing to do with that. But your mom told me." A few words shuffled around in his mind: *Congratulations? Good job?*

Eventually, he said, "You're feeling alright, then?"

Alex said, "It's not a big deal."

John reached out a hand to put around his daughter's shoulders, but realized that his fingers were smelly and stained with fish blood and soil from the bait container, so he just patted the concrete between the two of them.

Back at the shore, Rae had settled into a beach chair with her book, Lisa was doing some yoga stretches in the shade of the umbrella, Kimmy was making a drip castle at the water's edge, and Ryan and Poppy were floating on their backs in the ocean.

"Hey," Poppy said, creating a gentle current with her palms in order to move closer to Ryan. "You weren't expecting any calls here this week, were you?"

"Huh?" Ryan grunted, but otherwise his posture showed no discernible reaction to the question. He was facing the sky, eyes closed, expression blank, body stiff as a board, like a mannequin that had been tossed to sea.

Poppy said, "Nobody would be calling the house phone for you here, right?"

Ryan's brow twitched once: up, down. "No. Why?"

When Poppy didn't answer, it was quiet between them for a bit, then Ryan said again, "Why?"

She said, "Oh, a weird call came in this morning. Like a . . . a guy, a man at the other end, sorta breathed heavy into the phone . . ."

"Ew," Ryan said, sinking in the water, then moving to stand so that he could fully face his mother. He flicked a piece of debris on the surface near him, sent it soaring. "Seriously?"

Poppy waved a hand casually to indicate, *Maybe, maybe not.* She said, "It's no big deal, not really clear who it is, nothing to worry about. I just wanted to make sure it wouldn't be somebody trying to reach you."

"Nope," Ryan said. He was quiet for a while, then said, "Nobody knows anything about the caller?"

Poppy shook her head. "I'm sure it was a misdial."

"Sure."

Satisfied with this conversation and eager to speak of other things, Poppy said, "How's your crab coming along, anyway? You ever figure out what killed that little guy?"

Ryan shook his head. "Not a clue."

15

SCOTT WAS ON his way back from Beaufort (well, Beaufort by way of Ashdale, Burton, and Port Royal) before eleven o'clock that morning, and he was in some deep shit.

Already this morning, Scott had driven to all six banks within a thirty-mile radius of their beach house, withdrawn the maximum amount of cash, and was still $380 short of what he needed by noon today. At the last bank, a Wells Fargo in Port Royal, his debit card had been declined altogether. He spoke to a teller who explained that suspicious activity had caused the account to be frozen. She made a call to a headquarters and said that the problem had been corrected, but it would take forty-eight hours for his funds to become accessible again.

"Forty-eight hours?" Scott stared at her. "You friggin' *kidding* me? Did you say *forty-eight hours*?"

The teller shrank as she nodded to confirm this information.

Scott experienced a brief out-of-body moment as anger overtook him. He grabbed a deposit slip from the counter before him and ripped it to pieces. Then he hightailed it out of the bank, recognizing that he might well get himself arrested if his temper got the best of him.

Now he was on his way back to the beach house with just over three grand in cash, but what he really needed was thirty-five hundred even, to get himself out of this mess. Three grand was close, and he was lucky he'd gotten that much before his account was frozen, but *close* didn't cut it with these kind of guys. And he couldn't just not show up at their place at noon—he had already ruled that out. Not showing would be the worst possible thing he could do. The guys had the address of the beach house where Scott was staying, so not appearing at their place would almost certainly mean they would come looking for him there when the family was around. There would be a scene. Things would get ugly.

Scott's current plan, adapted since he hadn't been able to withdraw the full amount, was to take them the cash he had and offer up his watch, which was worth twice the remaining $380 balance. Still, he might end up with a black eye—it would depend on what sort of mood they were in and if they'd been drinking. A black eye wouldn't be the worst thing in the world; he'd say he got whacked with a stray golf ball or had gotten into a fight with some drunk at the car show. Scott wasn't a fighter, Lisa knew that, but it would probably fly. His biggest hope was that even if a black eye was involved, these guys wouldn't demand his diamond-encrusted wedding band, like they'd threatened to the day before, because Scott knew that showing up at the house without his wedding band would send Lisa into absolute hysterics.

Scott knew his wife already suspected an affair.

If only it were that, he thought. Wouldn't that be easy? You could end an affair with some lame excuse and a snap of the fingers. Right? Scott had never cheated in all their years of marriage, but he imagined it was easy to cut it off with a mistress, bada-boom, some tears, some insults or threats, some guilt trips, then it was done. But the sort of mess Scott was in . . . And it was a brand-new mess every few weeks, to be fair, depending on the size of the debt, and each one entirely his own doing, but still, a gambling debt wasn't the sort of trouble you could weasel out of with a dozen roses.

Shit, shit. Scott pounded the steering wheel with his palms as he waited in line to cross the bridge onto Fripp Island. *You dumb shit. Why couldn't you quit when you were ahead?* He had been up twelve hundred dollars after an hour and a half of poker the first afternoon at the beach, when he'd met these guys. Four of them, trashy real-estate hotshots, down from Newark for the week. They had rescued Scott from the golf course before the storm that afternoon, had him back to their condo, couple cocktails, couple hands of poker. Everything great, all good fun. Scott had suggested playing for money, nothing serious, fifty dollar buy-in. Everyone had been on board, and Scott had gone up quick.

Before parting ways that first day, Scott had suggested playing for money on the golf course the following day. He was being cocky, of course, just wanted to ride out the win. Couldn't *stand* to call it quits while he was ahead. That was the disease, wasn't it? That's what they called it in the meetings: a disease. Scott had been to only a few meetings over the past few years. They made him feel real shitty. Because he *knew* this was bad, *knew* this made him a bad man, and if he allowed himself to dwell on it for more than two seconds, it crushed his heart. He'd broken so many promises to himself, he'd lost count. He didn't want to hurt his family, didn't want to be this bad man. But the impulse overcame all logic, all thoughts of family and future, when it took hold. A disease.

All of this had started about three years ago, with a buddy's bachelor party in Atlantic City. *Who had bachelor parties for their second marriage?* Anyhow, that was the start, and it had been a riotous affair ever since. Once he reached his mid-forties, Scott didn't expect to feel anything new — he thought he'd pretty much done it all, seen it all, felt all the things he was going to feel. But when he got that first whiff and then that first real taste of gambling that weekend in Atlantic City, it brought with it a new kind of adrenaline that knocked him upside down, socked him silly, sucked him right in. He was powerless, instantly in love with everything about it: the games themselves (it didn't matter if it was blackjack online, roulette at the casino in Germantown, throwing a grand at the Redskins game, or Aces and Deuces on the golf course with some dudes from New Jersey), the smell of cash, the big wins, the wildly fluctuating bank account . . . It was, quite frankly — and it brought Scott no pleasure to admit this — better than the best sex. And along with all of this came the rush of trying to hide it all from Lisa, which was the highest-stakes game of all. God, it was *brilliant,* some of the maneuvers he'd pulled, some of the disasters he'd worked his way out of. He had to cover his tracks when it came to his internet activity, the happy hours at Monnetti's to meet up with the bookie, and the occasional weekend at the casino, but so far Lisa was still completely in the dark. There had been a few times when she'd gotten close to catching him in a lie about his whereabouts, but even then, all it took was a bit of convincing and Lisa ultimately bought the lie and let it go.

Scott had noticed a decline in his sex drive when he first started gambling, and worried at the time that this would arouse suspicion. But Lisa seemed fine with it, perhaps even favorable to the new, less frequent routine. Scott didn't like to dwell on this too much. And when it came to the money, gambling had required Scott to create secret accounts, make transfers that wouldn't raise red flags, and be sure that he always had enough in the joint account to cover the bills and Lisa's credit card spending. He tried hard never to touch this joint account, and so far had done it only once, dipping in for a hefty loan that he was able to replenish the very next day. Some way, somehow, Scott had always been able to pull out a big win when he needed it most. It was almost like somebody up there cared and was looking out for him.

That's what made this whole golf situation so annoying. Thirty-five hundred dollars was nothing to Scott, really. At present, he had millions in the bank. But he'd planned poorly —it hadn't crossed his mind to bring a bunch of cash with him because he knew Poppy and John wouldn't be down to gamble, and he hadn't anticipated making friends on the island who were. When they set the stakes before golf yesterday, it never occurred to him that he might lose as badly as he did.

Of course, as bad luck would have it, he'd played the worst round of his life. He had a few excuses—lame, but still. First of all, in his enthusiasm to gamble, he had forgotten his golf glove in his room that morning. He'd forgotten his club pass too, for crying out loud—fortunately, one of the other guys had an extra to lend him. But no one had an extra glove, so Scott had a blister to contend with by the fifth hole. Also, it was a relatively unfamiliar course, he was nervous, could have been something in the air . . . Regardless, he was in a pile of shit by the tenth hole, and when he didn't have the cash on him at the end of the round, those guys were drunk, pissed, and just about pounded him then and there. New Jersey trash, all of them. Scott knew the score, though: it was terrible form to enter a game with strangers if you weren't prepared to pony up on the spot. Jesus, he had been stupid. Sloppy.

Scott had tried to deescalate. They weren't humored. He explained that he'd just have to hit a few ATMs to get the cash. "Just give me until tomorrow," Scott had pled with them. "Noon tomorrow, I'll be at your place with the money." They had demanded the address of his beach house, and they almost took his wedding ring as collateral, but Scott was able to talk them out of that, thank goodness —things were bad enough with Lisa as it was.

He thought he'd be able to produce the cash, no problem, but had neglected to consider the fact that here on this godforsaken island, he was a five-hour drive from the closest branch of his bank, and of course there would be with-drawal limits at any other institution ... No checkbook, and he obviously couldn't ask John for a loan without it getting back to Lisa ... Christ, what a mess. What a stupid, stupid mess. *What the hell is wrong with you?* Scott slammed his palms on the steering wheel. *What's it gonna take to quit? A divorce? A bullet through your skull?* He was consumed by shame.

It was 10:48 now, the clock was ticking, bridge traffic backed up, and he had to get to the beach house to pick up his watch before he went to those guys' condo, due there at twelve o'clock sharp. He could only hope they would ac-cept three grand and an eight-hundred-dollar watch in lieu of thirty-five hundred all in cash. They'd be fools not to take the watch and call it even, but Jesus Christ, *New Jersey,* who knew what to expect from New Jersey?

Bridge traffic started to improve at 10:55. Within a few more minutes, it was moving at a good pace.

Scott made it back to the house by a quarter after eleven. Now he just had to hope that everybody was still either out fishing or on the beach, so that he wouldn't encounter any-one and have to make any small talk, answer questions about the car show in Beaufort, where he had allegedly spent his morning. The Omni was gone—that was a good sign. As he parked his car, Scott ran his hands over his scalp, not sure if his sweaty palms were dampening his dry hair, or the other way around. Everything sweaty now, hot and tense and tight as a drum. *Everything shit.*

• • •

Scott entered through the front door of the house and jogged up the stairs that led to the kitchen and main room, connecting to the bedroom hallway. He was halfway up the steps when he heard a voice, and he froze instantly. Only one voice. Male. With the Omni gone, most likely it was Ryan. Only one voice, so . . . on the phone? Scott would make a beeline for his room, he decided, give a friendly nod to Ryan on his way to and from the bedroom, in and out . . .

But when Scott, on the stairs, peeked up over the floor level so that he could see Ryan, something stopped him from proceeding. Scott stayed where he was, eyes level with the floor, so he could see Ryan, but Ryan wouldn't see Scott unless he had reason to turn and look his way.

Ryan was hunched over beside the refrigerator, phone at his ear. He spoke with a palm over his mouth and was facing out to the patio, presumably so that he would see anyone approach from the beach before they saw him. The air of secrecy — Ryan clearly did not want to be heard, did not want anyone to know he was on the phone at all. Scott was intrigued. Illicit girlfriend? Illicit *boyfriend*? Still facing out toward the beach, Ryan hissed, "That was my *mom* who answered this morning, you moron," and a little chuckle escaped him, despite his obvious agitation with the person at the other end of the line.

Scott stayed perfectly still.

When Ryan spoke again it was at full volume — seemingly confident now that no one else was in the house. "Anyway," Ryan said, "like I said, it went fine." He was quiet for a bit. "Don't worry about it, nobody's gonna ask any more questions if you don't call again, so just *don't call again,* dude." Ryan paused and then snorted laughter into his fist. "My mom said you like breathed heavy or something?" Whatever the guy at the other end of the line said in response made Ryan laugh even harder. Then he got quiet. "Anyway, it ended up being twelve hundred. Yeah, all cash." Ryan was quiet for a moment, then he said, "I'll see you in a few days. Don't call here again, you mouth-breather." He hung up the phone.

Scott froze in place, formulating a plan in case Ryan came his way once the phone call had ended, but Ryan exited the kitchen in the opposite direction almost immediately after hanging up the phone, heading out to the patio.

Scott dashed up the stairs. Still pressed for time. He stood in the kitchen to watch as Ryan crossed the patio and walked toward the beach.

Scott paused briefly to observe the boy. *What the hell is that kid up to?* Had to be drugs. A "stash," he had said. Twelve hundred dollars. Well, it was kind of nice, really, to consider that the whiz kid with the full scholarship was into some shady shit, carrying around what sounded like a hefty wad of cash, conducting some sort of drug business on the family vacation. It was quite nice, everything about it. Perfect, actually. Because—and Scott couldn't believe he was so distracted by wondering what precisely Ryan was up to that the critical detail had almost escaped him—the kid had said twelve hundred in cash. That's what he'd said, right? *Too good.* Couldn't be, could it?

Scott just had to find it. He didn't have much time to spare, but how hard could it be?

He crept into Ryan's bedroom, where the door was several inches ajar. The room had a pleasant, soupy, lived-in smell. His eyes darted around. Clothing everywhere. Dirty towels. Backpack. *Backpack?* Nah, too obvious. Glass full of bright blue water on the dresser, a dead crab on top. *Weird.* Bed stand. He tried to home in on his own instincts, realizing that with all the experience he'd had hiding cash from Lisa, this ought to be easy. *Where would I stash twelve hundred dollars?* He entered the bathroom connected to Ryan's room and opened the cabinet beneath the sink. His eyes immediately fell on the toilet plunger, tucked in the back corner of the cabinet. He knew it, he knew it before he even lifted the thing.

He tipped the plunger back an inch off the plywood surface and there it was, a neat little wad of hundreds, halved and held together with a paper clip.

Scott could not believe his luck. He smelled the cash and kissed it. Then he counted out four hundreds — no use robbing the kid for all he was worth, he'd only take what he needed.

He folded up the remaining eight bills, clipped them, slipped them back beneath the plunger. He left the room with his heart in his ears and glanced out the kitchen window to confirm that Ryan was at the beach with the others, before dashing outside to his car.

It was 11:31. He was going to make it to their place with

the full payment and time to spare. And he wouldn't have to give up his watch! Scott pulled out of the driveway and up the street, the sun on his face, and he was so happy, he sang. He fingered the crucifix at his neck. He didn't particularly like to invoke the Father, Son, or Holy Spirit in his gambling unless it was an absolute emergency, but he also wanted to give credit where credit was due. He lifted the gold piece to his lips and kissed it.

Before he was five minutes down the road, Scott began to steel himself against the inevitable temptation he knew would rise within him the moment he was in their presence. The disease. The urge to ride it out a little bit longer. Propose another round of golf or an hour of poker. Or even just a single hand. *No.* He wouldn't do it. He pictured Lisa's face, Rae's, and Kimmy's. *No more,* he commanded himself. *Never again. This is where it ends.*

16

SCOTT, JOHN, AND Alex all returned to the house around the same time, half past noon, as the sky was darkening to charcoal and everyone from the beach was rushing in, supplies in hand.

The storm hit with a violent crack, the sky split, warm rain pounded the house in sheets and bursts. Poppy got out the blender for frozen margaritas and started melting butter for the fillets John and Alex had returned with. Lisa set the table and assembled BLTs — "just in case there's not enough of that fish to go around" — and she also sliced up some pears and tossed them in a bowl with berries and cream.

Alex and Kimmy raided the game cabinet and pulled out a floppy, falling-apart yellow box containing Guess Who? They set up the game on the coffee table in the main room, where Scott was watching a *Jeopardy!* rerun on TV.

John emerged from his bedroom in jeans and a clean T-shirt, hair freshly combed with a neat side part that was sunburned pink.

Poppy said, "Fish looks great, hon," as she tossed the fillets into the butter. She had a lime-green, icy margarita mustache, and John kissed it and licked his lips. "How's your back?" Poppy said.

"Seized up a little while I was cleaning the fish," John said. "Doc said I'm fine to take an extra half-pill when it does that. I'm thinkin' about it."

Poppy said brightly, "Let's not."

John stared at her, annoyed at both her words and the chirpy tone. He gestured toward the hallway, and she followed him to their bedroom. He pulled the door shut behind him, spun to face her, and said, "We've been over this. It's fine, I know what I'm doing, swear to God. Your paranoia is starting to get to me. Don't think I haven't noticed you counting my pills day in and day out for the past three months. You're about to give me a complex."

"Shit," Poppy said. "I thought I was being sneaky." She swallowed. "I know it seems like I go overboard, but we know too many people who've gone down that path. I get scared sometimes. Doesn't mean I don't trust you."

"Interesting," John said. "Can I trust *you*?" He paused for a few seconds, and when she didn't respond, he said, "You think I didn't smell cigarette on you when you got back from your run yesterday morning?"

Poppy's eyes rounded with surprise, then went narrow, trapped and defensive. "You didn't say anything," she said. "You're supposed to say something when you catch someone."

"I guess I was waiting for the right opportunity." John laughed at this and offered a hug of reconciliation.

Poppy stepped briskly aside and out of reach. She knelt

to pick up a sock off the floor, then rearranged her things on the top of the armoire: sunglasses, magazines, sunscreen.

John's arms were still outstretched. "Oh, come on. Don't do that, not while we're on vacation."

"Do what?" She picked up a damp towel from the floor and flung it over the TV cabinet door to dry.

"That thing you do when you're mad. Start cleaning, all fast and furious. Yes, just like that."

"Well I *am* mad," Poppy said. "You made me feel stupid."

"How come?"

"Because you knew I was counting your pills all this time and you let me keep doing it. And then you catch me red-handed, smelling like smoke, and you don't even say so. You just save it to use as ammo . . ."

"Pop. I let you keep counting my pills even though I knew you were doing it because it makes me feel safe. OK? I get it, even if it bugs the hell out of me. I just hate to see you so worried and so wound up all the time."

Poppy tossed the sock in her hand into the suitcase at her feet. Irritably, she said, "I wish I loved you less. I really do. Then I could probably relax and enjoy this world a little more."

Back in the main room, Rae was standing at the sliding glass door that overlooked the patio and the path to the beach. She was wearing a white crop top over denim shorts that were frayed to shreds, and glittery flip-flops. She held a bottle of electric-blue Gatorade. Rain slashed the glass before her.

On the couch behind her, Alex and Kimmy were playing Guess Who? Alex said, "Does your person have black hair?"

"Nope," Kimmy said.

Alex flipped down the yellow squares displaying the faces of three black-haired people on her board. *Click, click, click.*

The episode of *Jeopardy!* had ended, the theme song played, Alex Trebek left his post to shake the hands of the contestants as the credits and disclaimers rolled. Scott tipped his head back and forth in time with the song and harmonized above it. *"Doo-dee-doo-dee-doo-dee-doo . . ."*

He added a flourish with his hand at the cadence.

Kimmy watched her father, imitated the flourish, then returned to the game. "Is your person making a face like this?" Kimmy said to Alex, and she scrunched her face into a pursed-lipped grimace, brows drawn, eyes narrowed.

Alex looked down at her own board and laughed. "Yes."

Kimmy asked, "Bernardo?"

"You got it *again!*" Alex said. "You are really good at this. You know all the people."

Kimmy said, "I play it at my friend Ashley's house all the time."

Alex said, "Who was your person?"

"Maria. She's my favorite. She's *so* pretty, isn't she?"

Alex said, "I guess so."

"I think she looks like Rae," Kimmy said. She was quiet for a moment, then she said, "There's a few kids at my school who call me Bugsy, like because of my teeth?"

Alex said, "I wouldn't worry about them. I think you're really pretty."

Kimmy sighed. "Thanks."

"You want to play another game?" Alex said.

Kimmy nodded, and she stared at Maria for a little longer before flipping all of the faces on her board upward for the next game.

In his bedroom, Ryan was doing some quick math on the back of a *National Geographic* magazine. The deal had been so easy. He was still tingly at the thought of that fat wad of cash stuck under the plunger in his bathroom. Now that the deal was done, he couldn't help himself from dreaming up next steps. A bigger operation. He considered how much more product he could grow in the limited space he had available, how much more quickly he could grow it, and how much more money they could charge for it. After all, those people had said that it was the best weed they ever smoked.

Ryan had spent the past six months perfecting the hydroponic setup in his bedroom closet. It was a large closet, conveniently constructed in such a way that a single jacket on a hanger would conceal the whole operation unless someone was looking. And no one came looking. Ryan was tidy enough that Poppy barely set foot in his room except to give it a quick glance now and then. John wasn't one to pry. Alex had never been a snoop.

A classmate who went by Ham had introduced Ryan to marijuana while working together on a group project for science class at the beginning of their senior year. The two of them would smoke shitty joints out of the bed of Ham's pickup truck after they had finished their work. Ham had come up with the idea of growing and selling their own weed once he saw how proficient Ryan was with the simple hydroponic setup required for their class project.

It ended up making the most sense for Ryan to grow and Ham to distribute. Ryan would harvest and package the weed in the privacy of his bedroom and deliver it to Ham, who lived a twenty-minute bike ride away, in the evenings or on weekends so that he would never have to run the risk of bringing product to school. Ham took care of the money side.

Ham wisely decided to sell to kids at the university rather than their high school, and had an easy connection with an older sister and two cousins who were students at WVU. It was a neat and profitable little venture. Six months in and they hadn't had so much as a close call with parents or law enforcement.

The Fripp Island deal came about when Ryan had mentioned to Ham that he would be gone for a long weekend on a family vacation there. Ham said, "In South Carolina? You're shittin' me, dude." He made a quick phone call to confirm, and sure enough, Ham's older brother, Keller, was on Fripp Island for the summer, working as the caddy for some professional golfer who had tournaments and workshops lined up on the island. Keller had been complaining to Ham at every opportunity that he had no access to weed for the entire summer, since he was stranded in a place where you had to have a pass just to cross the bridge, which pretty much kept all the yuppies in and the dealers out. Ham had arranged the drop: Ryan would meet Keller up the beach around midnight on the first night of vacation to swap a couple ounces of weed for twelve hundred in cash. The deal seemed like a piece of cake and worth the extra stress on Ryan to be the in-person hookup, because Ham rarely sold broke college kids more than thirty bucks of weed at a time. To sell that much in one night, all in cash, to someone they knew and trusted — it was a no-brainer.

Ryan was planning on a quick handoff, not a full-on party, but when he met Keller at the agreed-upon location up the beach, that's what he found. A whole wonderful mess of people in their twenties and thirties on the patio of a ginormous beach house, a twenty-five-minute walk from where Ryan was staying. Handsome, rich people, athletic people, beautiful and charming people, drunk people, some of them in swimsuits and hatching a plan to go skinny-dipping. It was hot, even at this midnight hour, and the air on the patio was sticky and breathless. The sky vibrated with the alien greenish glow of heat lightning.

Ryan quickly identified Keller, who bore a strong resemblance to his brother. They did the handoff right there in the middle of the party, like it was nothing. He invited Ryan to stay and party with them. Ryan obliged, rolling up a few joints, which got lit and passed around, so that soon the air was a dense fog, and the green world slowed.

Keller introduced Ryan to others at the party, calling him "Bryan" — Ryan didn't care. He met the golf pro that Keller was caddying for, and other golf pros, and their hot girl-friends. Everyone sparkled. The group eventually went for a late-night swim. They drank more, smoked more, shivered in the ocean, laughed, sang, and returned to the house, where someone loaned Ryan a towel. He was loose and dizzy with pot and beautiful people. He shared a kiss with a gorgeous dark-haired girl whom he would pass the next day on the beach while walking with Rae. Ryan had shared kisses with several girls from his high school, nothing more. Ryan would have loved for it to go further with this dark-haired girl, but when she was on his lap, he suddenly felt too silly to kiss. Aware of the size of his tongue. He giggled and she pulled away. Ten minutes later, she was kissing another girl at the party—a much longer and more passionate kiss than she had offered Ryan. Ryan laughed. He felt a great sweetness for the world.

Somehow, the night edged toward the blue of morning, and Ryan was stunned to realize it was five o'clock. Someone at the party gave him a partially smoked joint on his way out. Ryan trucked it back to his beach house with twelve hundred in cash and a damp stubby joint in the pocket of his backpack.

Ham had called the house this morning—Ryan had given him the number in case of an emergency change of plans—having not yet been able to reach his brother, just to make sure everything went smoothly. Stupidly unprepared for anyone other than Ryan to answer, Ham was stunned to an awkward silence when Poppy picked up the phone. That single phone call, which hadn't amounted to anything, had been the most stressful part of the entire ordeal.

Ryan sat on his bed, scribbling numbers on the magazine in his lap. He thought that he and Ham could increase their price thirty percent without losing any business. He could probably reduce the time from seed to sale by a week or two. The main question was whether it was worth looking into more space at a location other than his house, and that was what he planned to propose to Ham when he got back home.

After lunch, the adults continued to drink margaritas, and when these ran out, they switched to piña coladas. Everyone was in good spirits.

Kimmy and Rae had been getting along well. In fact, Kimmy had finally been able to interest her sister in playing a game by first getting Ryan to commit. The four kids set up Monopoly on the coffee table.

Poppy observed Lisa as she floated around the kitchen, serving up tiki cocktails and looking like an angel in her white linen shift dress, lips freshly stained red, hair sleek, laughter pretty and song-like. Poppy felt free and easy goodwill toward her best friend. Lisa would divorce Scott. That was clear now. Lisa would land a hefty settlement, probably remain in the house with the girls, mourn the end of her marriage for a few obligatory months, then start going on blind dates with friends of friends. Maybe the recently divorced real-estate agent she kept running into at PTA functions. Maybe her podiatrist. Maybe a retired plastic surgeon whose wife had died of cancer or a yogi from her breadmaking class. Maybe a twenty-five-year-old bartender with a ponytail and a degree in photography. Or maybe a fancy equestrian who trained at the stable where Rae kept her horse and went for lessons. Poppy could totally see it. Lisa would fall in love with some fine blueblood with a family estate, move herself and the girls out of D.C. and onto forty acres of farmland, tend a rose garden, bake pies . . . The possibilities were endless. Poppy allowed herself to feel only mildly guilty for imagining Lisa's bright future without Scott, while seated on a barstool right next to him.

She glanced sideways at him, trying to assess the level of sadness she would feel when he was no longer in her life. It was not considerable. He looked as self-satisfied as ever, Ray-Bans perched on top of that expensive haircut. *Eh, good riddance,* Poppy thought. Scott was *definitely* having an affair, anyway. He had returned from the "car show in Beaufort" in a strangely ecstatic mood, and when Poppy asked him what sort of cool cars he'd seen, he balked and ho-hummed before offering up the most generic answer. Whether or not Lisa would ever have the satisfaction of catching him in the act, it was obvious that's what was going on, and so Poppy would not mourn the end of their marriage.

It was still raining heavily when the Monopoly game petered out, so the group put on a movie. They went back and forth between a few before settling on *Independence Day*. Rae didn't contribute to the movie debate, but once the decision

had been made, she grabbed the VHS box to check it out
—she couldn't remember if she'd seen the film before and
wondered if the cover would spark recognition. As soon as
she glimpsed the stills on the back of the box, her groin became so hot she had to look down to make sure it wasn't
glowing from within. Andrew Keegan, the long-haired guy
in that movie, with the shoulders and the lips and the eyes
all swollen like he'd just done sex things . . .

Rae had to set the box aside and think of other things.
This was all too much. It was too much to be vacationing
with Ryan, who bore a striking resemblance to Andrew Keegan, now that she thought about it; too much that her bedroom shared a wall with his, that she'd had to spend the past
forty-eight hours watching him go from tanned to more
tanned, watching him sweat and laugh and roll a toothpick over his lips, which were so juicy they looked like they
wanted to be popped. And now she was supposed to sit next
to Ryan on the couch and watch the actual Andrew Keegan
make out with a girl onscreen . . . Rae's body ached like she
had been Tasered with currents of desire and injustice.

Before Rae knew it, the movie was on, the light was off.
Lisa and Poppy were sharing the loveseat, and Alex and
Kimmy were laid out on the carpet before them, with chins
cupped in hands, bare feet in the air. John was at the far end
of the sectional couch, looking like he was about to enjoy a
good nap, and Scott was at the kitchen table, typing on his
laptop. This left Rae and Ryan in the middle of the couch
with two feet of space between them, but gravity seemed
to pull them both toward the crack between cushions at

the center. The fierce need inside Rae was so powerful that her throat felt like it was pure blood. She felt like life was impossible, and she was certain that nothing would ever be enough.

The rain had passed by the time the movie ended, and almost unbelievably to Rae, she and Ryan had not drawn closer to each other on the couch; they maintained their distance for the entire movie.

They all stepped out onto the patio together, and the early-evening sun seemed to amplify the humidity. The clouds had disintegrated into feathery crescents scattered unevenly across the sky, as though they had been tossed there recklessly by someone in a rush. Lisa fanned her face with a takeout menu from inside. Beads of sweat lined her upper lip and glittered in the sun.

Poppy fanned her face with her shirttail. She directed everyone's attention toward the beach, where the sand was saturated, stained dark with rainwater. She told them the story of the Gray Man, how he stalked the beach for heartbroken women, longing to protect them from impending doom.

Kimmy said, "Ghosts can be good like that?"

Rae said, "Ghosts aren't real, dummy."

"I know." Kimmy didn't say more, but she thought on this for a while. She knew Ryan was really smart, but she wasn't sure she agreed with what he'd said the other day about ghosts and God, how believing or not believing was all totally in your head. Kimmy thought that *surely* there had to be proof one way or the other; there was no way that not one person on this whole huge earth could either prove or disprove something, even if that something was as slippery as a ghost. Kimmy realized suddenly how desperately she wanted someone to just tell her how the world was, so she could be sure. She wanted answers. Proof. It seemed so unreasonable to exist without it.

"There's no Gray Man," Poppy was saying. "Don't worry." She seemed concerned that Kimmy had fallen quiet, and she reached over to touch Kimmy's head gently. "It's only a silly story meant to scare people."

Suddenly, Kimmy was afraid she had been believing some really stupid things for quite a long time.

They decided to order food in rather than cook dinner.

They ate pizza on paper plates, then went for a walk on the beach before it got dark. Lisa brought along a camera and a mai tai, and Poppy brought a daiquiri. John brought a Frisbee. Scott brought a flask. They rolled up pant legs and waded into the water. Crabs skittered across the sand, and Alex and Kimmy swatted after them and told private jokes to each other. Rae accumulated a handful of pretty shells. Lisa and Poppy linked arms. Lisa rested her cheek on the crown of Poppy's head, and they talked about how they ought to plan an annual family vacation together. They did not discuss the likelihood that Scott would be part of this. John and Ryan threw the Frisbee back and forth. The sky was gauzy, the color of orange sherbet, the sun a shivering coin.

Back inside, they turned on the oven to reheat leftover pizza. They got so involved in playing Pictionary that they forgot about the oven and burned the pizza, which set off the smoke alarm. They rushed to open all the doors and windows so the draft would clear out the smoke. They made popcorn in place of pizza. Kimmy said she wanted to try to make caramel corn by dumping some of the caramel ice cream topping in the fridge onto her bowl of popcorn, and to her amazement, Lisa said, "Sure, give it a try."

After eating the popcorn, they switched from Pictionary to Mouse Trap and played this around the kitchen table until Scott complained of a headache. They sacked out on couches and put the TV back on. Ryan found a documentary on unique flora in the Himalayas, and Poppy sank into John's armpit.

Scott and Lisa retired to their bedroom five minutes into the documentary, yawning and apologetic at being the first party poopers.

John announced that he would go to bed too. He tried to rouse Poppy, whose head was in his lap, but she resisted, murmuring in sleep that she was still "wide awake" and "watching Ryan's show."

John chuckled, got up from the couch, and placed a throw pillow beneath her ear, to replace his thigh.

Alex and Kimmy went to bed next, around midnight. Earlier in the day the two of them had discussed sneaking out again tonight, but they were so exhausted that as soon as their heads hit their pillows, both were ready for sleep.

Rae managed to make it to the end of the documentary, silently willing Poppy to wake and go to bed, leaving herself and Ryan alone in the main room, but this did not happen: Poppy remained, snoozing peacefully, feet crossed on the couch, pillow at her cheek.

The credits rolled and Ryan rose to turn off the TV. He gently shook his mother to wake her.

It was almost one o'clock.

"Bedtime," Ryan whispered, and he offered Rae what she interpreted to be an apologetic look as he ushered Poppy down the hall, then he disappeared into his own room.

Rae stayed in the main room and listened for the door to his bedroom to shut behind him. She listened for the flush of his toilet. Then she heard the faucet—brushing teeth. Well, she figured, that was it, he was calling it a night. This was disappointing, but they still had one more night on the island. And after all, he had just walked his own mother down the hall to her bedroom. It would be a little weird, Rae rationalized on Ryan's behalf, for him to turn right around from his own mother, come back to the main room, and share an intimate moment with Rae. Even if he was developing feelings for her, Rae thought, he was probably still uncertain about making the first move. Well, she thought, that was OK. Her hormones were surging far too intensely for her to feel ready for sleep, but she would go to her room for now even if it meant lying awake or practicing her looks or reading her book for another two hours before she became tired. She could also scavenge the boozy remains of the various tiki cocktails now that she had the kitchen to herself.

She was annoyed that she had endured that entire mind-numbing documentary in the hopes that it would result in some alone time for her and Ryan, but all was not lost. They still had one more day and one more night, Rae consoled herself. She would make a plan. She already had some ideas. If Ryan couldn't work up the courage to express his feelings to her, then she would be prepared to make the first move, because one thing was for certain: Rae was not going to go home the same unkissed, untouched girl she had been upon arrival.

17

KEATS AND ROXIE were woken by a phone call around midnight. Keats answered the call on the phone that lived on their bed stand, grunted a few questions, hung up, and sat upright in bed. He yawned mightily, arms stretched overhead, sleepy muscles shifting and warming.

Roxie had an elbow tented over her face to block the light of the moon, which felt severe at this hour. "What now?" she mumbled.

"Emergency call," Keats said, rising from bed and making his way to their closet for clothing.

"At this time of night?" Roxie said.

"Couple guests out on the bay," Keats said over his shoulder. "Taking a late-night bath, faucet on the Jacuzzi broke off and started spittin' like a fireman's hose. They called the homeowner in a panic, he called me. Scared it's gonna flood so bad the floor caves in if it waits till the morning."

"You can't catch a break this week."

"Can't complain," Keats said. "We need the money." He sat on the bed while he pulled on his socks.

"How long you think it'll take you?" Roxie said, shifting in bed.

"Won't have a clue till I get there."

18

IN HIS BEDROOM, Ryan wasn't tired yet—his mind was spinning with new information from the documentary. He got out the books he'd brought along and did some reading, took some notes. He tried to remember the name of the little blue flowers from the documentary; he wanted to look them up in the library when he got home. His back was sore, so he got out of bed to do a few stretches, and this was when his eyes fell on the dead crab.

The solution in the glass hadn't provided any sort of information on the cause of its death, and Ryan had forgotten about the crab on the dresser for a day or two, but now . . . well, surely he had been mistaken when it first caught his attention. He moved closer to the glass so that he could peer down into it. No *way*. It couldn't be. He almost shrieked. His eyes hadn't deceived him: that dead crab was *not dead*.

Ryan stared at the crab in disbelief. It was gently treading its back legs, drumming up a small current, swimming around the glass in a lazy circle. Ryan gazed at it, then stirred the water with his finger to make sure. *What the* . . . Ryan couldn't take his eyes off the thing. There was no question the crab had been dead three days earlier when he'd brought it in. Was it possible something in that solution had somehow revived the crab? Ryan stared and paced and pulled the crab out of the glass by balancing it on a piece of cardboard, allowed it to flit across the carpet, then he scooped it up and put it back in the glass. He stared and marveled and poked and thought that surely he must be losing his mind.

When he next looked at the clock, Ryan was startled to realize it was almost three in the morning. He *really* needed to try and get some sleep, but with this resurrected crab business, he was nowhere near it. What could he do that would ready him for sleep? Stupidly, he had left his *Playboy*s at home.

He remembered that he still had the soggy joint, wrapped in a Kleenex and stuffed into the small pocket of his backpack. He had almost forgotten about the joint entirely, but tonight was definitely the night for it. It was late — everyone else would certainly be fast asleep. He'd sneak out through the rec room downstairs, take a seat beneath the patio, have a peaceful outdoor smoke, then come in and hope sleep would find him.

Ryan put on a T-shirt and shorts, retrieved the joint from his backpack, and got the lighter from his suitcase. He also took his large beach towel and draped it across his shoulders. He crept along the hall, down the stairs, through the rec room. He left the sliding glass door unlocked behind him, made his way out, went underneath the patio and to the far end of it, where he could spread his towel and be out of sight of anyone who might amble to the kitchen for a snack.

Ryan lit the joint and lay back on the towel. The stars were mostly obscured by white-gray cloud cover overhead, but the moon, low above the water, was a magnificent butter yellow. The world grew impossibly placid and good after a single hit. But then a noise from the house startled him.

He licked his fingers and pinched the lit end of the joint to snuff it out and frantically waved at the dense cloud of smoke that encircled his head. He looked back toward the house. A figure was exiting through the sliding back door, and it took his eyes a moment to identify size and angles and posture in the dark, the shadow beneath the patio, but he soon realized it was Lisa. Her red hair was tied up in a messy, high bun. She wore a loose-fitting pink silk pajama top over capri-length pants of the same material.

She closed the glass door behind her and started to make her way out toward the beach, directly in Ryan's direction, but she suddenly stopped and froze.

He'd been spotted.

He didn't move. For a moment, she didn't either. She squinted to make out who he was in the darkness, then she held a palm over a silently laughing chest. *You scared me!* she mouthed. She offered a friendly wave as she grew closer, and she sniffed the air.

Ryan's stomach surged and hissed. Well, now Lisa knew that he smoked pot. Was it worth trying to persuade her not to tell Poppy?

Lisa said, "May I?" pointing down at the large towel where Ryan sat upright now.

He scooted to the side to accommodate her. She nodded to his left fist, which was clenched around the joint.

Lisa wore a mischievous expression and she whispered, "What're you doing, putting it out? Spark that thing back up."

Ryan stared at her. "Really?"

"I haven't smoked since I was nineteen, with your mom." Lisa brushed sand from her toes and curled them on the towel.

"You and *my mom* smoked pot?"

"Now and then. So are you gonna give me a drag or what?"

Ryan reached for the lighter and relit the joint. He took the first puff to start it, then passed it to Lisa.

She took a confident drag and a cough sputtered from her. She covered her lips with her fist to muffle the noise. When she had stopped coughing, she giggled and lay back on the towel, her skin milky in the bald light of the moon.

"That'll do it for me," she said, her smile so wide it looked like her face might crack in half. "I feel . . ." She paused. "I'm in a nest."

Ryan laughed. His airy buzz was returning, after the fear of getting caught had caused it to instantly vanish.

Lisa murmured, "Hell of a sky."

Ryan gazed up. The clouds were parting, and now many stars were visible directly above them.

Lisa patted the towel next to her, indicating that Ryan should lie back and enjoy the view too. He did. His hair was touching her hair.

She said, "I was just gonna go for a little walk. I couldn't sleep."

He said, "Me either."

"What's got *you* wide awake at three o'clock in the morning?"

Ryan took another puff on the joint and said, "You'd never believe me if I told you."

"Told me what?" Lisa said.

Ryan half laughed and said, *"Huh."* Then he said, "I swear you're gonna think I'm crazy. But." He slapped at a bug on his thigh. "You know that dead crab I brought in a couple days ago? Had it sitting in a glass of solution in my bedroom?"

"Yeah."

"It came back to life."

Next to his head, he felt Lisa move to partially face him. "What?" she said.

Ryan said, "Thing's been dead and floating in there for days. But tonight I happen to glance over, and I am not kidding you, it's swimming around, looking up at me, looking as healthy, as *alive,* as can be."

Lisa stared at him saucer-eyed for a moment, then shook with silent laughter. She moved to prop her head up on her elbow, facing him fully. She giggled some more, wiped away a tear, her eyes sweet and full.

Ryan laughed. "Crazy, right? I'm serious, though. I'll go get it if you want to see it."

Lisa said, "Oh, hon, oh, hon," and she waved the air between them. Through snorting laughter, she explained, "Earlier, when we were on the beach, I overheard Kimmy and Alex hatching a plan while they were trying to catch a crab. I only overheard bits and pieces, didn't bother to listen closely at the time. They were whispering about *Take it inside,* and *I'll sneak it into his room,* and *When do you think he'll notice?* And they were giggling up a storm. I think those little stinkers caught a crab and stuck it in there. I think they pulled one over on you."

Ryan's mouth dropped open. "Those little shits," he whispered. Then he felt a bubble of joy work its way up and out of him, and he collapsed onto the towel in laughter, incredulous at the success of the girls' trick. He and Lisa lay there on the towel, laughing as softly as they could, sniffing and wiping at tears. The joint was still lit and a thin string of smoke rose from the tip. Ryan had wasted a few good hits. Didn't care. Lisa reached for it and took a pull, released smoke from her nostrils. She drew the rubber band from her hair so that it fell in thick auburn waves to her shoulders. She scratched and gently massaged her part.

Ryan said, "So what's got *you* up at three o'clock in the morning?"

Lisa rubbed her eyes. Her face was still flushed and lively from laughter. "I've got stuff on my mind."

"Mm." Ryan was quiet for a bit. He knew he oughtn't say

anything, but the pot and the night air and the euphoria of sharing such a good, long, hard, genuine laugh with Lisa had him feeling warm and brave and open. He said, "I shouldn't say anything."

She gazed at him, her head cocked and resting on the heel of her hand. "Shouldn't say what?"

"I heard you and my mom talking on the beach yesterday."

"About what?" Lisa crushed her bottom lip with her top teeth, then released it.

Ryan couldn't help noticing that she wasn't wearing a bra beneath her pink silk pajamas. Her breasts were heavy, pointing down at the towel beneath her. His mind felt like it was covered in a greasy film.

He was quiet for a bit longer, then he said, "I heard you saying yesterday how you think Scott's cheating."

"Oh." Lisa grimaced. "On the beach? You were there?"

"I was sleeping," Ryan said, "but I woke up."

Lisa scratched her nose and stared out toward the water. "Well," she said, and then fell silent for a moment. "There you have it."

Ryan said, "I think he's an asshole."

Lisa gave him a sad smile. A spider that was attached to the underside of the deck was descending in measured little jerks, and her eyes followed it, like a cat with a toy.

"I'm serious," Ryan said. Words tumbled from him. "I'm serious. Cheating on *you?* I think he's an asshole and he doesn't deserve you. You are perfect."

Lisa blinked. Her face was lovely. She leaned toward him first. At least that was how he perceived it. It was hard to say because suddenly something turned lusty and desperate in the air, inside Ryan, and the sky swelled toward him. She came with it, and suddenly her lips were on his. Then her hand was on the back of his head, fingers hungry, spidering through his hair, her tongue in his mouth. His fingers scooped greedily at the back of her neck and knitted through her hair.

Then she was on top, her full weight on him, straddling him, and they kissed there, lips and tongues searching and soft and muscular and reckless, four hands moving frantic and grasping here, rubbing there, the whole world pulsing with need all around them.

That was as far as it went. Lisa was the one who pulled away first, her crotch still on his, two layers of fabric, one silk and one cotton, the only barriers between their flesh, but Lisa pulled away, gazed at his face, and murmured, *"No,"* and she rolled off of him with great effort, panting, her eyes wild.

Ryan couldn't speak. The whole world was in his throat. He lay on his back, and she lay there next to him, both staring at the sky, two wild hearts vibrating loud with lust and fear.

Lisa said in a breath, "I am so sorry."

Ryan swallowed. "Me too," he whispered.

It was quiet for a long time, until the night felt like a dream.

Finally, Lisa said, "Do you think it's possible that that didn't happen between us?"

"Yes." Ryan nodded. "It was just a dream."

Lisa got up first.

Ryan stayed outside a while longer. When he finally made it back to his bedroom, it was after four o'clock. He was sick over what had happened. He stared at the living crab in the glass of blue water and it stared back.

19

I heard him leave his room around three o'clock in the morning. Sleep was nowhere near me. I was full of alcohol, young blood, hormones, and stupid ideas about the world.

Earlier in the night, just after Ryan had gone to bed, I went to the kitchen and emptied the contents of the blender into a plastic cup and took this to my bedroom. It was three inches' worth of melted daiquiri. I'd been doing this for over a year now, wait for my parents to have their fill and become loopy and weary and inattentive. I'd swipe the bottom few inches of whatever they had been sipping on, transfer it to a different cup, and take it to my bedroom. Or if I was certain that it wouldn't be noticed, I would pour myself a glass of wine straight from the bottle, as I had done the night before, when Kimmy caught me. I was still learning how much I dared drink before I got too stupid or too sick.

That night, the melted daiquiri was so sugary and thick with pulp that I couldn't detect the amount of alcohol, but it must have been at least a few ounces of rum. Soon the drink was gone and the room was spinning. I held a trash can between my bare sweating thighs in case it all came back up. After a few minutes, the early blast and intensity of the buzz had passed, as had the nausea, but I was still wide awake, hot as blazes, mind zooming, each thought like a thunderclap. I tried to adjust the air conditioning in my room to cool it down, but that didn't seem to make a difference. When I heard Ryan leave his room, I figured he was going to the kitchen for a snack, so I listened for his return. I knew it was him because our bedrooms shared a wall. I waited two minutes. Five minutes. Ten.

I didn't hear my mother leave her bedroom because it was at the other end of the hall, although I imagine she left her room shortly after he left his. I didn't know this at the time, of course. As the minutes passed and Ryan did not return to his room, my curiosity and courage multiplied. It occurred to me as I lay there in bed, short of breath, my cheeks hot, that perhaps he was waiting for me. Perhaps I would not have to wait until tomorrow night to find out if I was to be an unkissed, untouched girl. Perhaps, I thought, Ryan was silently summoning me from elsewhere in the house. He was too timid to come for me directly, but he had intended for me to hear him leave his room, and was now waiting for me to come find him. See, this was the sort of thing I read about in my books —this was the sort of miracle that could exist for a girl like me, who had never been kissed.

I had removed my pajama pants, and now I put them back on as I crawled out of bed. The elastic waistband of my panties was damp. The hair around my face was damp. My face was damp. The clock read 3:08 a.m.

I left my room and went to the living room. He was not there, but when I glanced out at the patio, I noticed something . . . A plume of white smoke, twirling as thin as a vine, rose from beneath the patio. A little gasp escaped me. I understood now. He was outside, on the far side of the patio, on the beach and out of sight of anyone in the house, smoking a cigarette that was meant to communicate his location to me and only me—the smoke was a beacon. We were going to kiss, and maybe, probably, more. Concerned that opening the patio door might wake someone else in the house, I crept back through the hallway to the staircase at the far end. Down the stairs. Through the rec room. My heart thrashed against my thin pajama top. I felt like I might cry, but of course I wouldn't.

I paused at the sliding glass door, which was pulled shut but unlocked. He might have already seen me, I realized, since I would be illuminated from behind by the light over the utility sink across the rec room. I hesitated, letting my eyes adjust to the night before me, and then prepared myself to go out into it.

That's when I saw her hair. She was on top.

The universe blinked shut like an old-fashioned flashbulb. A hiss, and everything was gone. Then everything was back. I saw them in color, her red hair, his tanned arms, then in black and white, then in an oozing, inky nightmare. I hiccupped and swallowed back a rush of hot, sour nausea. They never saw me. They moved like aliens. Like monsters.

I ran. Back through the rec room, up the stairs, through the bedroom hallway, and out the front door of the house. Silent that whole way, not by willpower but by necessity; my throat was full of wasps. My desire to thrash wildly, to run and wake my father, to scream into his sleeping mouth what I had seen, to do some terrible violence to my mother, all this was overridden by my desire to get away from that house, as far as I could, and as fast. I took a left out of the driveway, pounding in bare feet up the sandy sidewalk, which was still damp from the rain. Tears were now slime that coated my face.

I ran and wheezed, my body feeling strangely insufficient.

Then I decided where to go. Yesterday afternoon, after the jellyfish, I had walked up the beach by myself to find it. There was no guarantee; the only way to identify the house would be to see either the man himself or his brown Labrador with the red collar entering or exiting. But luck was on my side, and the ten-minute walk proved worthwhile, because suddenly Leo and his handsome owner were in view as they made their way up the beach. I used my binoculars to confirm their identity. Leo's long, pink tongue hung limp as a noodle from the side of his mouth. The owner had a leash and a towel in hand. I drew a little closer and watched as the man brushed sand off Leo's paws. They entered, not a house but an apartment above a garage, through a side door of the garage. A light appeared inside a moment later.

Although I had lacked the courage in broad daylight that afternoon to go any closer to his home or make my presence known to him, I noted the location of the place. My focus had been on Ryan in the hours since; I'd barely had a second thought about the man and his house. But now that I'd seen what I'd seen . . . now I was determined to find this man, to make him mine and to make myself his.

Eventually, I found myself on the sidewalk in front of a set of similar-looking homes, and I gathered, through my wildness and several ounces of rum, that I was in the right area. I decided to go down to the beach so that I would have the same view that I'd had yesterday from the shore. I crept stealthily between houses, jogging over sand that was cool between my toes. I made a beeline for the beach, where I would be outside the reach of the safety lights that most homes had installed above their garages. From the water's edge, I would be both protected by darkness and able to view the homes from yesterday's vantage point. As I moved between houses and then through a marshy patch, I crashed through some brush and wet, soupy sand, then over something prickly that hurt my foot. I hopped on one leg, long enough to extract the small, thorny thing that had pierced the bottom of my foot, then I ran over sand that felt like silk. I ran and ran toward the water, toward the moon, my thin yellow pajamas sticking to my sweating body.

I should mention that I have no recollection of what my exact intentions were at this point. Everything was a confused blur, and I was completely alone. The world had just proven itself to be an absolute terror, yet I feared nothing. See, I understood now that my mother wasn't protecting me when she chased this man away from me on the beach; she wanted him for herself, just like she wanted Ryan. I knew now that my mother was my enemy—I felt this truth coursing through me.

Difficult as this may be to accept, I would say it is a small blessing in death to be freed from the great burden of feelings and the belief that everything that originates from within you is true, can be trusted, and must be acted upon.

20

WHEN ROXIE WOKE for her run at 3:30 in the morning, Keats was still gone and hadn't checked in. This was not un- usual. Roxie didn't imagine she'd see him until the Jacuzzi repair had been completed, and she guessed something like that could take many hours. Coffee was brewing and bread was in the toaster by 3:35; she wanted to be out the door by 4:00 so she could have the whole circuit done before sunrise. She decided to take Leo down to the beach for his morning pee while the coffee brewed. Leo was slow to be roused, but as soon as he was fully awake, he was ready for a swim. Outside, the moon was low and blurry and the air was thick, with some pockets of strange heat.

Roxie and Leo had been down at the water for only a short time when she spotted the girl.

She was short, couldn't have been more than twelve years old, Roxie guessed, and she was tearing down toward the water, wearing yellow pajamas, a crazed look on her face.

Roxie held Leo by the collar so he would stay at her side. He wouldn't hurt a flea, but Roxie was afraid he would run at the girl, thinking this was play, and leap at her in some fearsome way. She held the dog and stood still, her heart vibrating in her eye sockets, waiting to see what the girl would do. She wondered if the girl had just been attacked. She wondered if the girl was suicidal. Roxie took a few steps forward with a friendly arm half raised, hoping she wouldn't startle the girl.

Whatever was going on, Roxie was already formulating a plan, figuring out how she could help the girl. Comfort her. If the girl was in some sort of trouble, she could wait in Roxie and Keats's home until help arrived. The girl could have the coffee and toast Roxie had prepared for herself if she was hungry or wanted a hot drink. The girl could borrow a pair of pants and a sweater if she felt exposed in her pajamas, she could take a shower or a warm bath. The girl could sleep on their couch. It crossed Roxie's mind that perhaps the girl's parents were fighting, as Roxie's parents had fought when Roxie was a girl and they had vacationed on Fripp Island. Sometimes Roxie's parents' fighting was enough to make Roxie want to flee the house at three o'clock in the morning. Whatever was going on with the girl, Roxie could help.

21

Before I reached the water's edge, an instinct alerted me to the presence of someone else on the beach. I stopped at the water and raised both hands to my chest, where my sternum felt tight and angry and sharp, like it might be trying to escape my body.

She was staring at me. She had a long blond braid that glittered silver in the moonlight. White T-shirt and blue running shorts. She was very pretty.

Leo was at her side, wet like he'd just been in the water, and he was staring at me too. She held his collar. As soon as I stopped running, she made a gesture indicating that it was safe for me to approach. When I didn't, she said, "I didn't know if you were gonna stop before you got to the water! You had me scared, kid. Are you OK?" Her eyes were bright and wide with concern.

I said, "Is that your dog?"

She nodded. She wore a wedding ring and held a tennis ball. She patted Leo's head and said, "He's very friendly," and she looked at me warmly, expectantly, like it might make everything better if I could pet this friendly dog.

I said, "Where's your husband?"

She cocked her head at me, curious but not necessarily upset by the question. She didn't answer, though.

I was still panting. I said, "What are you doing out here?"

"I'm about to go for a run," she said. She gazed at me for a moment, then said, "What are you doing out here?"

I coughed, and it seemed to rattle something loose inside me; it set free something mean and stupid. I still can't explain precisely what drove me to say what I said. "He came up to me on the beach yesterday and talked to me. My mom had to chase him away."

The blond woman's whole pretty face changed in one instant. Her eyes darkened and her brow closed in. Her chin seemed to grow. She stared straight at my face and didn't speak or blink.

I waited for her to react. To call me a liar. Or to beg me to tell her the details of my interaction with her husband—maybe she would say, I knew it! Maybe she would weep and confess to me that she knew he had tried to pursue me. But she still didn't speak, only looked at me with a face that was hard and sad and confused.

I said, "He told me to come meet him here at night."

22

WHEN THE GIRL said this, Roxie's brain went black. Something went screaming through her entire body as fast and fiery as a rocket launch. Her heart froze in an instant.

She lunged at the girl, driven by the sense that this was not real, none of it. Not the moon or the ocean or the girl in the yellow pajamas, not the things the girl was saying about Keats, or the possibility that Keats might find himself in the position of needing to defend himself *again*—none of it was real to Roxie in that moment, and she knew that it was not real because the moon was too low and strange and bright. This entire scenario was not real, and therefore, for her next actions, there could be no consequences. This was just a dream that needed to end.

Her first impulse was not to kill the girl but simply to silence her.

But once the girl was thrashing under the water, Roxie knew she had to go the whole way. The moment she forced the girl's face down into the surf was the moment that she sealed her fate. Allowing the girl to live after assaulting her would have ended Roxie. And so the girl had to die.

Because, of course, if the girl lived to tell her story, the police would believe it. Keats was, after all, on the registry. They would believe every single one of the girl's lies—from Keats approaching her on the beach, to Keats instructing her to meet him there in the middle of the night, to Roxie lunging at her out of jealousy, or whatever twisted psychosis the girl might dream up to explain it. They were monsters, Keats and Roxie, at least that's what the police and the girl's parents and the community would believe. Their lives would be over, while the girl would be given years of counseling for her trauma and would be applauded for her bravery in exposing the monsters, for escaping their trap, and providing all the information the prosecution would need to make sure Keats and Roxie would never see the light of day, or each other, again.

Roxie's eyes watered but her muscles did not tremble or flinch as she put her full weight onto the girl's back. Each of her movements was strong and true, purpose and necessity guiding her hips as they bore down on the girl's tiny waist. Roxie's knees sunk deep into sand along the girl's sides, and she applied pressure to the back of that small skull with the heels of her hands instead of grabbing with her fingertips, in order to avoid bruising. Roxie vomited the contents of an empty stomach, bile and saliva, into the ocean when the girl stopped struggling, when her whole small body suddenly went as soft and pliant under the water as a handful of hair.

· · ·

Once the girl was dead, Roxie acted quickly, knowing that the longer it took her to decide on her next move, the more likely it was she would be seen.

The dead girl floated easily through the water, like an oversized inflatable.

Roxie pulled the girl by her arms, moving smoothly and with the current to avoid bruising, farther out to sea. Farther, farther. They reached a sandbar, the ocean so shallow that Roxie had to roll the girl over the sand instead of pulling her through water. She rolled clumsily, hip bone, shoulder bone, hip bone, shoulder bone, the girl's head lolling back and forth. Roxie avoided looking at her face. Leo was at her side, splashing happily, thinking this was all great fun.

Out past the sandbar, farther, farther, then swimming with the girl's neck tucked in her underarm like a dummy, farther, farther, until Roxie could almost not touch ground. She assessed the current. They were past the break, so the girl would likely be carried north a little way, but would remain at this distance from shore until the tide came in around dawn. At that same time, the tide would cover their footsteps in the sand, and any evidence of the struggle. Assuming no one noticed the girl's disappearance between now and then, it would be very difficult for anyone to assess exactly where she had entered the water.

Roxie left the body and swam to shore with Leo at her side. He shook out his coat, which turned his dark hair instantly to spikes. Roxie ran to the house, shaking violently now, not from cold but from the knowledge of what she had done. The proficiency with which she had performed the murder and pulled the body out to sea had used up every calculated survival instinct and given way to the warm beating human heart of her. She was filled with horror.

Once she reached their house, she pulled Leo in the door, even as he stood waiting outside to be dried with a towel. She yanked him in soaking wet by his red collar, locked the door behind him, and went directly to the bedroom. She removed her wet clothing, threw it into the shower, and got into bed, completely naked, where she began to cry in strange bursts.

Not understanding why he had been permitted to enter the house with wet, sandy paws, Leo decided to push his luck and crawl up onto the bed with Roxie. She allowed him to stay, wet sandy paws and all, and he nuzzled into her. He watched and listened to Roxie's crying and felt simple and confusing emotions. Already, the encounter with the girl was gone from Leo's memory.

Roxie was still nude in her bed, wet dog at her side, when a sudden panic jolted her upright as she happened to glance at the clock on the wall of their bedroom. It was 4:45.

The run . . . Poppy . . .

Roxie had promised to meet Poppy outside her house at the same time this morning, which was around 5:30. Dare she not go? No, unexpectedly breaking plans with Poppy could eventually cast suspicion in her direction. In fact, it occurred to Roxie, showing up was the only way to definitively exonerate herself if anything should happen to put her in the purview of the police. If she upheld her plan to meet up with Poppy, both she and Keats, still on his house call, would have perfect alibis.

Poppy was wearing a green baseball cap and doing a deep quad stretch against the mailbox when Roxie approached. A misty rain swirled around them. No actual drops, although there had been some on Roxie's way over. Roxie was wearing a hat as well; she had blow-dried her hair before leaving the house, to avoid the appearance of having recently showered or been in the water, but had done so in a rush, and her hair was not entirely dry.

Roxie offered a meek wave and said, "Hope I didn't keep you waiting."

"Nup," Poppy said. She smelled of coffee, and her eyes in the shadow of the hat were haggard and red. "I'm quite hung over," Poppy confessed immediately.

Roxie said, "No pressure to join. I'll be fine on my own if you wanna crawl back into bed."

Poppy said, "I think I can make it to the magnolias again. I'll probably just walk the whole way back."

The run was a blur. Roxie's mind cycled wildly over images and terrors, dream-like and indistinct. She did her best to respond appropriately as Poppy chattered on about how much fun last night had been. Pictionary, movies, frozen cocktails . . .

They parted ways at the magnolia grove.

Roxie felt ill. Her heart was a hummingbird thrashing against her ribs.

She said, "I'll be back at work tomorrow, stop in for breakfast if you want. Tomorrow's your last morning here, right?"

Poppy nodded. "I just may," she said. "Drag the whole crew down to Gram's, I think that'd be nice. So, this isn't goodbye."

"Exactly," Roxie said. "See you tomorrow, then."

When Poppy had made it nearly back to the house, she was surprised to see Lisa out front on the porch in her pink silk pajamas, her chin high in the air and wagging up and down the street. Poppy waved at her, impressed that Lisa had also gotten up so early after their late and boozy night.

Lisa returned Poppy's wave, but it was a mad and panicked gesture. Both arms.

Then, behind Lisa, the front door opened and Scott came out onto the porch. He was followed by Alex and John, then Kimmy and Ryan.

When Poppy got close, she felt a sudden, nameless dread settle over her. She said, "What's up, guys?"

Scott said in a voice that was tight and stricken, "She's not with you?"

Alex said, "Mommy, we hoped she was with you."

Poppy said, "Who?"

Lisa's face was stretched long, white, and corpse-like. She said, "Rae is gone."

23

UNABLE TO SLEEP, Lisa had gotten out of bed for an early morning cup of tea. This was when she noticed that both the door to Rae's bedroom and the front door of the house were slightly ajar.

Rae's body was found by surfers around seven thirty that morning. She was still wearing her yellow pajamas.

A homicide investigation was launched, but it was soon abandoned when tests indicated a high level of alcohol in Rae's blood, coinciding with the empty glass in her room. No signs pointed to forced entry or a struggle. The early-morning rain had erased any potential trace of footprints, but no physical evidence either in their home or on Rae's body suggested foul play. No sexual assault. No blunt force trauma. And there was that powerful riptide to consider.

In a fit of desperation, Lisa offered up the name of Keats Firestone to investigators, pointing out that he was a local sexual offender and explaining that they'd had several encounters with him, including one between him and Rae. But the investigators quickly confirmed his alibi: Keats had been working on a hot tub on the far side of the island from midnight until eight o'clock the next morning. The houseguests with the hot tub were there the whole time.

Scott offered up the names of the guys from Newark; they knew where he was staying, he said, and he didn't get a good vibe. But investigators were able to confirm that these guys had left the island around three o'clock yesterday afternoon. There was video surveillance of all of them in a car passing a toll bridge into New Jersey that night, many hours before Rae disappeared.

The most likely scenario, the investigators concluded and gently explained to her parents, was that the girl had left the house in the early-morning hours in a highly intoxicated state, made her way down to the water, gone for a swim, been overtaken and dragged out to sea by an undercurrent, lost control, and drowned. Scott and Lisa conceded that she was not a strong swimmer.

When they asked Lisa if her daughter was emotionally unstable or upset about something, if there was anything that had occurred that same night that might have set her off, Lisa did not allow her face to convey the horror that chilled her body to ice.

There was, of course, the possibility that Rae had witnessed Lisa and Ryan together outside, and that this was what had propelled her to flee the house in such a state. But Lisa wouldn't say this aloud. Not to the investigator, not to her husband, not to Poppy, with whom she shared nearly everything.

No, Lisa determined, the secret of what she had done that night, and the possibility that Rae could have seen it, could never, ever be made known. She would have to hope that Ryan would reach the same conclusion—she couldn't risk communicating with him to confirm this—that he would have the good sense to let his own memory of that night die within him as well. After all, he'd been the one to say it: *It was just a dream.*

When the autopsy results came in, the coroner listed the cause of death as asphyxia due to aspiration of air passages and hemoconcentration. In other words, accidental drowning.

Lisa moved through the days following Rae's death in a shell-shocked state, as delicate and easily confused as a patient just released after decades in a psychiatric ward. She forgot the word for "cup" and "door." She allowed herself to be led by Scott and Poppy, who were both constant and loving, through offices and interviews and the attention brought by the local press covering the tragic drowning of a young vacationer, and then back home to Warrenton. Scott and Poppy helped her through phone calls with family, through conversations about the preferred casket and the benefits of different methods of embalming, and through Kimmy's questions: *Why didn't she change into her swimsuit if she was going to go out for a swim?*, Kimmy wondered. *Did she know she was drowning while she was drowning?*

24

RYAN DISMANTLED THE hydroponic setup in his bedroom as soon as his family returned to Wheeling. He cleaned out his cartons of materials and flushed the last of his weed down the toilet. He gave Ham his cut of the Fripp Island deal and told him he was out of the game. He was sickened and confused by thoughts of the Daly family and everything associated with the vacation, including the cash that had gone missing from his stash beneath the sink. He remained deeply unsettled by this, and by the idea of adding to the lies and secrets that were already sewn inside himself.

Poppy traveled back and forth between Wheeling and War-renton to care for Lisa's family following Rae's death. John had to return to work immediately upon their return, so Ryan spent lots of time with Alex in the days and weeks following their time on the island. He took her fishing and biking, to the Blockbuster to check out movies, and to the post office to buy stamps, so that she could send letters to Kimmy. Lots of hotdogs. Lots of TV. Alex was very som-ber. She didn't ask questions. She seemed to have little desire to know anything beyond the very basics of what had happened to Rae.

Ryan had great difficulty sleeping. Thoughts of his moment of intimacy with Lisa became the most vivid after dark, when the memories wrapped themselves around his mind like hard rope, and all night long they squeezed. Nothing brought relief except the first blue whispers of morning, which did nothing to diminish his guilt but simply assured him that even if there was little hope that it would be any better, each day was something new, and perhaps the newness of a day—if nothing else—could make it worth living.

When Poppy returned from her final extended trip to Warrenton, she provided positive updates on how Scott and Lisa and Kimmy were doing. She kept Ryan and Alex busy around the house with tasks and fun plans, and she stuffed them full of comfort food. She scheduled visits for both of them to see a counselor, but Ryan begged out of it, and when Alex realized this was an option, she did the same.

Ryan started college in the fall, and he lived on campus but came home nearly every weekend. Poppy and John worried about him. It seemed strange that Rae's death had had such a profound impact. Of course it did on all of them, but Ryan seemed the least engaged with the Daly family of any of them, so they were confused by the darkness that seemed to consume him even months later. Sensitive kid. Poppy was relieved when eventually Ryan's trips home became less frequent, and still more relieved when he introduced them to several new friends from school.

After Rae's death, Poppy's nightly negotiations with Death ended. Life was cruel and death certain, and there was nothing to do but accept it; she hadn't had any say in the matter of her own existence, so what use was there to question or rage against any of the rest of it? On the other hand, it was this same rude bastard of a universe that had brought John into Luigi's to work on renovations to the patio all those years ago, when the owner of the place easily could have gone with any other construction company and Poppy might have never once in her life laid eyes on the man she was to marry. If there was anything in this lifetime as certain as death, it was Poppy's love for John. It was maddening, how it gave and took. With a universe like this, how the hell was a reasonable person supposed to believe, or not believe, anything?

John's back slowly improved with more intensive physical therapy after the trip, and eventually he weaned himself off the pain medication altogether and there was no need for a second surgery. Yet Poppy's fear of losing him did not diminish. Over time, she accepted the fact that the price for this great love was this great fear. Love's unfortunate alter ego.

Fear, she came to realize, was utterly enamored with love. Obsessed with it. Vying for its attention, modulating its own particularities to suit love. And love was equally accommodating to fear: creating space, ushering it in, giving it a home, the two of them operating in comparative measure and perfect synchrony, clinging to each other like warm bodies in the night.

25

FOR LISA, SCOTT, and Kimmy, the weeks and months following Rae's death were like being pressed slowly through a sausage grinder. Mangled. All three came out different.

Scott quit drinking and gambling, cold turkey. Instead, he shopped for groceries and cooked simple meals and took care of logistics around the house. He politely turned away well-intentioned visitors when he could tell Lisa was not up for it. He scheduled appointments for therapy for all three of them. He brought home books and movies on coping with loss and trauma.

Scott stopped attending mass after Rae's death. Her funeral was the last time he ever set foot in a church, and on the way home from her service, he ripped the crucifix from his neck, breaking the 14-carat gold chain, and threw it out the window. In the back seat, Kimmy watched him with huge eyes and a low jaw, but she didn't say a word.

When they were back home and Kimmy was out of earshot, Lisa said, "I wish you wouldn't have done that."

"Who cares? I'll be glad if I never have to say any of those stupid prayers or see any of those stupid people ever again. Won't you?"

Lisa was quiet for a bit, then she said, "I was actually thinking of going to mass tomorrow morning."

Scott stared at her. "I thought you hated going. Spent the last twenty years complaining about it."

"Today, what Father Patrick was saying about hope and the afterlife . . . it made me feel a little better."

"*That's* interesting," Scott said, "because it made me want to puke."

"I think you should keep that to yourself," Lisa said. "It'll confuse Kimmy. And throwing your crucifix out the window? Seems disrespectful."

"*Disrespectful?* To who, exactly?"

"I don't know. To God."

Scott barked out a single guffaw. "So after twenty years of naysaying, you suddenly want to will Him into existence now to make yourself feel better? By all means, you go right ahead. Enjoy the fantasy."

Lisa blinked. "You don't mean that. You've believed in God your whole life."

"Well, *not anymore*," Scott said harshly. "And on the off-chance that I'm wrong and He *does* exist, well . . . good riddance."

Scott grew quiet, and he watched his wife as she stared out the window, white sun on her cheeks, her posture low and weary, arms of cement.

"Lisa," Scott said. He released a long exhale. "I'm sorry. I'm not trying to be difficult. It's not you I'm mad at."

"I know."

Scott crossed the room to hug her. She rested her head against his.

Scott said, "You do whatever you need. That means going to mass, that's fine and I'll shut up about it. Whatever you need."

Lisa nodded and caught delicate tears with the back of her index finger. "Same goes for you," she said. "Whatever you need."

Later that day, they asked Kimmy if she wanted to go to mass the next morning with her mother or stay home and cook breakfast with her father. Having never before been presented with this choice, she did not take it lightly. After mulling it over she decided that she would prefer to stay home.

So Lisa went to mass by herself, and she faithfully kept going by herself every single Sunday, not just to the service but to Sunday school as well, and she began to attend Wednesday-evening mass too. She never pressured Scott to join her, and he did not mock her newfound faith again.

Carol insisted on going down to Warrenton for an extended stay, despite the fact that it meant her own treatments would be interrupted, since her health insurance wouldn't apply out of state. Her oncologist in Wheeling disapproved, but recent scans hadn't shown promise anyway; it was unclear if the treatments, which made for fevered, nauseous days and sleepless nights, were having any effect. Lisa lacked the will to fight her mother on this, though she disliked the idea for various reasons. Carol arranged her own travel, and arrived with many frozen casseroles stacked in a cooler, books and candies for Kimmy, and some thoughtful cards from family friends in Wheeling.

The moment Lisa set eyes on her mother, something that had been rock hard inside her for decades suddenly buckled and gave way and was gone. Carol's face was grayish and wan beneath a knitted cap. Lisa ran to her mother and wept into her warm neck, which smelled different than it ever had before, yet so much like home that every cell in Lisa's body responded with recognition.

Carol stayed for over a month, finding herself energized by the ways she discovered she could make herself useful. She finally learned her way around their kitchen, mustering the courage to use their fancy appliances. She woke when she heard Lisa make her way into Rae's room in the middle of the night; she joined her there and they cried together. She helped with laundry, sorted the abundance of cards that arrived in the mail, brewed fresh coffee for visitors. She hadn't felt so healthy or industrious since long before her diagnosis.

Carol decided it was time to go back to Wheeling when she retrieved the messages from her answering machine at home indicating that she was delinquent on her utility bills and in danger of being disconnected. She also listened to multiple concerned voicemails from her oncologist, neighbors, and friends from church. Lisa was saddened to see her mother go. They had shared so much in these weeks. Lisa felt she had been stripped down to muscle and bone and little more that resembled humanity; no hope, no dignity, no will to carry on. She was a raw body housing a broken heart, and nothing more. Carol saw it all and she didn't flinch.

A few months after Rae's death, Scott left Raslowe & Associates, taking a major pay cut to work in the legal department of a nonprofit in D.C. that provided counseling resources to families who couldn't afford health insurance.

Lisa and Scott clung to one another desperately and hard; it seemed like a powerful gravitational field had attached them. They reached for each other involuntarily. They watched for glitches in one another's daily consciousness and gently corrected them: a shirt put on backwards or mismatched socks, an extra packed lunch, dinner reservations made for four instead of three. They finished each other's sentences when a train of thought became unclear, interrupted by something dark and deep within. Shock waves of grief kept them wary and turbulent, dubious of the world and nearly everything in it. But for one another, they were soft and steady and certain.

Kimmy and Alex spoke on the phone often—in fact, it seemed Alex was the only person Kimmy had much interest in talking to at all. The two of them also kept in close touch through letters written in a secret code they developed. At the girls' request, Lisa and Poppy planned a weekend in October when they could meet up at a cabin in Shenandoah National Park. Poppy wondered if they should bring the husbands, and Ryan if he had any interest, and Lisa quickly responded that she thought just the girls would be best.

Kimmy changed. It was hard to watch. Terrible dreams woke her so often throughout the night that she was dark and sluggish and sometimes disoriented during the day. Other times, it wasn't dreams that woke her but constant racing thoughts that prevented her from falling asleep at all. A therapist suggested: "Have you tried turning your thoughts off at night? Picturing them in a box and closing the lid? Or cutting each thought off, stopping it in its tracks before it goes anywhere?"

Kimmy thought this was the stupidest thing she'd ever heard.

She misplaced her set of Lip Smackers and made no effort to replace them. There was no joy at her first period. No celebration when she got braces to fix the rabbit teeth, or when she got the braces taken off two years later, when people commented in hushed and pained tones about how much she looked like Rae. Kimmy grew increasingly hostile and cynical to many who tried to help. She rolled her eyes and scoffed openly when people spoke of Rae waiting for them in heaven or receiving signs from Rae in a butterfly or a bird, or when therapists referred to the five stages of grief and the possibility that Kimmy had gotten tripped up somewhere between denial and anger. Kimmy felt so far from the person she was before Fripp Island that sometimes it seemed to her that she was operating on a completely different plane of existence, like the universe had performed some sort of uncanny swap.

When Kimmy thought back on the days at Fripp Island, her memories were cloudy and indistinct. One time not long after Rae's death, in an attempt to share some happy family memories at a therapist's recommendation, Lisa said to Kimmy, "Remember how we all played Crazy Eights together? Or when you made caramel corn?" Kimmy stared at her mother blankly and said, "Huh?" There was no caramel corn in Kimmy's memories, no Crazy Eights. There were no facts from those days, from that house on Fripp Island, only feelings.

Alex remained her closest confidante as Kimmy's school friends fell away. Among one another, Kimmy's former friends said that Kimmy had gotten quiet and weird and sometimes mean. When their attempts to engage her fell flat, they took it personally and withdrew. Alex was the only one who seemed willing to accept who Kimmy had become after her sister's death, rather than trying to cajole her into the person she was before. She was unbothered by Kimmy's silent spells and her sharp tongue.

Carol went into remission not long after her extended trip to Warrenton. She lived several healthy years in Wheeling and enjoyed frequent visits from Lisa, Scott, and Kimmy.

The cancer eventually returned, and this time it was apparent that it would not be worth attempting to treat. Lisa insisted that Carol come to live with the family in Warrenton, so she could provide full-time care. Carol stayed in Rae's bedroom, which had been transformed into a sparsely decorated but comfortable guest room. Lisa did her best to make her mother comfortable as the cancer spread. They gave Carol medications to manage the pain and help her sleep. She grew very weak, and the medications muddled her mind so that conversation swirled over and around her and she found it impossible to keep up or contribute. Impossible, too, to move her eyes at will; they drifted and rolled, seemingly independent of each other and the muscles that had once brought things into focus. The world was garbled, yet not harsh or unpleasant. She enjoyed the presence of her family but couldn't follow their comings and goings. Everything felt like sleep except sleep itself, which was as dense and colorless as wet concrete.

Carol passed away on a bright winter morning while Scott was at the grocery store and Lisa was cooking breakfast in the kitchen. Kimmy was at her bedside. Kimmy, fifteen years old now, was reading aloud from *Great Expectations,* which was assigned reading for her literature class. Lisa had encouraged her to keep talking to her grandmother, explaining that even when Carol could no longer respond, she would find comfort in familiar voices. The sun was shocking on the fresh snow outside, and it burst through the windows like a scream. Kimmy paused her reading to reach over and adjust the curtain so her grandmother's face was shielded from the light. This was when she noticed a difference in Carol's breathing. It was quiet but raggedy, a little wet. Her eyes were closed.

Kimmy said, "Grandma?" The book fell from her lap as she leaned forward. "Grandma?"

Carol's lips were parted and her expression was untroubled. There was a very long break after her next exhale, and when the inhale finally came, it was shallow, noncommittal. Kimmy thought to call out to her mother but didn't want to disturb her grandmother's rest. She also realized that there wasn't time; Lisa wouldn't make it up the stairs before it happened. She held her own breath as a powerful *whoosh* seemed to suddenly flow not in or out of Carol's mouth, but through the air all around them, and when this sound dissipated, Kimmy was alone in the room.

Alex and Kimmy remained close through high school. They attended summer camp together, and their mothers coordinated visits. When they got their driver's licenses, they drove to see one another for long weekends. When the time came to consider college, they applied for the same ones. Both were admitted to WVU in Morgantown, where Ryan was in the PhD program, and they were roommates for all four years.

Alex was offered a full-time coaching position with the university's archery team upon graduating. Like Ryan, Kimmy had majored in ecology, and after she graduated,

Ryan helped her get a job at the research center where he was doing his postdoc. In field research, Kimmy spent nearly all her time outdoors and by herself, classifying flora in George Washington National Forest, assessing regrowth after forest fires, and studying the impact of new agricultural practices in the region.

26

IT WASN'T UNTIL Kimmy (who now went by Kim) and Alex were in their forties that they finally managed to plan a vacation for their two families together. It was something they had talked about doing for many years, but scheduling and logistics were tricky to coordinate with work and all the kids' camps and extracurriculars. Alex's husband's work had taken them to the West Coast, whereas Kim and her family had settled in Warrenton, just a few blocks from Scott and Lisa, so a joint vacation would mean flights for at least one of the families.

Kim and Alex cleared the dates far in advance and settled on a week's rental on Fontana Lake, nestled in the Smoky Mountains.

The house was a newly renovated timber A-frame that sat right on the water, with its own dock for swimming, a motorboat called the *Barbara Marie,* a fire pit, a hot tub, fishing equipment, hammocks, tetherball, a roomful of novels and board games—something for everyone.

Kim and her husband had twin boys, aged twelve, and a nine-year-old daughter. Alex and her husband had two girls, one thirteen and one ten.

Although the children had never spent time together and Kim and Alex didn't know quite how it would go, they all got on even better than expected. The house was soon vibrating with laughter, bare stamping feet, card games, plans for fishing and water-skiing if the *Barbara Marie* had enough horsepower, opinions about dinner and a late-night movie.

One evening midway through the week, the men decided to take the boat out for a sunset spin, and all the kids joined. This left Kim and Alex alone at the house for the first time since they had arrived. They gazed out the kitchen window to the west, where the *Barbara Marie* could be seen snaking its way across the lake in smooth, wide arcs, and the bright sky seemed to crash into the mountains. They finished loading the dishwasher, then took a bottle of red out to the dock.

They sat with their toes dangling in the water, which took on a strange black-gold hue in the dusk light and was entirely still except for the ripples created by their feet. Far away, some hound was belting out its sorrow. The sun had just set into a cleft between two mountains, and the V-shaped western sky, flanked by deep blue mountain land, was still fiery and glorious.

They sipped their wine and looked out across the water in silence. Kim rubbed out goosebumps on her thighs.

Alex said, "Ryan and I were texting earlier. He said to tell you hi."

"How's he doing?"

"Fine, I think," Alex said. "Haven't seen him since the holidays, and he's not great with keeping up. Did I tell you he moved back to Wheeling after his divorce? He got a job at the university there; she kept the house and stayed in Philly. Far as I can tell they kept it civil. That's how it was with his first wife too. I don't really know what went wrong either time—he doesn't get into that kind of thing with me. Keeps it all close to his vest, he's always been that way. Sort of makes me sad. Anyway, he's just a few miles from my folks now, so he sees a lot of them."

"That's good. Your mom's been in remission now for, what, three or four years?"

Alex nodded, then shook her head. "What a scare. She's been clear for almost four years, but I still get nervous as hell every time she goes in for a scan."

The sky was darkening, star-filled and navy overhead, purpling into a thin strip of fuchsia to the west.

Kim created small circles in the water with her toes and said, "You know, Rae was actually a really good swimmer."

Startled, Alex felt her head lift as though jerked upward by a string. Rae's name hadn't come up in conversation between the two of them for many years.

Alex said, "What do you mean?"

Kim was quiet for a bit, her eyes sweeping across the horizon. Her hair color had deepened in adulthood to a rich, dark mahogany, and it was long, tied back into a braid that reached her waist. She swatted a mosquito on her bare shoulder. "Before Fripp Island," she said, "this would've been the previous summer, our family was on vacation in Florida. Rae and I were in the ocean. All of a sudden I got pulled into a riptide and carried farther out. In no time at all, the water was over my head and I was terrified. Helpless. I panicked, flailing and screaming, gulping in water. Rae was sort of far away, but she swam over to save me, and she did it like it was *nothing*. She didn't hesitate — as soon as she heard me calling, she paddled over and pulled me up to the surface. I looped my arms around her neck and she swam me in to shore. She was fighting that current, but she was so strong, she just barreled through."

Alex stared at her. "Did your parents see?"

Kim shook her head. "They were far enough up the beach that they hadn't heard me, or maybe they weren't paying attention. And once Rae had got me to safety, I begged her not to tell them, because I was afraid they wouldn't let me swim by myself anymore."

"She didn't tell?"

"No, and I don't think she and I ever talked about it again either. She didn't seem to think it was a big deal, what she'd done. But the way she saved me was really something, not what you'd expect from a girl her size. And the way she came for me without a moment's hesitation . . . She could've easily gotten herself in the same trouble I was in — it could've easily ended with us both drowning. But she threw herself right into that danger, heard me cry, and a moment later she was right there next to me. I remember thinking . . . Well, from then on, she was like a *god* to me."

Alex considered this and said, "When . . . Fripp Island . . ." She hesitated. "Didn't they say Rae was a weak swimmer? That and the riptide and the alcohol? Everyone kept saying that."

Kim nodded. "And I remember thinking, 'That's not true. I've seen Rae swim.'"

"You didn't want to say anything?"

"It didn't seem important, I guess. Wouldn't have made any difference to what anybody was feeling." Kim paused. "I never mentioned any of this to a soul, not until you, now. But I think about these things sometimes . . . I wonder."

Alex gazed at her. "You're not sure her death was an accident."

Kim rubbed her eye sockets with the heels of her hands.

Alex said, "Do you think someone . . . or do you think Rae . . ." Her voice shrank.

Kim sniffed, leaned back, and placed both her hands on the dock. Her eyes were bright with fresh moisture, but her voice was steady. "I have a hard time remembering much at all from that week, but when I try to think really hard about who Rae was, the feeling I have, the memory, is that she was . . . teetering. Right on the brink of something."

"She was fourteen, so she *was* on the brink of something. Everything, really."

Kim scratched at an old, scabbed-over mosquito bite on her neck. "I'll never know what actually happened that night. But . . ." She gripped the damp wood on the underside of the dock and felt algae or mildew or some other sort of muck wedging deep and soft into her fingernails. "I think maybe some part of Rae wanted to die. Or at the very least, some part of her wasn't so sure about the alternative. She wasn't totally sold on it."

It surprised Kim that she could say such a thing aloud and

yet all around her the world simply carried on: the bullfrog belched, insects thrummed away, reeds shuffled and whispered against one another. No dark cloud appeared, nor any celestial ray of light. Kim felt calm and unspeakably weary. A few tears limped down her cheeks.

Eventually Alex asked, "Is that what's been keeping you up at night?" In the months leading up to this vacation, Kim had mentioned to Alex several times that she felt tired and disorganized on account of sleeping poorly. Ever since she was a kid, really; it was nothing new, although she went through spells that were better or worse, and lately it was worse.

"Not entirely," Kim said. "The real trouble I have with sleeping is that when I'm up in the night, I have to think every thought to its end. Not just about Rae, about everything. I have to take every single thought to its weirdest, wildest, furthest-away end. A thought won't go away until it's got nowhere else to go."

Alex said, "Can you ever make it through all of your thoughts in a night? Do you ever empty yourself completely out?"

Across the lake, a single yellow light suddenly came into view. The *Barbara Marie*. The light winked gold against the horizon, then grew larger and brighter.

"Sometimes I do, yes," Kim said. On the nights when she made it through all her thoughts, when she reached all their furthest-away ends and it felt like her whole mind had been scooped out clean, she would shuffle out of bed, blank and witless as a newborn, make her way to a window, and look outside. In these moments, when the world shimmered like a miracle and nothing obeyed time, she could believe in all sorts of things. Fake moons. Gray Men who roamed beaches in search of broken girls.

Soon, voices could be heard, skimming bright and clear across the surface of the water. The *Barbara Marie* was a black silhouette, and small, shadowy figures bobbed and danced within it. One of the twins was hollering about fish guts, and the girls were laughing. Someone tooted the horn. It struck Kim that the difference between seeing through the dark and imagining that you could was so indistinct that perhaps there was no difference at all. Like the difference between opting into life versus not opting out of it. Though the children were still too far away and it was too dark to make out their faces, Kim lifted both her arms and waved.

Kimmy never stopped wondering if I knew I was drowning while I was drowning. Over the years, she asked it of our parents, her therapists, her friends, her boyfriends. She never got out from under it; she asks it to this day. The answer is, only for a moment. After I became aware but before it actually seized me, my mind went scuttling backwards, depositing me in a faraway time and place. If I could reach her now, I'd explain:

You were a scream before you were a face.

You were thrashing, purple, and wrinkled like a raisin. Not cute.

Mom said, "This is your little sister," and asked if I wanted to hold you.

I hesitated, even though I had been eagerly anticipating your arrival for many months.

I said, "I'm scared."

Mom laughed because she thought I meant that I was scared of you. But I wasn't scared of you, I was scared for you. Already I knew that there were all sorts of ghastly, fearsome things in this world, and you were so small, I couldn't imagine how you would ever survive them all. But I reached for you anyway—this was the last thought I had, the last feeling I felt before death, how in one instant the universe gave up all its secrets, showed its full hand, pulled back the curtain, and laid itself bare right before me.

ACKNOWLEDGMENTS

Thank you to my wonderful agent, Michelle Tessler. Thank you to Helen Atsma, for your encouragement and guidance in raising and refining this manuscript, and to Larry Cooper, Jenny Xu, Emma Gordon, Lisa McAuliffe, Chloe Foster, Emily Snyder, Kimberly Kiefer, and Mark Robinson at Houghton Mifflin Harcourt. Thank you to Vi Dutcher and Eastern Mennonite University for a lovely office and supportive community. Last, my deepest gratitude, as always, to my friends and family, for the immense joy of sharing life with you.

Rebecca Kauffman received her MFA in creative writing from New York University. She is the author of *The Gunners* and *Another Place You've Never Been,* which was long-listed for the Center for Fiction First Novel Prize. Originally from rural northeastern Ohio, she now lives in Virginia.

The novel is structured with a mystery and a death at its heart, yet there's also humor and irony throughout. Can you tell us a little about how you created such a unique emotional contrast in the narrative and in the characters? Are there any favorite moments that you particularly enjoyed writing?

The most intense emotions — ecstasy or grief, for example — often seem to carry contrary impulses for me. Joy is quickly cut short by fear of its inevitable end, or the absence of its source, and grief is mediated by laughter and moments of inexplicable euphoria. I have a hard time looking death directly in the eye. I imagine most people do, but the specter of loss is such a profound part of existence that it plays a natural and perhaps even essential role in most stories. Death being something that we are rarely prepared for, and that never happens in a vacuum, it seemed important to fill the pages leading up to the death in this novel with moments that capture the humor and irony of life.

The alligator scene was my favorite to write. It never ceases to amaze me how some passages can take ages and be painstaking to complete, and other scenes seem to erupt fully formed in a single sitting, as was the case with the gator scene. I was laughing maniacally the entire time as I wrote it — though I wouldn't expect most readers to find it very funny. It was one of those rare and blissful writing moments that feel like riding a wave. You don't understand the mechanics; you just try to keep up and enjoy yourself.

How and why did you choose to set this story in the 1990s instead of the present?

Technology changes so much and so fast nowadays that I struggle to feel rooted enough in the present to capture it on the page. I'm especially clueless about how *today* looks and feels to younger generations. In the 1990s I was in grade school through early high school, so it was easier for me to imagine the lives of the children in the book in roughly that timeframe. I don't know what it would be like to have a Facebook account at age thirteen, but I do know what it was like to operate a VCR. Once I started writing the story in that time period, various logistics became important to the plot. For example, characters don't have cell phones but are able to dial *69 (for Caller ID), so the nineties ended up feeling both right and necessary.

Your descriptions of Fripp Island are stunning! There are the fancy golf courses and swimming pools, but the natural beauty of the island also comes through and is integral to the book—the crabs and gators, the beach, the ocean, the swamp. Can you tell us about your own experience with Fripp Island and what inspired you to set the novel there?

Thank you! My mother-in-law has family roots in South Carolina and an aunt who had a home on Fripp Island. That house is no longer in the family, but the island has remained a beloved destination, and we spent a week there several years ago. I was absolutely enchanted! Also, I learned right away that when crossing the bridge to enter the island, you have to either be a homeowner or provide some sort of proof that you're an authorized guest, which instantly gave me a sense of intrigue and isolation and *story*. The island is extraordinarily beautiful; the Vietnam War scenes from *Forrest Gump* were filmed there, as was *The Jungle Book* from the 1990s.

The book's narration is occasionally overtaken by a ghost—throughout the novel, too, there is a sense of haunting, of the Other, with characters pondering the existence of ghosts, sharing folk stories, conspiracy theories, and lore. How did you decide to include a ghostly narrator? Are any of the Fripp Island–specific tales real?

Nope! Well, they're "real" ghost stories, but not specific to Fripp Island.

I'm intrigued by the conflict and overlap between facts and feelings, especially as they pertain to memory, and this theme is explored in the book by both the living and the ghost. The ghost mentions at one point that the living are trying to recall the facts and feelings of their lives, and later mentions that it is actually a relief, in death, to be freed of the burden of feelings and "the belief that everything that originates from within you is true, can be trusted, and must be acted upon." I don't necessarily believe that intuition or emotions are what separate us in our human form from the Other, but it's something I enjoyed considering as I created the ghost voice.

In terms of the characters, you introduce such a range, in terms of age, class, and life experience. Was it tricky bouncing between so many different perspectives? Were there any that felt particularly difficult to write?

I get bored quickly, so it's best if I have several minds and hearts and sets of eyes to bounce between as I'm exploring a scene. I find it harder to write males, so you may notice that although I'll include insights from male perspectives, I tend not to linger there. The three girls, Rae, Kimmy, and Alex, were the easiest and most enjoyable to write, as all three contain specimens from my own childhood, from the swimsuit made to look like acid-washed denim to baiting hooks with night crawlers.

This is your third book. In what ways was the process different this time around?

The manner in which I became acquainted with my characters was different with this book, which is more of an ensemble story.

In my first two novels, there was a clear protagonist from the outset, and my goal was to chase the story surrounding that character, with their emotional life at the helm of every decision I made. In this book, I started off with a cast of characters and a central mystery, which is introduced in the prologue, but when I started writing the first draft, I hadn't yet decided how it would shake out. So I was unearthing multiple characters as I wrote (while they were unearthing one another), without a preordained hierarchy as to which narrative and whose voice would prove most critical to the story. Also, my first and second books both spanned several decades, whereas ninety percent of the action in this book takes place over the course of three days, give or take. One of the early challenges was learning how to draw out time without decelerating the pace of the narrative. In other words, I needed to figure out how to make time become slow without letting it *feel* slow to the reader, which was a new skill to consider and develop.

Do you have any hobbies, and if so, do they contribute to your creative work in any way?

Hiking, running, reading, fly-fishing, Dungeons & Dragons, cooking (or, more often, watching my husband cook), houseplants, fantasy football.

My experience has been that nearly everything I do away from my computer has the potential to enrich creative thinking. Solitary outdoor activities are when I'm best able to quiet my mind and focus on one thing for a very long time. Dungeons & Dragons sharpens my understanding of story and helps me approach problem-solving differently. Any scenario where I'm challenged — socially, physically, intellectually, or otherwise — helps me become more adaptable, which is absolutely essential to novel-writing. I'll concede that fantasy football adds nothing to my creative life but is merely an exercise in weekly self-flagellation.

1. Much of the conflict in this story is centered around wrong-ful assumptions and/or a fundamental misunderstanding of people who are different. How do characters navigate their misunderstandings successfully, or unsuccessfully? What are the ripple effects of either outcome?

2. How are class, gender, or age differences conveyed in the dia-logue and thought processes of each character? How does the author emphasize differences or similarities in perspective?

3. The author includes many memorable physical descriptions of people and places. Talk about the way they're woven into the text, and how they affected your understanding of the characters.

4. Two very different marriages are represented in this story. How are both of these relationships impacted by the events of the book? How do both relationships affect the lives of their children, and their children's relationships?

5. "She wanted to know that her life could be her home." Fripp Island becomes a temporary home to the visitors, but for Keats and Roxie, the island is a home they look forward to leaving. In which ways do the characters find what they

think they want in a home and in their lives on the island? In which ways do they feel unsettled?

6. There is a strong current of anxiety throughout the novel. Lisa feels a sense of "doom," and Poppy is "consumed by thoughts of her husband's death." Compare and contrast their worries about themselves and their relationships.

7. Kimmy is keenly interested in issues of faith and seeks information and answers from those around her. How do you see her spirituality change over the course of the book? How does spirituality shift for other characters?

8. "Over time, she accepted the fact that the price for this great love was this great fear. Love's unfortunate alter ego." This realization is from Poppy's perspective, but does the inextricable link between love and fear ring true for other characters as well? If so, which ones, and how?

9. This novel wrestles with the possibility that people are often punished for the wrong acts and/or for the wrong reasons. Which characters suffered on account of events that were not their fault, and which characters evaded punishment for real acts of wrongdoing? What does redemption and forgiveness look like?

10. The epigraph and various passages in the book allude to the feeling of being somehow ill suited for this world or at odds with one's own existence. In what ways do you believe this dynamic factored into the story?

11. Much of the novel takes place over the course of three days—yet time moves differently toward the end, and even

jumps into the future, beyond the island. Discuss why you think the author may have chosen to do this, and what are its effects on the narrative and on the emotional arc of the novel?

12. The epilogue includes this phrase: "in one instant the universe gave up all its secrets, showed its full hand, pulled back the curtain, and laid itself bare right before me." What do you believe this is referring to?